Praise for
Necessary Arrangements

"Written with unflinching honesty, Tanya Michna tackles a heartbreaking situation with grace and empathy. *Necessary Arrangements* is a novel about the power of love in a broken world. Tanya deftly captures the complications of finding joy in the everyday acts of love, life, death, and sisterhood. This is a poignant story that will touch the heart and make one wonder, 'What would I do?'"
—Patti Callahan Henry, author of *Between the Tides*

"A well-crafted and moving journey into the bonds of family and the hearts of sisters, a story of embracing what is and finding the strength to confront what might be."
—Lisa Wingate, author of *A Thousand Voices*

Necessary Arrangements

Tanya Michna

NAL Accent
Published by New American Library, a division of
Penguin Group (USA) Inc., 375 Hudson Street, New York, New York 10014, USA
Penguin Group (Canada), 90 Eglinton Avenue East, Suite 700, Toronto,
Ontario M4P 2Y3, Canada (a division of Pearson Penguin Canada Inc.)
Penguin Books Ltd., 80 Strand, London WC2R 0RL, England
Penguin Ireland, 25 St. Stephen's Green, Dublin 2, Ireland (a division of Penguin Books Ltd.)
Penguin Group (Australia), 250 Camberwell Road, Camberwell, Victoria 3124, Australia
(a division of Pearson Australia Group Pty. Ltd.)
Penguin Books India Pvt. Ltd., 11 Community Centre, Panchsheel Park,
New Delhi - 110 017, India
Penguin Group (NZ), 67 Apollo Drive, Rosedale, North Shore 0745, Auckland, New Zealand
(a division of Pearson New Zealand Ltd.)
Penguin Books (South Africa) (Pty.) Ltd., 24 Sturdee Avenue, Rosebank,
Johannesburg 2196, South Africa

Penguin Books Ltd., Registered Offices: 80 Strand, London WC2R 0RL, England

First published by NAL Accent, an imprint of New American Library,
a division of Penguin Group (USA) Inc.

First Printing, September 2007
10 9 8 7 6 5 4 3 2 1

 REGISTERED TRADEMARK—MARCA REGISTRADA

LIBRARY OF CONGRESS CATALOGING-IN-PUBLICATION DATA
Michna, Tanya.
Necessary arrangements / Tanya Michna.
p. cm.
ISBN: 978-0-451-22207-7
1. Sisters—Fiction. 2. Cancer—Fiction. I. Title.
PS3613.I3455N43 2007
813'.6—dc22   2007001151

Printed in the United States of America

Jill and Melissa, you are remembered with love.

Acknowledgments

My deep appreciation to Pam Hopkins, who believed in this book so much, and Ellen Edwards, for helping me make Lucy's and Asia's stories even stronger. Thank you to the cancer survivors and relatives of patients who helped me with research; I hope I've managed to capture a measure of your courage and class.

As is the case with the fictional Swensons, cancer has had a definite impact on my family. I support groups working toward a cure and, in the meantime, applaud foundations, such as Teens Living with Cancer, that seek to improve lives.

For every manuscript, I develop a "sound track," to which I listen continuously. I can't imagine having written *Necessary Arrangements* without the music of Jann Arden, the alternately poignant and bawdy folk songs of the Brobdingnagian Bards, and The Fray's "How to Save a Life."

Finally, and more than I can express, my love and gratitude to Jarrad, Ryan, Hailey, and the other family and friends who have blessed me with emotional support, abundant patience, and laughter.

One

Though Asia Swenson had rarely been in trouble as a child, her third-grade teacher had once berated her for calling the playground bully a fart-face. "Some words," Mrs. Larkin had admonished, "are very ugly and should not be used." Now, at thirty-four, late one afternoon in September, Asia had just been slapped with one of the ugliest words of her life.

Metastasis.

If only Mrs. Larkin were here. She could wash the doc's mouth out with soap. The absurd image almost made Asia smile. Almost. It was tough to grin when you'd been told the cancer had not only recurred but spread. She'd known it was a possibility. Every cancer patient always knew it was a possibility, but the reality . . .

Shifting in her seat, she rubbed her fingers over her cheeks, her disjointed thoughts as rapid as hummingbird wings. If only she could focus! Her mother boasted that Asia had been goal-oriented from the womb, born a week early, walking by the time she was eight months old. Where was that drive now, when she needed it most? Instead of this surreal, trying-to-run-underwater paralysis, she just had to redirect her energy back to battling cancer. The same war she'd begun waging two years ago, the war she'd briefly dared hope she'd won. She felt as if she'd struggled to the summit of a mountain, only to be flicked off by a gust of wind, doomed to make the climb all over again when she was already exhausted from her previous efforts.

"I know it may not feel like it now," Dr. Klamm said, his voice seeming to come from a distance greater than across the mahogany desk, "but we still have options, courses of treatment."

This small space with its dark furniture was so much cozier than the bright and chilly exam rooms that sometimes just being here soothed Asia. The masculine decor was oddly, irrationally reassuring after all the time she'd spent with other women who had her disease, after all the ubiquitous pink fight-breast-cancer products and gifts. But that was stupid. Men got cancer too, even breast cancer. Maybe the confidence she'd felt here in the past was simply her confidence in the oncologist himself.

The oncologist who was now unwillingly betraying her by admitting that the optimism that had been building for eight months was a lie.

After the original diagnosis, Asia had said to her sister and mother, "My life is in the hands of a man named for a shellfish. Should I worry, since they don't actually *have* hands?"

Lucy had laughed. Mrs. Swenson had looked pained. In the past, when their mother had overheard Lucy and Asia giggling at a bad pun or obscure inside joke, she'd often remarked, "There's something slightly wrong with you girls."

Or in my case, very *wrong. Damn mutating cells.*

"Asia?" The doctor peered at her, his eyes concerned through the lenses of his wire-rimmed glasses.

"Sorry. My mind . . . wandered."

"No apology necessary." He leaned back in his leather chair with a sigh, and it struck her how difficult a doctor's job must be some days. Despite the quiet stillness here, despite the brightly framed inspirational sayings hanging in the hallway, despite the fresh-cut flowers in the reception area, there was no disguising that this was a site of illness and frequent unwanted news. But her sympathy for Dr. Klamm's plight was eclipsed by worry for her own.

With renewed effort, she marshaled her thoughts. "It's in a new place, but it is still the same, primary cancer?" Breast cancer. Ironic, for a woman who hadn't had either of her breasts in over a year. *Guess I'll be postponing December's reconstructive surgery.*

He nodded. "I know this is a lot to take in. My advice is to go home, get some rest. We'll schedule another appointment for later in the week, after you've had a chance to make a list of specific questions, maybe on a day when one of your family can come in with you?"

As if she wanted to do that to someone she loved. Nothing ruined a day like being dragged to the medical complex north of Atlanta to have yet another cancer conversation. This she knew from experience.

God, they'll be so disappointed.

The Swensons were a close-knit family; her sister and parents had stuck by her during the rounds of treatment and two surgeries. When last fall's double mastectomy had been tentatively deemed successful, when her blood tests had come back clear, when she'd finally started to shed the lingering fatigue of her completed protocols and grow her hair back, when the port in her chest had been removed, everyone had been ecstatic to see a light at the end of the tunnel. *Chugga-chugga-chugga* ...

She swallowed, blinking away the imagined locomotive hurtling at her. "I'll see the receptionist about that appointment."

"Asia, you're young and strong. You've always been a fighter. If you'd like, we can put you in touch with some support groups that deal specifically with recurrence."

The déjà vu of the situation angered her. The suggestion of a group, the gentle reminders to stay positive. She'd worked to keep her spirits high the *first* time. She'd been an anticancer cheerleader, stopping just shy of goddamn pom-poms. Yet the disease was back anyway, like some money-borrowing distant relative who told offensive jokes and always showed up at the worst possible time. Too bad Asia couldn't turn off the lights, pull the curtains, and pretend not to be home. That sounded preferable to more chemo.

But she didn't dread the drugs as much as telling others. She vividly recalled the shock of everyone who had heard her news before, the horror and sadness quickly masked with brave faces. Her, trying to make each new medical update sound as encouraging as possible, even when she was frustrated and anxious; her loved ones trying to act as if they didn't think for a minute she might die. A truly bizarre dance, with all the participants trying to follow an unnatural rhythm without stepping on emotional toes.

Hoping none of them would have to endure that again, Asia hadn't mentioned her recent joint pain and other miscellaneous medical woes that didn't necessarily add up to cancer. But now that bone scans and biopsy results confirmed her unspoken fears, telling them was inevitable. *Tomorrow.* If she waited until tomorrow night's family dinner, that would give her twenty-four hours to rehearse what she would say.

There would be confusion, after she'd been so healthy for so many months. There would be tears her mother couldn't quite stifle; questions from her dad, who would want hard facts to bolster his own hopes. There would be awkward pauses with coworkers, sidelong glances from friends at the gym as they tried to figure out what to say.

Maybe it would be best if she took the day off work tomorrow to meditate and prepare. As a portfolio manager responsible for other people's money, she'd probably be too distracted to give her clients the attention they deserved. Lord, she missed the days when she'd thought of margins only as a securities term and not another way to gauge cancer growth.

Just call in sick. She clenched her hands into tight fists. Sick. It had been too much to hope that word would never apply to her again.

$\mathscr{D}$

Curled up inside a condominium on one of Atlanta's ubiquitous roads named Peachtree, Lucy Swenson felt as if she were floating, as light as the velvety rose petals that still dotted the foot of the bed.

September tenth was officially her lucky day. This time last year she'd attended a local arts fund-raiser when her friend Cam's husband had caught a cold and couldn't go with his wife. They offered Lucy his ticket, and it was at the gallery that she'd first bumped into Michael O'Malley, quite literally. He was an attorney for a downtown firm that specialized in labor law and contributed to several community causes. More impressive than Michael's position or devastating good looks was the fact that he'd kept a sense of humor when Lucy spilled red wine across his button-down shirt. She'd been horrified, but he'd gestured toward a framed canvas on the wall splattered in splotches of bold color.

"I'll tell everyone my shirt is an artistic statement," he'd told her with a smile. "Can I buy you another drink?"

"Anything that doesn't stain," she'd agreed as her friend slipped down a nearby corridor to give Lucy and Michael time to chat.

Technically they didn't have an anniversary for when they'd started dating, because their relationship had developed in a watercolor blur involving chance encounters and mutual acquaintances, casual dinners that had blossomed into intimate time together. So Michael had used the anniversary of the date they'd met—tonight—to propose.

Snuggled between cotton sheets that bore the warm fragrance of Michael's sandalwood cologne, Lucy held her hand above her, marveling at the diamond that winked in the freesia-scented candlelight. She'd brought the jar candles for him on a whim, so that it could always be spring in his condo no matter the season. The second she handed them to him, she'd realized what a girlie present it was for a broad-shouldered Irish charmer, but he'd thanked her with kisses and made love to her many times in the flattering glow.

If she didn't stop grinning like this, her face would ache

soon, but she couldn't help it. She was giddy, effervescing with goodwill. Everyone should be this happy!

Briefly, her thoughts strayed toward her best friend and older sister, Asia. She, more than anyone, deserved joy. Their mother had fretted only last week that Asia wouldn't slow down enough to find true happiness, by which Mrs. Swenson meant a husband and children. "She works too hard," Mrs. Swenson had complained, but with as much pride as worry.

"She's making up for lost time," Lucy had said. Asia wanted to prove something to her colleagues and clients, although what she could possibly have left to prove after all she'd already endured and conquered . . .

When the time was right, Asia would find her personal Prince Charming. Meanwhile, Lucy could hardly wait to share her own happy news! Because of the six years between the sisters and their very different personalities, some people underestimated how close the two were, but there was no one Lucy would rather have standing beside her as maid of honor on her big day than Asia.

Lucy stole a guilty glance at the phone on Michael's nightstand, tempted to call Asia now and spill the incredible news while Michael was in the shower. *No, we're waiting to tell the family at dinner tomorrow, in person.* Even Lucy wasn't so much of a screwup that she'd break their first agreement as a betrothed couple mere hours after making the decision.

The white noise of running water ceased. She scooched further down beneath the comforter, wiggling her bare feet in happy anticipation of Michael rejoining her. He'd merely angled the bathroom door, not shutting it all the way; now he emerged from the other side, his well-muscled, five-eleven frame clad only in a low-slung tan towel.

His gaze immediately went to hers. "I missed you. I was hoping you'd change your mind about joining me."

Propping herself up on her elbows, she indulged in a leisurely ogle, from his damp black hair down a lean body kept fit with squash games and faithful jogging. *Mine.* Also: *Yum.* "I was afraid if I got out of bed, the whole evening would turn out to be a dream."

He cast an amused glance at the floor, where the clothes they'd pulled off each other lay discarded and entwined. "Are your dreams always so naughty?"

Only since she'd met a man who made her feel this genuinely desirable. She flashed a flirtatious grin. "I plead the Fifth, counselor."

"Well, you know I respect your constitutional liberties," he said, coming toward her.

"You'd be a lousy attorney if you didn't."

"On a strictly personal note"—he dropped the towel—"how do you feel about my trying to seduce an answer out of you?"

Yes, please. "You can try, but I'm afraid it might take a long time." She arched an eyebrow. "If you're up for that."

He rolled across her, pressing a quick kiss to her collarbone on his way to her mouth. "Smart aleck."

"That's one of the things you love about me, right?"

"One of many." He dragged away the sheet that separated their bodies. "I can go through the list if you've got the rest of the night."

She cupped his face, pulling him closer. "I've got the rest of my life."

❧

Alimento con Amore, an Italian restaurant in Roswell, was a long-time Swenson favorite. They all enjoyed its casual, quietly festive atmosphere and homey, family-style menu. The hardwood floor, red-topped tables, and strands of white twinkle lights overhead should have been as familiar to Asia as Marianne Swenson's kitchen. Yet tonight, everything seemed oddly foreign.

The place *isn't different*, Asia told herself as she approached the teak podium. *You are.*

Because the family ate here so often, she had many memories of evenings that began with her walking in hungry and smiling. Tonight, however, there was no happy anticipation. No appetite. She vaguely recalled choking down some oatmeal for breakfast. Had that been the only thing she'd eaten since leaving Dr. Klamm's office late yesterday afternoon?

Catching sight of herself in the mirrored wall behind the hostess, Asia was relieved to see she looked more normal than she felt. Her family would expect her to be coming from work. Since Monroe Capital Group had barely embraced casual Friday, much less pioneered a casual Wednesday, she'd changed from the sweatshirt she'd worn all day into charcoal slacks and a matching jacket over a pale pink shell.

Although Asia had styled her dark hair long and sleek for most of her life, the woman in the reflection managed to make the short cap of curls look like an intentional choice. When it had become clear that her particular course of chemo was going to cause hair loss, she'd bought a wig, a high-quality natural-synthetic blend that reflected her normal style. But it hadn't been worth her vanity to wear it during Georgia's sweltering summer months. At the end of her treatment, she'd eagerly donated the hardly worn piece to someone else, counting the days until her own hair started to fill back in.

Strange how in some ways losing her hair had been even more difficult than losing her breasts. Maybe because she'd always been fairly flat-chested and hadn't had a lover at the time of the mastectomy. She'd been casually dating a divorced bank manager when she was first diagnosed, but gave him an easy out by telling him she needed to concentrate on getting well. Or maybe the baldness had made her feel so vulnerable because it was a more publicly visible sign of her disease.

Losing her hair wouldn't require as big an adjustment this time, since she'd already survived it once and her hair was short. But the thought of seeing that smooth skull in the mirror again . . .

This is life or death. Surely you're not so shallow that you're going to obsess over your hairstyle?

If it had been anyone in her former support group having this reaction, she would have reminded them that it was normal, *healthy,* to be angry about side effects. You didn't have to minimize or apologize. But she demanded more of herself than she did from others.

So find the positive.

"Right this way, please." The hostess had finished writing down a reservation and beamed at Asia. "I'll show you to your party."

Preoccupied, Asia followed the blonde through the anterior dining room toward the three stairs that led to a smaller second level and the horseshoe-shaped booth where Asia could see her parents waiting.

At the bottom of the stairs, the hostess told Asia to enjoy her meal. As Asia took the few steps, Marianne and George Swenson rose as one on the other side of the railing, their unconscious synchronization the result of being married for nearly forty years. Looking at the couple—George with steel gray hair and a wardrobe that consisted mostly of beige and navy; diminutive Marianne with her silky print dress and cubic zirconia earrings—even a casual observer could guess which one of them had come up with Asia's exotic name. Her father had tempered his wife's creative impulse by adding the middle name Jane, but that just made it more bizarre in contrast. Asia had remarked on her unusual name only once, in junior high; Marianne had seemed wounded her daughter didn't appreciate it more.

"You're so uncommonly gifted," Marianne had protested, "a common name wouldn't have suited you." Which sounded nice in theory, but thank goodness they'd chosen something more traditional for Lucy. The sensitive girl had been picked on enough as a kid.

Marianne, on the outside of the booth, kissed Asia's cheek. "How are you? Make any millions today?"

Didn't even make my bed. Asia returned her mom's embrace, then stretched across to give her dad a one-armed hug.

Through a kid's eyes, she'd viewed his average height as tall. She had a memory from her early childhood of his squashing a spider for her beneath a large, booted foot. Asia had been so relieved, so secure, thinking that surely her dad was big enough to stomp bad guys if he had to, big enough to protect her from anything that huddled in the shadows waiting to get her. Now both her parents seemed smaller and more frail. Her last bout with cancer, a saga with several complications and two surgeries, had taken its toll. Beneath the cosmetics no neighbor had ever glimpsed her mother without, Marianne had aged a decade in the past two years.

I can't. The courage Asia had been trying to gather all day wilted. *I can't tell them.*

She cleared her throat. "Where are Lucy and Michael?" Although Lucy still came to the odd family outing alone, more often than not Michael accompanied her.

Michael had told them he'd been to Ireland only once, the summer after his high school graduation, but his father, a partner in a Kentucky horse farm, had been born in County Kildare. With the exception of the oldest brother, who had inherited a gift with horses, the five O'Malley siblings had scattered across the southeast, following different dreams. Asia was glad she and Lucy had always lived near each other.

As much as Asia dreaded telling her family about the latest grim development, if anyone could help her cope, it was Lucy. With her infectious smile and enthusiasm for life, Lucy artlessly lightened the burdens of those around her.

George Swenson laughed. "After all these years, you actually expect your sister to be on time? For Lucy, anything less than fifteen minutes late is early."

Asia managed a grin as she slid into the booth. Lucy wasn't irresponsible, merely disorganized. Simple actions like getting in the car became marathon events as Lucy realized she had to go back for her wallet, couldn't find her sunglasses, or had left her headlights on and run down her battery. At least the little house Lucy rented had a covered carport and not an actual garage. The only "accident" Marianne Swenson's now-retired Ford station wagon had ever been in was the time Lucy had been running late for an all-state choir audition and threw the car into reverse without raising the automatic garage door. During holiday get-togethers and family reunions, the occasional joke was still made if Lucy was the one to grab a set of keys to move a car or take a quick trip for more ice. Lucy was a good sport, usually the first to laugh at her own exploits. Still, it seemed too tall an order to hope that Lucy could raise everyone's spirits tonight once Asia's bomb was detonated.

"Honey?" Across the table, Marianne had lost her smile. "Are you all right?"

Asia couldn't say yes without lying. "I'm distracted. I have something to talk about, but I'm waiting f—"

"We're here!" Lucy's cheery announcement wafted across the high-ceilinged room, over the metallic clatter of other diners' eating, as she hurried up the stairs. "Sorry we're late."

"What late?" Their father made a show of studying the gold-plated wristwatch he'd received at his retirement party. "I didn't expect you for another ten minutes. Michael, you must be a good influence."

"It's nice that you think so," Michael said politely. "I keep waiting for everyone to realize I don't deserve her."

It might have sounded horribly kiss-ass from another boy-friend, but Michael's indigo eyes radiated sincerity. *Good,* Asia thought fiercely. Her sister was too special not to be loved with devotion.

"I'm starved," Lucy declared as she slid in next to Asia. She grabbed a menu but didn't bother opening it. "I vote for the shrimp arrabbiata."

"Seafood sounds nice," Marianne said. "Your father loves shrimp."

Lucy grinned. "Me, too, but mostly I just like saying 'arrabbiata.'" She rolled her Rs with gusto.

They gave the exotic name to the wrong kid. The thought clicked into Asia's mind. She was married to her job and wore suits, while her sunny younger sister treated even the most mundane activities as if they were fun adventures. Asia's eyes stung. Why couldn't she be more like that? For a little more than six months, she'd labored under the delusion that she was healthy again. Why hadn't she done something wild and impetuous to celebrate? Book a cruise, backpack in Europe, fly to New York just to see a play on Broadway?

She'd seen a musical at Atlanta's Fox Theatre with Lucy, if that counted for anything. Besides, Asia *enjoyed* her job. Returning to the normalcy of a daily routine, one that didn't involve medical professionals, had been a celebration of sorts.

"Hey." Lucy nudged Asia's knee under the table. "You okay?"

"She was just about to tell us something," Marianne said as a waiter approached. He was relatively new but had served them before. Roberto, or maybe Romero?

Michael, seated on Lucy's other side, cleared his throat. It was the first time Asia had ever heard him sound nervous. "We have something to tell you, too. Lucy's so antsy to let you all know, I thought she was going to call you from the car! Roberto, can you recommend a bottle of champagne?"

George was looking at his youngest daughter with interest, asking her about her job. Lucy had surprised and delighted her parents last year when a temp assignment had led to permanent employment and a position in lower management.

Dad's nuts. Asia studied her sister. No raise or promotion had stamped that rosy glow on Lucy's round, pretty face. It was so obviously love. But that wasn't exactly breaking news, unless—

Oh, hell. "He proposed," she breathed in an almost inaudible undertone. Not tonight. They couldn't both do this tonight.

Only Lucy heard the whispered realization, and she nodded, grinning even as unshed tears glistened in her green eyes. She turned to include everyone else in the moment. "Mom, Dad. Roberto. Michael and I are getting married!"

Two

Lucy supposed she could have found a more eloquent way to tell her family, but blurting was more her style.

She squeezed Asia's hand, thrilled that everyone was here to share the joy. "You'll be my maid of honor, of course! Say you will. There's no one else in the world I'd want to do it."

Asia's fingers were cold, her expression . . . stricken? She couldn't be *that* shocked, not when Lucy and Michael had been dating since last year's holidays, serious since before spring. It was as if a switch had been thrown, Asia finishing the last of her just-in-case chemo right around the time Lucy had been offered a permanent placement and started dating Michael. They'd been on a steady climb away from the dark times and toward happiness. Lucy grinned inwardly at the climbing analogy; hadn't they assured each other that a Swenson sister was capable of tackling Everest if she put her mind to it? Despite the refrain, deep down Lucy had always thought that, of the two of them, her sister was far more capable of scaling mountains—*moving* them even. It had taken a few months for

Lucy to trust that her good fortune in finding Michael wasn't a temporary aberration. Asia had been the one to quietly predict wedding bells back when Lucy still wondered if the good-looking lawyer would eventually drift to greener, size-six pastures.

Why didn't Asia look happier?

Lucy searched her sister's eyes. Last time she'd checked, Asia liked Michael. And Asia was far too secure to be one of those I-can't-be-happy-for-my-baby-sister-because-I'm-over-thirty-and-still-don't-have-a-man women. Although mere seconds had passed, Asia's lack of response had alerted their parents, whose congratulations trailed off into wordless questions.

Lucy's own voice came out in a squeak. "Sis?"

"I'm fine," Asia managed, her gaze darting around the table but not meeting any one person's eyes for long. "I'm ecstatic for you both! So happy, I was speechless."

The gaiety in her tone sounded closer to hysteria. Even Roberto, who'd returned with a bottle and champagne glasses, looked momentarily concerned.

Either Mrs. Swenson was less observant than the olive-skinned waiter, or she wanted to believe her daughter's reassurance. "This *is* a lovely surprise, isn't it? Although I suppose we should have—"

"Asia." Their father's baritone was graveled with affection and worry. "Earlier, you said you had something to tell us."

"Another time." Asia reached for a glass. "This is Lucy and Michael's night. My news can wait."

Could it? Lucy felt her body tremble, her subconscious realizing what she wasn't letting herself think. Isolated fragments from the last few weeks suddenly fit themselves into a complete picture.

Asia had seemed more tired lately, her hazel eyes shadowed with fatigue. Maybe even pain? She had been slower to return Lucy's calls, but Lucy had been so caught up in her romance with Michael, it hadn't bothered her. She'd thought perhaps her sister was still just reveling in the space now that the . . . now that the cancer was gone and people were no longer hovering. Had Asia instead been avoiding her family because she didn't want to burden them?

Was it back?

No. That is not going to happen to her again. It would be too cruel for someone to triumph over something so monstrous, only to—

"Lucy?" Michael was trying to hand her a glass. "Darlin'?"

She ignored him, her eyes locked on her sister in silent interrogation. At first she thought Asia would look away, but after a moment and a muttered curse, she gave a slight nod.

All the air was crushed out of Lucy's chest, dread taking its place like a noxious substance she couldn't breathe. Her vision blurred with the hot threat of tears. Was she really so weak that *she* was going to fall apart when it was Asia, pale-faced but composed, who would be the one suffering?

Not the only one, a selfish inner voice pointed out.

Asia had unquestionably suffered the most, in ways Lucy couldn't—didn't want to—imagine, but the cancer had ripped at them all, leaving even happy occasions like Christmas jagged with bittersweet edges. It was tough to deck the halls when you were terrified one of you wouldn't be around for the final fa-la-las. Not that any of them would have voiced the possibility. They'd all tried to follow Asia's brave example, but none of them had her innate courage and grace. Ever since Asia's illness, Marianne had grown increasingly childlike, deferring to her oldest daughter, seeking out her opinions and company as if her clinging could keep Asia with them.

Ordering herself to be strong, Lucy swallowed and stole a glance at Marianne. The woman looked troubled in an innocent, confused way, but not yet truly upset. She was worrying the slim gold cross around her neck, twisting it with arthritic fingers.

George Swenson, however, watched his daughters. And he knew. Lucy witnessed him have the realization, then quickly lower his head to the menu. He wasn't going to press the conversation.

Because he and Asia don't want to ruin tonight for me. The thought almost drew a hollow laugh. Her father had always been a protective teddy bear, but this wasn't like grilling his daughter's date or trying to help her get a better deal on a car.

George cleared his throat. "I think we could all use a bit of that bubbly, huh?"

"Absolutely," Michael said. Lucy doubted that the others, who didn't know him as well, caught his hesitation. "So, the way it works here is that we order an entrée or two and all share? What's good?"

"Oh, everything," Marianne prattled, listing her favorite pasta dishes and recounting some of the events they'd celebrated here: Lucy's high school graduation, George's retirement from his longtime job as an airline mechanic, Asia's thirtieth birthday.

Lucy clasped her sister's hand beneath the table, both of them holding on so tightly they were probably damaging their circulation. *Please, God, let her have dozens more birthdays.* The tears Lucy wanted to be tough enough to stave off spilled down her cheeks.

"Honestly." Their mother paused in her reminiscing and scowled. "What is going on?"

Swiping at her eyes with one knuckle, Lucy sniffed. "You know me. The tiniest little thing and I bawl like a baby. I think I'll just excuse myself to the—"

"It's okay." Asia gave her sister's fingers one final squeeze. Then she let go. "Mom, Dad, I'm afraid I do have something to tell you, and I wish it were as joyous as Lucy's announcement. I wish there were another time to tell you. I wish there'd never be a need to tell you at all."

George dropped his arm around Marianne, pulling his wife closer, as if bracing her for impact. The woman's breathing had grown shallow, and her eyes were wild with what she hoped her oldest daughter was not about to say.

"The cancer has returned," Asia said simply. "And metastasized."

A single keening sound erupted from Marianne before she pressed her hands to her mouth.

"I'm so sorry." Michael spoke first. "We'll all help you beat this. Just let us know what we can do."

I love this man so much. His calm, determined tone was a balm to Lucy's splintering spirit.

Asia nodded. "Thank you. I'm sure I'll be taking you up on that."

Silent tears snaked rivulets over Marianne's wrinkled jaw, but she kept her voice admirably composed. "Remind me what exactly that means, 'metastasized'?"

"Spread beyond the initial site. In my case, into bone. But Dr. Klamm says we have options. Focused treatments, whole body care, maybe hormone therapy—"

"And people have overcome it before, right?" George Swenson's bluff tone made him sound like a football coach trying to convince his team, down twenty to zip in the last quarter, that the game could still be won. "What statistics did the doctor give you?"

"Dr. Klamm and I aren't getting into numbers," Asia said. "If the odds are against a person living out the year, it doesn't help to dwell on that. Conversely, even if only one person in a million ends up with a fatal case, the odds aren't a comfort to that one person."

Though Lucy saw the truth in what her sister was saying, she suspected that, were their situations reversed, she wouldn't be able to resist logging on to the Internet to research her chances, trying desperately to find some magical guarantee in numbers. *Forget the numbers. Asia beat it once, and she will again.*

Except . . . she hadn't beaten it, had she?

Roberto chose that moment to reappear, a pen poised over a small pad as he asked if they were ready to order.

Five pairs of eyes stared blankly.

At the long pause, the waiter smiled toward the champagne

bottle. "You were all too busy celebrating to decide! This is a happy occasion, no?"

Lucy's heart sank. *No.*

~

It was a shame that screaming obscenities into the cloudy dark wouldn't actually make her feel better, because Asia had some real doozies on the tip of her tongue. Sweet Lord. The night of her sister's *engagement.* Since she'd gotten home and changed clothes, she'd been pacing her apartment and torturing herself with what a train wreck dinner had been.

She'd thought going out on the balcony would help, but all it had done was limit her room for pacing.

Why didn't she call me last night? A cold breeze rippled over her skin like a full-body goose bump, but did nothing to soothe the hot anger Asia felt as she recalled watching Michael's and Lucy's happiness wither in the wake of an announcement Asia was too late to stop. Lucy had never been able to keep secrets, at least not from her sister, and it just *figured* the one time Asia could have used some damn warning— What the hell was she doing?

Gripping her hands around the railing and glaring up at stars that were hardly visible this close to downtown, Asia took a deep breath. If anyone should be mad, it should be Lucy. This evening was supposed to have been special for her, a memory in the making.

She'll live, retorted the cynical part of her. *Will you?*

Asia turned back toward the sliding glass door and the living room, decorated in warm earth tones. Her parents had offered to see her home or let her spend the night in her old room, but she'd insisted on being alone. She wasn't sure she could handle her mother's naked distress and her dad's questions. Still, now that she was here, she felt lonely, a rarity for someone who'd always enjoyed her own companionship. Someone who just this time last year—despite being grateful for the dozens of health care professionals who had saved her life, a large company of colleagues who had worked to pick up her slack and still make her feel part of the team, and a family who'd wanted to be there for her twenty-four/seven—had craved some solitude.

Then again, her circumstances had changed since this time last year. Or, worse, hadn't. She was once again the cancer patient who would depend on strangers to keep the cells in her own body from killing her.

The bitter fury she'd wrestled all day felt like an extension of the disease, multiplying and spreading through her. She hadn't touched either the manicotti or chicken saltimbocca tonight, instead choking down the temptation to lash out. Rage wouldn't help. *Calm down.* She insisted on having at least that much control over her body.

Inhaling and exhaling in a yoga-inspired rhythm, she sank into the plush fabric of her cocoa-colored sectional; though she hadn't known it at the time, this had been one of her most brilliant furniture purchases. The sections on either end opened into recliners that were comfortable enough to sleep in and, during the worst of her treatments, easier to get in and out of than the queen-size bed that sat so high off the ground on its antique-replica iron frame. Marianne had fussed about the sofa, claiming that Asia's furniture was too dark, too blocky to be feminine.

"What about some pretty lace curtains, dear?" her mother had asked. "At the very least, more color."

The most colorful thing in the room was the framed Georgia O'Keeffe print Lucy had bought Asia when she signed the lease here. *Red Cannas*. Not truly Asia's style, but unwilling to hurt her sister's feelings, she'd given the poster a place of prominence on the living room wall. Asia had to admit it was striking, surrounded by the dark-wood furniture, the cream carpet, the chocolate and caramel fabrics. Lucy fondly called the apartment Asia's cave.

Much as Asia respected Lucy's attempt to decorate on a budget by throwing coats of bright primary colors over secondhand furniture that had seen better days, if Asia lived in Lucy's house, she'd start wearing sunglasses indoors. Nor could Asia see herself selecting the ruffled curtains Marianne had hung in the Swenson family home, to say nothing of the plentiful knickknacks. Since the girls had moved out, taking with them the normal childhood risks of knocking over the crystal collectibles, Marianne had filled corner curios and shelves with figurines, sparkling but fragile. *Just like Mom.*

The thought startled Asia. She felt disloyal, but the description fit her mother. Marianne had grown up in an affectionate lower-class household, dreaming of surrounding herself with lovely things, while George was the only son in a family that traced its roots back to Confederate generals and antebellum mansions. His sister, Asia's aunt Ginny, had been a bona fide debutante. Asia had girlhood memories of her mother trying hard to impress Grandma Swenson, but Marianne's love of anything bright and dazzling did not match her mother-in-law's preference for subdued elegance. In making her own opinions known to her daughters, Marianne had been more charming than austere Grandma Swenson had been, always acting out of a sincere desire to help.

Suddenly Asia realized her mother hadn't offered one helpful comment in months. *She's handling me with kid gloves, even when they thought I was healthy again.* Asia found herself missing the mom who'd fretted that she didn't wear skirts often enough and was letting herself get too skinny.

Considering the latest diagnosis, however, her family's shaky ability to relate to her would get worse before it got better. And what about her friends and colleagues? Ever since Asia had left a voice mail that morning saying she wouldn't be in the office that day, she'd managed to put aside thoughts of work. Her more optimistic half wanted to put off telling her coworkers and clients, wanted to cling to the myth that maybe her condition wouldn't be noticeable at first. But chemo was a cumulative poison, sometimes more hard-hitting the second time around. Plus, there were the necessary appointments that would cut into her work schedule.

People would notice she was sick . . . people who'd only recently stopped looking at her as if they wanted to offer her a better stock deal, or were scared she'd brush up against them in the elevator and pass along her disease. It was amazing how *stupid* educated and successful adults could be, but cancer aroused fear, a primal emotion not easily defeated by logic.

That potential fear had kept Asia from notifying a very special group today, her Internet sisters. While researching her mastectomy last year, she'd happened across another cancer survivor's blog. Asia herself was not the type to write a journal, much less make it public, but the faceless woman on the Web had described situations so eerily familiar that Asia couldn't resist commenting. Soon, there were five of them who'd met online, women at similar stages of their breast cancer treatment who'd begun exchanging enough e-mails to draw up their own loop for chatting.

Those candid conversations among people she'd never met face-to-face had been much more helpful to Asia than larger, in-person groups. All five women had finished treatment within a few months of one another, and until Asia's diagnosis yesterday, as far as she knew, all of them had successfully reclaimed their lives. At first, weekly updates were the norm, followed by monthly highlights that were friendly but increasingly impersonal, holiday alumni newsletters to sisters who'd been in the same unwanted sorority.

Kappa Kappa Chemo?
Phi Beta Gamma Ray?

As they'd each grown busier and healthier, the e-mails had slowed even further, the only real activity on the loop occurring when one of them had remarried. Perhaps they would be the best people to understand how Asia was feeling right now, and one click of the send button would reestablish the bond that had helped see her through before. Or maybe her bad news would only make it harder for them to go about their normal, healthy lives. Maybe she would be the harbinger of fear that they, too, might be facing a relapse right around the corner. Then there was *her* fear that the bond would no longer be there, at least, not in the same way.

E-mails could wait until she had a better handle on what her medical situation actually was. Work was a more immediate concern.

Tomorrow she'd go into her boss's office, head held high, and give him the simple facts, explaining that she would continue to do the high-quality work he'd come to expect from her for as long as physically possible. Maybe if she kept her own fear under control, others could do the same. Huddling into her sweatshirt, she felt exhausted by the prospect of putting on her game face once again. She didn't want to be the cheerleader for everyone else. Right this moment, she wanted someone to hug her close and tell her it would all be fine.

Though she'd always had the love of family and the respect of colleagues, tonight she wanted a big, strong man like Michael. Or maybe not. Maybe a lover would only be one more person she felt she should apologize to, then hate because of it.

When she'd looked into her sister's eyes tonight and seen Lucy piece together the truth, her first emotion had been relief. Thank God Lucy had figured it out, because Asia hadn't had the first clue how to break the news. But the relief had barely bloomed before it was replaced by the need to protect; she'd wanted to take Luce in her arms, kiss her brow as their mother had done when they were kids, and tell her not to cry. That she would be all right, that she was sorry she'd ruined Lucy's night. Then, of course, had come the resentment, the reminder that *she* was the victim here, the one who would be heaving her guts into a plastic bucket while the rest of them were planning a wedding and doing holiday baking.

You are a victim only if you let yourself become one.

She couldn't control the disease, but she could control the way she faced the coming months. Asia Jane Swenson would not spend precious time feeling sorry for herself or being secretly, selfishly angry that others were healthy. Lucy deserved happiness and a picture-perfect wedding. As big sister and a member of the bridal party, Asia's responsibility was to help with that . . . and hopefully distract herself from the less pleasant aspects of her current situation.

Tomorrow she would talk to Lucy, and dammit, cancer or no cancer, she would be the best maid of honor there ever was.

Three

"You know I'm happy to stay, or leave you alone, or even take you to your parents'." Michael wrapped his arms around her from behind. "Whatever you need tonight."

Lucy stood at her kitchen counter, staring at the spice rack that hung slightly crooked on the wall. For the life of her, she couldn't remember why she'd come in here. Maybe for something warm to drink? Just that morning—a surreal lifetime ago—she'd said that it felt too hot for nearly autumn, but now she felt frozen through.

She let herself fall back into Michael's hug. "Stay. Definitely stay."

Tendrils of guilt snaked through her as she recalled how quickly and deliberately she'd said her good-byes tonight, leaving with Michael before her mother had a chance to ask Lucy to come to the house. *She has Dad. And I wouldn't know what to say to her anyway.* Lucy would have willingly gone to Asia's place, but her sister hadn't wanted any of them. *She* was facing this alone, while Lucy leaned on Michael. It wasn't fair. Any of it.

He rubbed slow, comforting circles along her forearm. "I could make you an Irish coffee."

"No coffee. But I'll take the whiskey." When he let go of her to scare up clean glasses, she slumped into a bright blue cushioned chair of the mismatched dinette set.

Michael joined her moments later, dragging a yellow seat around so he could sit next to her. "Want to talk about it?"

"No!" There would be so much talking in the weeks to come.

She and Michael hadn't been seriously involved during the worst patch of Asia's previous illness, so he had only a distant, peripheral idea of what to expect. Even when they weren't discussing the cancer, it would be shaping their lives. The days Lucy and her parents juggled driving Asia to and from the medical complex and the radiology center; the days Asia might be too sick to come home and they'd take turns visiting her in the hospital.

Memories of how it was before overlapped with Lucy's sudden dread of the future, creating a fragmented, disorienting picture. For tonight, she didn't want to speak about it at all. Except maybe to address one concern.

"Michael? I know we didn't get around to filling my folks in on wedding plans, but you and I talked about a somewhat elaborate wedding next year." Two Christmases from now, a beautiful holiday ceremony.

She'd barely met any of his relatives, just his parents, who'd had dinner with them in Atlanta a couple of months after Michael and Lucy had started dating, and one of his brothers when he'd had a lengthy layover at Hartsfield. The O'Malleys were a sizable family, so a large ceremony had seemed a given. Lucy still had that perpetual little girl inside her twenty-eight-year-old self who wanted a full-blown fairy-tale event. *Princess for a day.*

It suddenly seemed such a shallow goal.

Michael assessed her quietly. "We might need to adjust our plans?"

"I don't know yet. Maybe."

On the one hand, waiting would give Asia time to cope with the upcoming treatment cycle, so that perhaps she could be a fully recovered participant. Then again, wedding preparations could give them all something happier to occupy their thoughts. Plus, from what she understood, a recurrence of cancer, especially so soon after the first instance, always meant a graver diagnosis. Delaying the wedding for over a year could increase the risk that . . . She downed a hefty swallow of the whiskey, gasping at the burn that didn't actually leave her any warmer.

"Ah, Lucy. You walk down the aisle to join with me, and that's all I need to make it a perfect wedding day. The details are entirely up to you, darlin'."

She tilted closer until her head rested on Michael's shoulder. His familiar scent was far more comforting than the alcohol. Maybe she could cling to him until reality left her the hell alone. Trailing small kisses along Michael's jaw, she whispered, "You said whatever I need?"

"Name it." His voice was husky with the desire to help and the frustration that he couldn't do more. Twin emotions Lucy knew all too well.

"I need you, Michael. I need you inside me." Lacing her fingers in the dark silk of his hair, she kissed him hard, thrusting her tongue with his and almost weeping with relief when sensation sprang to life inside her body. Michael could thaw her, drive out the icy fear.

They kissed hungrily, abandoning finesse as if they'd been separated for months instead of having made love throughout the better part of last night.

Gallant romance wasn't what Lucy needed now. Her muscles tightened, refocusing her body's tension toward a primitive outlet, a mindless coupling that would leave her too exhausted to dream. She yanked his shirt up over Michael's head, unsure when they'd stood up. Somehow they were against the wall, between the kitchen and the front door, her hands fumbling with the zipper on his slacks. His fingers were more deft. The buttons on her shirt seemed to melt away under his touch, as did the front clasp of her lace-trimmed bra.

Once, she'd been self-conscious about being so generously endowed, an anomaly among the slender women in her family. But Michael knew exactly how to caress her, making her feel like some wanton earth goddess whose form was too perfect to allow embarrassment or apology. Holding her pinioned with his kiss, he ground against her, the pressure of his erection sparking small explosions inside her. He lowered his head to her collarbone, tracing his tongue to the top of one breast. He circled his thumb around a nipple, not yet touching. Spasms of sharp arousal rocked her. His breath feathered over the opposite nipple, making her nearly frenetic with need. His sensual appreciation made her *very* glad to be curvy instead of flat-chested, like A—

She slammed the door on the unfinished thought, trying not to lose her grip on the edges of sexual anticipation. *Touch me touch me touch me.* He did, tweaking her nipple in a possessive motion that made her womb clench. But on the heels of the fierce pang of lust came a wave of shame she couldn't block. Small whimpers echoed through the modest ranch house, feeding the guilt. She didn't deserve to feel this good right now.

Asia faced the biggest struggle of her life, and Lucy's reaction was to have pounding sex up against a wall?

Ignoring the thoughts and trying to fall back into the groove, she lifted Michael's face to hers for another soul-searing kiss, but it tasted like desperation. When his hands cupped her chest, she batted them away, tears already leaking from her eyes and spilling down both their faces.

"I-I'm sorry." She tugged together the halves of her blouse. "I-I . . ."

"It's okay." He cradled her against him, sinking to the floor with her when the sobs made it nearly impossible for her to stand.

"No. N-no, I—" She broke off on a wail, unable to draw in enough breath to speak. Even if she could, what would she say? What assurances could Michael give her? What justification? Despite his eloquent lawyer's gift with words, what possible rationalization was there for a woman like Asia suffering through this illness not once but *twice*?

Growing up, Asia had been more than a friend; she'd been a protector. She'd glared bullies into submission on Lucy's behalf; she'd crawled into Lucy's twin bed on stormy nights to read to her until the frightening cannon bursts of thunder rolled into the distance. Asia always made Lucy braver. Except now, when the icy fear of losing her sister gripped Lucy so hard her soul ripped apart.

"Lucy, darlin'." Michael smoothed her hair and rocked her. "Go ahead and get it out. Just let it all out."

If only it were that simple.

The offices of Monroe Capital Group reeked of wealth and power in the most tasteful sense; the decor was classic and subtly expensive. James Monroe III, the semiretired president of the company, said he liked to attract older, more conservative clients with the environment and younger investors with his staff, which was made up predominantly of dynamic thirty-somethings, with the occasional wunderkind in his mid-twenties and several older employees in key positions. Customers of all ages and backgrounds could appreciate the company's mission statement and results. MCG had earned many people a lot of money, and Asia had been an integral part of that success.

When her supervisors had assured her during her first illness that they would work with her, giving her flextime and "donated" sick days to help pick up slack without affecting her salary, it had been in part because they hoped to keep a lasting relationship with one of their most productive employees. Asia had fantastic instincts on the job.

Those instincts told her now, as she sat ramrod straight in a chair the deep, dark half-past-red of a bloodstain, that the second time around would have a different scenario.

Morris Grigg, an intelligent man with a prominent nose and receding hairline, frowned, the picture of a supervisor worried for his employee. His shrewd gaze made her wonder if he was worried for *her*, or the reaction her clients might have upon learning their portfolio manager was critically ill.

"I can't tell you how sorry I am to hear this, Asia." Morris's features softened, injecting some humanity into the calculating expression and lending his words sincerity.

Not half as sorry I am. "Thank you."

"Is this meeting in confidence, or were you planning to make news of your relapse public?"

What, like take out an ad in the *Journal-Constitution?* "Telling people depends partly on your opinion. It's not yet critical for anyone to know, but there will be doctors' appointments and days I won't be at the office at all."

"Too sick to come to work."

"Possibly. All patients experience chemo differently, though. And there are measures that can be taken to alleviate the side effects. Antinausea meds." Dolasetron, lorazepam. Hadn't there been a time when the only pharmaceutical terms she'd known were ibuprofen and penicillin? Now she felt qualified to write a foreword for the next edition of the *Physician's Desk Reference*.

Morris rose, turning his back to her and staring out his window onto the fairway of a nearby golf course. She suspected he was having a legitimately sentimental reaction to her news and needed a moment to adjust. She preferred this to staring at each other in awkward silence as he deliberated over his words. Finally, he spun back to regard her with resignation.

Where was the rousing optimism, the "You can do it, and we'll be right behind you all the way"?

"Asia, I am truly sorry, and I can't imagine what you must be facing. But, cold as it may sound, James hired me to help run this business, and I have to keep that uppermost in my goals. Hundreds of employees and clients count on it."

"I understand." She folded her hands in her lap, hoping it wasn't obvious how tightly she was squeezing them together. He wouldn't fire her. Even without the rights she knew she had under various medical acts, he had more integrity than that. But keeping her on didn't mean keeping her job as it was. As she'd worked hard to make it.

"You're well aware of all the behind-the-scenes work that must be done in a firm like this," Morris said. "The paperwork, computer work, phone calls, which can be done almost as easily from home as at the office. We want to accommodate you. But you're in charge of several high-profile clients, people who expect and pay for more of our man-hours on a weekly basis. In the next few months, you're probably not going to be up for as many power lunches or meetings."

What he didn't add was that certain clients might be discomfited by the sunburnlike rashes caused by radiation, the baldness, and the temporary disfigurations that were often a result of steroid treatments.

"You're right," she admitted. "I probably won't."

He sat back down, seeming relieved that she'd agreed, and steepled his fingers beneath his chin. "We'll reduce your hours some but keep you at your current salary."

She should have been grateful. Instead, she was angry.

"While you are unquestionably one of my best portfolio

managers, Asia, this company has numerous top-notch employees. Brandon Peters, for instance."

Since that was nothing more than the expected truth, she kept her jaw from clenching. Barely.

She had nothing against Brandon, a charming (*slick,* her subconscious provided) golden boy about her age who seemed to thrive on friendly competition. But Asia couldn't view the work she did here as a game. It was a hard-earned privilege being pulled out from under her. Maybe a brush with death should have given her a new set of priorities, making work less important than it had been before, but somehow succeeding had become even more essential. She'd needed to demonstrate that she was strong, that she could rise above what had happened to her.

Brandon was on a hell of a streak, and while that was good for MCG as a whole and she didn't begrudge him his accomplishments—or tried not to—she felt too much as if she were starting from square one. Even in the last months, it had been brought repeatedly to her unwilling attention that she tired more easily than she had before rounds of chemo and the surgery. Concentrating was more difficult. Her short-term memory seemed as riddled with holes as a wool sweater locked in a trunk with hungry moths. Even returning to a task after an interrupting phone call was tougher.

Dammit. For all these reasons, Morris was exactly right. Her biggest clients *should* be given to Brandon. They deserved his finesse and unbeatable record, although it felt a lot like being kicked while she was down.

"Maybe the two of us could have a private meeting with Brandon this afternoon," Morris suggested. "After you've had a chance to tell anyone else you'd like to, such as your assistant."

Asia nodded, knowing that Fern, one of her closest colleagues, would take the news badly. She'd almost told her this morning, before the meeting with Morris, but had stalled, dreading the inevitable tears.

She forced a smile. What was that ridiculous philosophy—that if you faked happiness and confidence long enough, they'd become real? "You know, the lighter schedule will come in handy. My sister's getting married, and this gives me more time to help with the wedding. The maid of honor has a lot of responsibilities."

Morris's eyebrows shot upward. Possibly he thought she was demented to be chirping about fortunate timing, but what was she supposed to do? Sulk?

"Well, congratulations to your sister, then. I'm glad this works out to . . . your benefit."

Okay, so it was odd to try to spin cancer as if it were to her advantage, but with enough attitude, she might be able to counteract an outpouring of sympathy. Attitude, she reminded herself as she left Morris and returned to her own, much smaller office. Superheroes from Buffy the Vampire Slayer to James Bond were able to maintain a smirk in the face of danger and potential death.

I could be a superhero.

Asia Jane versus the Cancer of Doom.

❧

I'm a spy. Lucy was in the produce section on a mission. She glanced around with the questions on her client form in mind.

Clean floors, check. A cheerful floral display in autumn colors, no empty carts or cardboard bins lingering once the vegetables had been unloaded.

A guy who looked young enough to be in high school approached her. "May I help you, miss?"

Good job . . . She scanned his dark green apron and found the name badge right where it should be: KEV. *Good job, Kev.* They chatted for a few moments, Lucy taking mental notes for her report. When she'd gone on her first few mystery shopping assignments as a temporary worker, picking up some extra cash after her flight attendant roommate moved out of their small brick home, Lucy had worried about whether or not she could do a decent job. She wasn't what one would call detail-oriented.

Surprisingly, she'd done quite well, working as one of the company's anonymous shoppers and eventually taking reports over the phone at the corporate office. Now she oversaw the reporting department, a junior position in comparison to her colleagues who ran quality control, human resources and sales, but still an achievement for a girl who'd never excelled at school and had changed majors three times before dropping out of college.

She'd once admitted to Michael, "I can't believe I can remember whether or not a fast-food attendant asked me if I'd like to upsize my beverage last week, yet can't recall where I put the remote control."

"It's because you're a people person," he'd told her with a smile. "You genuinely care. You might accidentally lock your keys in the car, but you don't forget names or faces. You never fail to ask your neighbor Mrs. McCleary about her grandkids or to remember a scarf your mother once liked when it comes time for Christmas shopping. I wouldn't say you aren't a detail person, darlin', just that you might notice different details than others."

No wonder she was madly in love with him, Lucy mused as she accepted her change from the cashier and exited the store. "Checkout" was a separate section on the rating form Lucy would fill out later, and the woman working the register would not be getting as high a score as Kev. The nameless cashier, who had been without a badge and would be described in the report by her appearance, would be cited for taking a call on her cell phone that involved a dispute about the release date of an upcoming horror movie.

Softhearted Lucy would have overlooked the personal call if it had been, say, a family emergency. She blinked, freezing in the act of unlocking her car door, hit sideways by this latest mental collision with last night's events. *Stop trying to avoid it and talk to your sister.*

What could she say?

Asia, hey, it's Luce. Just wanted to say I love you. Also, cancer sucks the big one.

Hey, it's me. I don't remember what I could have possibly said the first time you were diagnosed, but let's pretend I said it again this time, with even more feeling and conviction that you'll kick ass.

Asia would kick ass. It was what she did. Never in a bullying or show-off manner, just with consistent, capable determination.

Other kids had occasionally picked on Lucy when she was in school—she'd been chubby and uncoordinated—but the second Asia got wind of it, she'd ended the trouble. As a teenager, Asia had saved enough money to purchase a car, whereas Lucy was often scrounging up her leftover allowance to buy fashion magazines that never featured models her size. In college, Asia had organized several student rallies and petitions and been cited by local politicians as an example of civic-minded youth with a bright promise for the future. After graduation, Asia had gone to work for a Fortune 500 company, where she continued to excel.

Lucy often joked, "If you weren't my sister, I'd have to hate you."

Asia invariably laughed. "Luce, you couldn't hate anyone or anything."

Bullshit. Lucy hated *this.* Hated what her sister had endured, would be forced to endure again. Lucy hated that she didn't know what to say, that she was sitting in the mostly empty parking lot of a grocery store clutching a bag of kiwis to her chest and sobbing.

Poor Michael. When he'd encouraged her to go ahead and cry last night, he'd had no idea the floodgates would officially open. Lucy had sniffled her way through morning coffee and lost it completely in the break room at work. (If they didn't want people breaking down there, they should rename it.) Luckily, her coworkers had spotted the diamond engagement ring and assumed she was crying tears of joy.

Not trusting that illusion to hold, Lucy had jumped at the rare opportunity to be out in the field today. Her company was hired by other corporations to send people in as regular shoppers, restaurant patrons, or hotel guests and carefully rate customer service based on preset criteria. Occasionally, the jobs were for nice restaurants, the city zoo, or other fun places, and were given to full-time employees like Lucy as a perk. Other times, the person scheduled to do the "shop" called in sick, or canceled because they'd found a real day job, and Lucy took their place. Mystery shopping could get you some extra cash and a few free groceries or blue jeans, but it wasn't steady income with actual benefits.

When a shopper had informed them this morning that he'd be unable to complete the assignment, Lucy had jumped at the chance to get away and use the time alone to find her composure. *You know you aren't going to feel better until you talk to her.* She dug her cell phone out of her purse. Dialing with one hand, she used the other to rub at the mascara streaks below her eyes.

Shockingly, her sister, who was usually either taking meetings or on the phone, answered on the first ring. "Asia Swenson."

Would anyone else detect the strain beneath her polished tone, or was Lucy simply listening too hard for it? "Hey. It's me."

"Thank God. I thought it was Mom again."

"How many times?"

"Eight. On the last one, she and my assistant set each other off. Fern's still in the restroom bawling. She hasn't been this emotional since the week she got back from maternity leave."

Which put Asia in the position of having to console other people about her own disease. "Guess not everyone responds to crisis as gracefully as you do." Lucy stared through the windshield at a paper bag blowing back and forth between two redbud trees planted to liven up the paved landscape. *I have to find a way to handle this.*

Asia sighed. "Trust me, I'm no expert either. I'm a mess."

Lucy rejected the idea that her sister could be anything other than strong and classy. "If *you're* a mess, I hate to think what that makes us mere mortals. You're practically a . . . a superhero."

"That's so weird. I was thinking this morning that I wanted superpowers."

Like the power to defeat cancer? *God willing.* "You definitely have the legs to pull off tights," Lucy said. "Need a sidekick? I'm no good in a fight, but I can stand around spouting things like, 'Holy robin eggs, Asia!' "

"Hey, you're a hero in your own right," Asia chided. "Remember when that varsity wrestler went out with a majorette behind my back when I had mono senior year? You, all of eleven, were going to sneak out, brave the dark, and toilet-paper his yard to avenge me."

"Yeah, but I screwed it up. I fell out my window and landed in Mom's rosebushes." Lucy felt the phantom sting of all those thorns. She'd suffer them again in a heartbeat—the fall, the painful landing, the rather loud lecture and three-week grounding—if any of it would help Asia.

"You have a heart of gold, Lucy Ann. That's powerful."

Ignoring the lump in her throat, Lucy kept her response airy. "Well, it's settled then. We're both Wonder Women. Heck, the only reason neither of us has scaled Everest is because it doesn't present enough of a challenge."

"Exactly." Asia was quiet for a moment, then said in a voice with less bravado, "There is one Herculean task you could undertake for me, if you can leave work a few hours early tomorrow. Mom's going with me to see Dr. Klamm. It would be better with you there, too."

"Absolutely." As reluctant as Lucy had been last night to get sucked back into the world of cancer treatment, it was actually a relief to help out.

She couldn't battle the disease in her sister's stead, but she could be on hand for moral support, and provide silly diversions. It wasn't much as far as superpowers went, but you had to fight your battles with the weapons God gave you.

"If any of you ladies have further questions, I'm happy to answer them now or by phone later," Dr. Klamm invited. "It's not uncommon for people to realize after our meeting that they forgot to ask something."

Asia knew it was also not uncommon for a family member to have a question he or she wasn't comfortable voicing in front of the patient. She cast a sidelong glance at her mother and sister, glad she'd been able to finagle it so that Lucy was sitting in the middle. She would have felt too claustrophobic between them. She had to admit, though, that Lucy and their mom had both done an outstanding job of holding it together while Dr. Klamm outlined systemic care, which they would use in conjunction with more immediate localized treatments, and possible experimental drugs if she qualified for test studies. Marianne was uncharacteristically calm, taking his comments in stride, and Lucy had cracked one or two jokes under her breath, including the speculation that perhaps their mom's lunch had consisted of supersized Valium.

Asia was a little dazed to think that by this time next week she would already have had numerous radiation treatments.

Last time she was sick, it seemed as though many more tests had been done, options discussed for longer periods before they'd acted. *Guess they don't like to wait around with repeat cases.* Radiation was comparatively easy; she was eager to start fighting back.

Dr. Klamm stood, coming around his desk to shake hands with all three women. He nodded toward the brochures he'd given Asia. "If you have any questions, please call the office. I hope you'll find the reading material reassuring."

Ah, yes, more supplements for her ever-growing "Cancer and You" library.

Nobody said much as they walked outside. They'd met at a nearby restaurant, then all taken Lucy's car, figuring they would save gas by driving together and could have dinner at the restaurant afterward. It had been rainy all day, making the afternoon abnormally dreary.

"I've always liked that Dr. Klamm," Marianne said as they reached Lucy's yellow VW New Beetle. "He seems very competent. And so handsome, too. Don't you think so, girls?"

Asia nodded noncommittally, hoping her mother was making conversation and not thinking in terms of matchmaking. *Asia Klamm? Ye gods.* She'd sound like some sort of seafood special. Besides, she was pretty sure doctors weren't allowed to date patients. And no offense to the man, but when this was over, she wouldn't want reminders.

Besides, when this was over, would any man feel comfortable dating her? Maybe some of the enjoyment she'd taken in her alone time over the summer had been a convenient way to mask her own uneasiness about getting involved with anyone.

Not that it mattered in the here and now. She'd bungee-jump off that bridge when she came to it.

Letting their mom ride shotgun, Asia climbed into the back seat and flipped through the assorted brochures, including one on coping with metastatic disease. A boxed quote in the bottom corner caught her eye, and Asia groaned. Bad move, since it caused Marianne to whip her head around, her green eyes wide with worry.

"Are you all right, dear? Is it pain, or maybe you're just hungry?"

"I'm fine, Mom. Honest. Just noticing something on this pamphlet. 'Some patients live with their metastatic condition for decades.' I don't actually find that reassuring."

"Take heart," Lucy said from the driver's seat. "You probably won't live with it that long."

"Lucy Ann!" Their mother's tone was horrified.

"Th-that's not what I meant," Lucy stammered. "Asia, you know that's not what I meant, right? I wasn't saying you wouldn't live another few decades, just that you'll probably have this beat soon. If anyone can—"

"I know what you meant," Asia interrupted.

"Okay," Lucy said.

But Asia caught sight of her mother's expression in the rearview mirror and knew Marianne wasn't entirely mollified. Her face was reminiscent of an appalled Morris Grigg's yesterday afternoon. She'd met with him and Brandon Peters in Morris's office.

Morris had explained Asia's situation in grim tones, offering Brandon her best clients in a manner that all but ordered Brandon to apologize for a situation that wasn't his fault. As if he'd just been presented a corporate gift but should spend the indefinite future feeling guilty about it.

Instead, the sandy-haired man had shot her a cocky smile, revealing a single dimple. "Be warned. When you're feeling a hundred percent again, don't expect me to hand your customers back on a platter. I may try to keep them. And they may want to stay. People who've been with me tend to like the experience." He'd punctuated it with a wink that would have had the human resources manager hyperventilating and handing out leaflets on sexual harassment.

"Brandon!" Morris had been outraged. "I don't believe that was the appropriate response to your coworker's condition or this turn of events."

"It's all right." Asia had actually been tempted to grin back at Brandon until she'd noticed their boss's expression. "I know he was joking."

No, I wasn't, Brandon mouthed at her with that same twinkle in his gray-blue eyes.

In part, he had been teasing, no matter what he claimed to the contrary. And in part, he was serious about giving her a run for the top clients. Perversely, she appreciated that. Recalling his audacious manner, Asia smiled to herself.

It took her a moment to realize they'd reached the restaurant where all three of them had parked their cars.

"You still feel up to eating out?" Marianne asked, her tone solicitous.

"Yes, I'm up to it. I'm fine," Asia repeated. Well, technically she wasn't. But she'd no doubt utter the reassurance another few million times before this was all over.

Inside, the three of them were immediately seated at a

booth, since they were still early for the Friday night dinner crowd. Marianne excused herself to find the ladies' room, and Asia slid in next to Lucy.

Her sister craned her head to the side, regarding Asia with serious eyes. "You do know what I meant to say in the car, right? It wasn't one of those Freudian slips or anything. Mom just mistranslated."

"Relax, Luce. I actually thought Mom's reaction was kind of funny."

Lucy looked as if she would protest this, but then bit her lip. "Okay, but don't tell *her* that."

"Are you kidding? I don't have a death wish."

This struck them both as ridiculously amusing, and they erupted into giggles—the kind you can share when the joke's not really as compelling as your desire to laugh together. Or when you've been up really late and are both punchy with sleep deprivation.

"We should stop before Mom gets back and asks why we're laughing," Lucy said.

"Poor woman. You just know she wonders where she went wrong, ending up with two daughters with warped senses of humor."

"Must be some loons a few limbs back on the family tree," Lucy speculated. "Every Southern family has a few, don't they?"

"I think it's like a law. But, Luce, seriously? There's something I want to say before Mom returns."

Lucy sobered instantly, as if dreading the worst. "Okay."

"I can't even remember if I said a proper congratulations on your engagement. You and Michael are fabulous together, and I couldn't be happier for you." She spied the telltale shimmer in her sister's eyes. "Do not well up! If you cry, you'll get me started, and then Mom will find us both in tears."

Lucy sniffled. "I don't know what you're talking about. I wasn't going to cry."

"Good. Back to what I was saying, then. By sheer coincidence, it looks as if I'll be easing off my usual sixty-hour work-weeks, so I'll have more time to go dress hunting with you, plan a raunchy bachelorette party, stuff like that. I want this to be the wedding of your dreams. And I want it to be a glad time for you. I'm so, so sorry about the dark cloud I've cast over it."

"Oh, Asia, no. You can't apologize for that. *I'm* sorry that you ... that you ... Dammit."

Asia swallowed, gulping back the tears they'd both sworn not to shed. She hadn't cried since Dr. Klamm had first given her the diagnosis. Maybe she should; maybe it would be cathartic, but not here.

When Lucy was eight years old and a bigger, tougher classmate was "suggesting" Lucy hand over her dessert each day at lunch, Asia had put a stop to it. When Lucy had come to breakfast with a hickey one summer when Asia was home from college, Asia had distracted her parents long enough for her little sister to change her shirt and hide it. Lifelong protective habits didn't break easily.

"Lucy, I don't want to talk about the cancer. Obviously there will be days when it's an unavoidable topic. But let's not bring it up if we don't have to. Let's focus on the wedding. Okay?"

Though she looked skeptical, Lucy eventually nodded. "Okay. If that's what you want."

Feeling less sure now that she'd made her impulsive statement, Asia nonetheless stuck by it, wondering whom she was really trying to protect.

Four

"This is the best thing I've heard in months!" Strawberry-blond Camelia Cameron, who'd been Camelia Barnerfield when she'd roomed with Lucy their sophomore year of college, leaned back in a plush chair that would have swallowed a shorter woman.

Cam gestured excitedly with her half-finished mocha latte; free beverages of the java variety were a perk, no pun intended, of being the manager here. If running a small coffee shop wasn't quite what Cam had expected to do with her BFA in art and design, she seemed content. Plus, her original paintings were displayed for sale on the walls. "Michael is a *dream*. I take total credit for your meeting him."

Lucy laughed. "Technically, it was Dave who caught the cold and gave me his ticket."

"So we're crediting his weak immune system for the best thing that's ever happened to your love life?"

Immune systems. Illnesses. Lucy scowled. It didn't take much of a reminder to bring to the surface what had already been lurking near the top. Ever since the night she'd announced her engagement, low-frequency guilt had become an electric hum in her ears, an ever-present buzzing no one else could hear and that Lucy mostly ignored but couldn't completely silence. *My sister wants me to be happy. I do not have to be sorry that my life is going well.* Yet she couldn't shake the feeling that it was unseemly to run around telling everyone her good news.

Cam set down her mug, uncrossing impossibly long legs. Falling for a man who worked at a gym had done wonders for the woman's figure. She'd always been tall, with a pretty face, but by the time she'd married Dave Cameron two summers ago, she'd become a stunner. She'd been asked to model nude at a local art center, but Dave's near apoplexy at the suggestion had convinced her to decline the offer. "Everything okay?" Cam asked. "For a minute there, your expression wasn't one of prenuptial rapture."

"Are you kidding? I'm thrilled about the engagement." Lucy held out her left hand for another admiring look at the ring. The princess-cut diamond sparkled with everything she should be feeling right now. "I'm the luckiest girl alive. No offense to Dave."

"None taken."

"And I came down not just to tell you the news but to ask a favor. . . . Will you be one of my bridesmaids?" Michael's sister had enthusiastically accepted over the phone, and Lucy had wanted to ask Cam before getting around to the cousins. If she didn't include Reva and Rae, Aunt Ginny would never forgive her (the woman's grudges took on a life of their own and grew over everything in their path, like kudzu), although

Lucy had never exactly been bosom buddies with the identical blond twenty-four-year-olds, despite countless holidays spent together.

Grinning, Camelia clapped her hands together under her chin. "Oh, I was going to be so annoyed if you didn't ask! It'll be fun to relive the drama of a wedding when I'm not actually stressing over the major details. Since I've already been through it, I have all kinds of recommendations, if you want them. If not, I'll butt out. I'm sure your mom and sister will be helping you a lot."

"Yeah. Asia's going to be my maid of honor."

"Naturally. How's she doing these days, by the way? One of the girls here is doing a walkathon, and I thought of Asia when I filled out the pledge form."

Lucy's lips twisted, as if they weren't sure whether to smile bravely or grimace. "She's . . . the cancer has come back. Spread."

"Oh."

"But we've already met with doctors, and her oncologist has pointed out how many treatments are available, how strong she is." How comparatively young, how incredibly healthy she'd always been. *You know, except for the cancer.* "Asia's like you. She takes really good care of herself."

Cam summoned enough cheer to wink mischievously. "Well, it's kind of cheating, being married to a personal trainer. But I'm highly motivated to look at least as good as the gym bunnies he sees every day. You're right about Asia, though. I've never met anyone so . . . If anyone can kick this . . ."

"Yeah." The sentiment, unfinished but unmistakable, was exactly what Lucy had been telling herself.

Cam cleared her throat, then steered the conversation back to its original topic. "So have you and Michael set a date?"

"Not exactly. Mom's waiting to hear back from the church on availability, but we're thinking sometime in January. What better way to start the new year, right?"

"Wow. This coming January? Three and a half months. Are you going to have enough time to make all the arrangements?"

Did anyone ever have as much time as they needed? "Well, I didn't want to give Michael a chance to change his mind."

Her friend scowled. "You shouldn't do that, put yourself down."

"I was kidding." Lucy moved on quickly. "What do you suggest I tackle first? The dress?"

"Well, that and a location."

"Given my parents' longtime membership at the church, I'm reasonably certain there will be an opening."

"For the reception, too? Or do you want to have that somewhere else?"

Good question. There was so much to absorb, from wedding details to Asia's situation to the house-hunting she and Michael had discussed. Lucy was looking forward to finding a place of their own, but the avalanche of change was overwhelming. She reached across to squeeze Cam's hand. "I'm so glad you'll be helping! Mom got married decades ago, and the last wedding Asia attended was yours." Not to mention how busy Asia would be with her own crucial health concerns.

The guilt flared again, briefly, but Lucy tamped it down with forceful optimism. By this time next year she would be a married woman, and, hopefully, Asia's challenges would be behind her.

✑

Asia walked away from her assistant's desk, dropping the smile she'd conjured in response to Fern's joke about rediscovering the joys of caffeine buzzing through her body after having her baby. In four weeks, at the end of her radiation treatments, Asia would start receiving all kinds of drugs into her body. Once the port she'd lived with for so long went back in, there would be a loading dose of chemo. And with the chemo that fought the cancer would come other drugs to fight the side effects of the chemo. It was like that song about the woman who swallowed the cat to get the bird, the dog to get the cat . . . Asia didn't care to think about how the ridiculous song ended.

One of the chemo treatments was a red liquid a nurse euphemistically called punch, probably to make it seem less scary. It had a hell of a punch to it, all right. Patients Asia had known called it by less innocuous epithets—Red Devil, Red Death.

With a shaky sigh, she turned the corner, absently swerving to miss a leafy plant in a large brass barrel and crashing into Brandon Peters standing in her office doorway. She steadied herself with a hand pressed against the doorjamb.

"Sorry about that," he said, taking a quick step back. He raked a brief but intense glance over her, as if seeking reassurance that he hadn't damaged her.

"No, I should have been watching where I was going." People should stop apologizing for circumstances that weren't their fault. With a malevolent glare, she jerked her thumb toward the planter. "That thing's a safety hazard. Is there some reason we can't leave nature *out*side?"

He laughed. "So, after you help me with my client questions, I shouldn't thank you with a plant of some kind?"

"God, no. Especially not flowers." The abrupt words were out of her mouth before she could temper them. She would forever associate the cloying scent of bright blooms with being sick. People had sent them to her in a sincere, considerate effort to bolster her mood. While she appreciated the thought, she'd be perfectly happy never to see another piece of baby's breath.

She forced a smile to soften her manner. "You caught me. I'm not a floral kind of girl. But I don't mind the occasional indoor plant as long as its smaller than Killer here. I have an aloe vera plant at home."

It had been a gift from Charlotte, a patient with advanced metastatic disease whom Asia had met after her lumpectomy, around the time her margins revealed that the cancer was worse than first thought and that removing her entire right breast, at the very least, was necessary. Before Asia's second surgery, Char gave her the aloe plant, nicknamed Al, and a pink T-shirt that proclaimed *Cleavage Is Overrated*. Though Char had been a fighter right up until the end, trying one treatment after another well into her last days, complications from a lung collapse had eventually killed her; the loss had made it impossible for Asia to return to the support group.

Certainly many people survived cancer. Personally she hoped for remission and another thirty years. But already shaky morale deteriorated when those around you, those you allowed yourself to grow close to, were defeated. Fallen soldiers on the battlegrounds of hospital rooms and chemo recliners.

Then there was the risk of guilt when treatments seemed to be working for *you,* while failing others.

At times, Asia simply wanted to distance herself from people with cancer. They were too painful a reflection of conditions and risks she was experiencing; she needed to visualize being healthy again, reclaiming her life beyond the IV bags and the tiny "tattoos" marking her radiation area. Once she'd decided to remain cordial but reserved, it had proven unexpectedly easy to stay superficially friendly with other patients.

Asia had always been respected and well liked among peers and colleagues, popular without the messy intimacy of relationships that could distract her from her goals. There'd been occasional lovers, and she considered her family a tight unit, but all in all . . . She sucked in a breath. Should she be disturbed that she'd honed an ability to keep people at arm's length, or was it an accomplishment that she did so without anyone thinking her cold?

"Asia?" Brandon's solicitous expression made her feel annoyingly delicate.

She snapped back to the discussion at hand. "You said something about client questions?"

He nodded, stepping aside to let her in the office. "I have some information I want to go over. I'm having a face-to-face meeting with one of the transferred clients Friday."

The transferred clients. What a neutral way to sum up the situation. "I keep fairly complete notes," she said as she slid into the chair behind her desk. "I'm happy to answer any specific questions, of course, but everything should be in the files."

"Not everything can be summed up in database fields. There are personality quirks and conversational approaches I should maybe know about." Ignoring the two available seats, he propped his butt onto the corner of her desk.

She raised an eyebrow. "Something wrong with the chairs?"

He cast a cursory glance over his shoulder, then met her gaze with a grin. "Not as far as I can tell."

"If there's something you need to know about, I promise it's in the file."

He raised his own eyebrow in challenge. She honestly couldn't tell if the action was a reflex or if he was mocking her. "Are you being uncooperative because you don't like having the clients reassigned?"

"*Temporarily* reassigned, and I'm not being uncooperative. I'm being protective of my time, which is already being encroached on." Radiation itself didn't take long, but she'd lose hours of work this week just in driving time.

"I don't think we got off on the right foot." He sounded apologetic.

Don't get soft on me now, Peters. "Possibly because you're obnoxious," she speculated. "Only child?"

"I have an older sister, but her husband got transferred to Germany, so she's not close enough to keep me in line." He flashed a smile. "Just think of 'obnoxious' as part of my multi-faceted charm."

"If you can charm the clients, you probably don't need my insight anyway."

Leaning forward as if about to confide a secret, he murmured, "It's rare, but occasionally I encounter some freak of nature who's impervious to the charm."

She laughed, a spontaneous, unladylike guffaw. She'd heard that medieval people believed a sneeze was a demon being expelled from the body; this laugh felt like that. Tonight, in the solitude of her apartment, there would be personal demons happy to haunt her as soon as she made the mistake of lowering her emotional guard. But for now, they'd been exorcised with Brandon's audacious if unsophisticated humor.

Lucy would like him. It was a thought from left field and apropos of absolutely nothing. "All right, you have twenty minutes to ask questions. Then I'm kicking you out to get some real work done."

"See? My charm is irresistible."

Maybe so. For a man who followed his gut more than careful market research, cracked juvenile jokes, and stole her clients, he was surprisingly likable.

"The second Saturday in January?" Thank goodness Lucy was already seated at her mother's cherrywood dining room table, dappled in the late-day sunlight streaming through lacy curtains, because suddenly her legs felt wobbly.

It was one thing to say she wanted to have her wedding as soon as possible, another to set an official date. She wished Michael were here. He didn't even know yet that on the second Saturday afternoon of January, he would become a married man. He was working late downtown tonight, preparing to mediate an employee dispute next week.

Currently, it was only Lucy and Marianne in the Swenson family home; George had left to get in a few rounds of practice before his league bowling. Asia would be joining them later, picking up a pizza after she left the radiology center. One week of treatment down; three more to go before she began the chemo.

"Are you sure you don't want a ride?" Lucy had asked when they spoke on the phone yesterday.

"Look, there's going to come a time in the next couple of weeks when I won't be able to drive myself, so you should probably save up the offers to chauffeur until then."

"Suit yourself, but I was offering for completely selfish reasons. If we don't start talking about bridesmaids' dresses soon, you could end up in something sporting so many ruffles that Scarlett O'Hara would have been offended."

Asia had laughed. "Don't even think about it, Blondie. I would hate to have to take down the bride at her own wedding."

My own wedding.

Lucy felt the prickle of tears and would have groaned at her ridiculously overemotional tendencies if she weren't so euphoric. By Valentine's Day, she'd be a wife! Mrs. Michael O'Malley. Lucy O'Malley. Cam had asked if Lucy, like some of their mutual friends, would hyphenate her name once she was married. Hardly. Swenson-O'Malley was a mouthful . . . although a potentially good name for a pub.

Marianne set down the tray she'd carried from the kitchen, laden with two glasses of iced tea and a warm loaf of home-made zucchini bread, and took her chair. "That's what Doreen said." Doreen was the part-time church employee who served as wedding coordinator, helping schedule the ceremony, run the rehearsal, and give direction on the big day. "The second Saturday, at four. She was pleased as punch to fit you in. So we just have to find a place for the reception."

"Now that I have the exact date, I'll call back some hotels and check ballroom availability," Lucy replied. Cam had joked that if all else failed, she'd close the shop to the public and give them a truly unique coffeehouse reception. At least they had the church secured, an all-important first step. *Just keep moving your feet until you get to the top.* "It means a lot to me that we'll be having our ceremony at the church."

Pastor Bob, the same man who as a young newcomer to their church had confirmed her in grade school, would now see her married.

Marianne patted her daughter's hand. "I'd always hoped both you girls would have your weddings there."

Lucy caught her bottom lip between her teeth, unsure how to respond to her mother's wistful tone or unspoken fear.

"Can I slice you some of this bread?" Marianne asked.

The pizza would arrive soon, and it wasn't as if Lucy needed the extra calories, but she'd never turned down her mama's award-winning zucchini bread. Between bites, they brainstormed. Tomorrow would begin the hunt for the perfect wedding dress.

"What about a theme?" Marianne asked. "For the wedding."

"You mean, other than becoming man and wife?"

"I mean like 'White Christmas.' I always loved that movie."

"Christmas is in December, weeks before the wedding."

Marianne shot her an exasperated look. "Since when are you narrow-minded? I didn't mean Christmas specifically, just the festive romance of the holidays. Lots of white and silver and sparkly snow imagery. Something joyous. That's just what the family needs," she concluded before launching into more suggestions.

Lucy sighed. Not to be melodramatic, but getting married was a sacred affair. She knew she could be a little ... goofy at times, but this was a formal occasion. The longer her mother talked, the more Lucy envisioned a high school dance in a gym decorated with Styrofoam snowflakes.

"Knock, knock," Asia called as she opened the front door half an hour later. "I have pizzas."

"Lucy, go help your sister," Marianne instructed. "I'll get the plates."

Real plates. Lucy had once pulled out paper plates for a pizza night with her mother and sister, and Marianne had fanned herself as though she found the scandal dizzying. *Michael and I will need to register for china.* Lucy grinned, slowing as she passed through the kitchen. They had so many decisions to make, each one bringing her closer to a lifetime with a man she still couldn't believe loved her. Asia met her in the front living room, balancing two large cardboard squares that bore the checkered logo of their favorite pizzeria.

"Hey, Earth to Luce," Asia said as Lucy shook her head to bring herself to the present. "I interrupt a good daydream?"

"I was envisioning shopping for silverware and china."

The disappointment on her sister's face was comical. "And I thought *I* needed to get a life."

Lucy laughed. "Well, Michael was in the daydream, too. That's the part that made me happy. Want me to take one of those boxes?"

As she reached for it, she heard Marianne's voice in her

head, as if she were nine again. *Be careful with that, dear.* The well-meaning reminders hadn't prevented Lucy from dropping things; if anything, they'd made her more jittery. But Lucy was an adult now, even if she and her mother hadn't grown into the relationship of equals that Asia and Marianne seemed to share. Marianne actively consulted her oldest daughter for her opinion, while Lucy sometimes found it difficult to express her own likes and dislikes.

She cast a furtive look over her shoulder, where Marianne was retrieving a head of lettuce and salad dressing from the refrigerator. "Asia, can I ask you something?"

At Lucy's whispered tone, her sister automatically leaned closer. "Sounds serious."

"Not exactly. Do you think I need a theme?"

Asia furrowed her brow. "Did I lose part of the conversation?"

"Mom wants me to have a theme, like snow. Or using lots of green, since Michael's Irish. I was genuinely afraid she might suggest a shamrock bouquet. But she's moved on to my wearing white and carrying a pot of red poinsettias while the bridesmaids do the reverse, all wearing bright red and holding white poinsettias."

"I'm not sure the bride wants to be carrying a 'pot' of anything. Seems less than delicate, doesn't it?"

Lucy sighed in relief. "Then you'll help me talk her out of it? You know she respects your input."

Well, who wouldn't? Asia had impeccable taste.

"Girls?" Marianne called. "Come sit down before the pizza gets cold."

"We'll be right there," they chorused.

Lucy had to remind herself that at work she carried respect and responsibility. Was it just being in this house that made her feel like a kid again? The two-story home with its white columned porch and aged but stately coffee tables and bookshelves, even the area rugs from Dalton (North Georgia's "carpet capital of the world"), held all her childhood memories. It was as if you couldn't truly age here, not with the giggles of adolescent sisters echoing in the silence and the smell of fresh-baked apple pies and spice breads permanently in the air.

"You're woolgathering again," Asia observed.

"Not really, just . . ." Lucy didn't know how to express the brief but sharp moment of nostalgia. "So, about the wedding?"

"I'll add my two cents if you think it will help; that's part of my job as maid of honor. But, Lucy—" Asia broke off, staring beyond to the family pictures that covered the back wall of the living room. Baby photos, holiday portraits, graduations, their lives playing out frame by frame.

"Yeah?"

"Nothing. I'm here for whatever you need."

Lucy followed her sister's gaze to a photo of a dark-haired six-year-old, not a single smudge on her Easter dress, seated on a blanket beneath an oak tree with a drooling baby propped in her lap. "You always have been."

Five

Asia watched her mom study a rack of formal hats. One was a pale pink cap with a long, graceful white feather sweeping down, secured by rhinestones.

Marianne grinned. "I suppose that would be a bit much for the mother of the bride?"

"A bit," Asia agreed.

"Pity. I rather like it." Marianne turned away from the hats. "I'm so glad you had today free to help us pick out Lucy's dress."

Asia looked toward the closed dressing room door. "I am, too, but Lucy would have found something beautiful even without my help."

The way Marianne had been deferring to Asia's opinions all day might have been appropriate if this were *Asia's* wedding. Maybe her mom was simply trying too hard to make Asia feel included, to take her mind off ... things. Ironically, Marianne's subtle and undoubtedly unintentional favoritism was making both her daughters uncomfortable. Every time she made an offhand comment to Lucy like, "If you'll stand straighter, dear, you'll feel thinner." Lucy ducked her head in faint embarrassment. Yet, at the same time, part of Asia was . . . well, envious.

When Asia was eleven, a couple across the street was the first in the neighborhood to get divorced. "They fought sometimes and it didn't mean anything," the couple's daughter had told her on the school bus. "But I knew it was going to be really bad when all of a sudden they let me wear makeup to school and stopped nagging me about studying harder."

The boutique owner emerged from the fitting room. "Here comes the bride!"

Lucy emerged, laced into a brocade bodice with a full skirt in a way that gave new meaning to the term *lift and separate*. She rolled her eyes in Asia's direction. "Well?" Her tone suggested she'd already vetoed the ivory gown.

Marianne goggled at the dress, and the vast acres of cleavage it created. "Lordy, your father and I will be banned from the church if you show up in that."

"I don't know," Asia teased. "I say if you've got it, flaunt it. Not like you're showing nipples."

"Asia!"

"Definitely no nipples at the wedding ceremony," Lucy agreed, returning her sister's grin. "On the wedding *night* . . ."

"Lucy Ann!"

Asia laughed. "Mom, it's her honeymoon. What do you think is going to happen?"

Their mother gestured toward the boutique owner, who was trying to hide a smile. "I don't know what is wrong with you two, but I did not raise my daughters to have these kinds of conversations in front of total strangers."

"Sorry," Asia said dutifully, her spirits lighter than they had been all day.

"I'll just take this one off and try another," Lucy said.

Marianne muttered something that Asia didn't quite hear. Her mother's annoyed tone, however, was gratifying. Like old times.

Several stores—and hours—later, they still hadn't found anything Lucy loved, and as much as Asia fought it, her energy was flagging.

"Perhaps we should call it a day," Marianne suggested as they left a bridal shop franchise in the mall.

Asia caught the look her mother and sister exchanged, the palpable concern between them. "I'll be fine. Might I remind you that Lucy doesn't have much time to find a dress?" No one had articulated why Lucy was determined to plan a wedding in just a few months, but Asia knew it wasn't solely her sister's eagerness to become Mrs. Michael O'Malley.

"We should at least rest," Lucy said. "Let's find seats in the food court, get something to drink, and flip through a few of these magazines I've picked up. Asia, we haven't talked at all about what you want to wear."

Since it was a winter wedding, Asia didn't have to worry about summery, strapless dresses that would reveal scars and send the flower girl running. And, of course, her port would need to be covered. But Lucy had never been one for low necklines, despite the earlier joking. "You just let me know what you have in mind, and me and my boobs-in-a-box will be there for the fittings."

Lucy scanned the atrium, trying to find an empty table in the weekend crowd. "We're not making very fast progress, are we? I feel like my mind just locked up at the prospect of all these decisions—flowers, reception, food, music." She shifted back to her mother and sister, her expression turning to one of self-disgust. Lucy had many talents; a poker face was not among them. "I'm sorry. I know none of those are life-or-death issues."

Marianne blanched at *death*.

"I shouldn't be whining when this is a happy occasion and I've been so blessed," Lucy said miserably.

"Luce. All brides get stressed," Asia said. "It's part of the deal."

If Lucy had been here with Cam or one of her other *healthy* friends, they would have commiserated over the long to-do list and it never would have occurred to Lucy to apologize. Asia had suggested to Lucy a couple of weeks ago that they not mar wedding plans with discussions about cancer, but not talking about it wasn't keeping it out of the conversation.

"Am I late?" Lucy asked as she sidled up next to Michael outside the ticket booth of their favorite movie theater. Her question was strictly rhetorical—of course she was late.

He smiled down at her, the twinkle in his dark blue eyes evident beneath the theater's outdoor lights. "You were worth waiting for. How was your day? The dress shopping a success?"

"Not remotely." She wrinkled her nose. "Would your family be appalled if the bride wore her favorite pair of comfy

jeans to the ceremony?" His family had all seemed ecstatic
about the news when they'd called to tell them about the engagement; his parents were planning a trip here next month in
order to congratulate the happy couple in person.

He laughed. "Jeans? I doubt it would bother any of the
O'Malleys, since we grew up around horse barns. But that
hardly sounds like a dress code for the wedding of your
dreams."

"That was before I saw what I looked like in a mermaid
wedding dress." She shuddered.

"So mermaids are out. That still leaves unicorns, phoenixes,
nymphs. . . ."

She socked him lightly in the arm, taking a step forward as
the line moved. The autumn evening air was crisp and fresh.
After being inside all day, she regretted that they couldn't lin-
ger out here longer instead of crowding into the theater with
everyone else, all eager to see the latest critically acclaimed
drama. In the past, she'd been satisfied with light romantic
comedies where the guy got the girl at the end and the audience was guaranteed a few laughs along the way. On an early
date with Michael, she'd seen her first ever foreign film, complete with subtitles, and later some abstract thrillers that really challenged her to solve the mystery—or even figure out
what the mystery *was*. Michael had broadened her horizons,
yet didn't take himself so seriously that he was above making
bad jokes.

"Your suggestions are worse than Mom's," she chided.
"Don't talk to her or I'll end up with some bizarre magical-
creatures theme and readings from Greek mythology instead
of First Corinthians. My wedding—"

He quirked an eyebrow.

"*Our* wedding," she amended, "should be . . . serious."

"Because we're solemn, upstanding people."

"I don't want to talk to you anymore," she said, managing to keep a straight face. "You're impossible."

"I make you laugh."

He did. Despite how intense he could be about work, he had a definite playful side. Funny, successful, modest. *The best kisser ever.* Honestly, at times he seemed so perfect that part of her was just waiting for the other shoe to drop.

He hugged her close. "Want to split an obscenely large tub of overly buttered popcorn with me?"

"Pass." She had an image of how she'd looked this afternoon in one of the more closely fitted gowns, unflattering ridges making her tummy and butt more pronounced where the fabric didn't lay smooth. "I'm hoping to lose a little weight before the wedding."

For a moment he looked as if he might respond, but he opted not to say anything. He didn't need to, not with the disapproving gaze he tried to lower before she could see. He thought she was too critical of herself. Maybe he had a point, maybe he didn't, but she was at least ten pounds heavier than her doctor would prefer. Whenever she stopped to think about it, Lucy tried to make good choices, but physical health often slipped so far down her list of daily priorities that she was getting ready for bed before she realized that she hadn't taken Cam up on yet another invitation to visit the gym for free and hadn't even done any stomach crunches at home. Maybe with the wedding as a motivator, she could finally turn her nebulous good intentions into a result.

Life made no freaking sense. Asia had always possessed the self-discipline to exercise and eat well. Even as a kid, she would come home on Halloween night, select one piece of candy to enjoy, then save the rest for another night and brush her teeth. *Unnatural.* And yet, years later, she was the one . . .

Lucy snapped her mind shut on the thought, trying to trap it in the dark box of her subconscious. Comparisons like that, regarding circumstances out of her control, weren't going to help anyone. And they certainly wouldn't make her a fun date.

Three hours later, however, as she sat blubbering in the passenger seat, blowing her nose into a napkin from a fast-food restaurant and listening to Michael's apology, she reflected that tonight she would have been better off home alone with a rented comedy.

The articulate lawyer in the driver's seat had digressed into rambling defense. "All I'd heard about the movie was praise about the acting and the writing. You know I don't like spoilers before movies, but if I'd known how it ended . . . Everyone's saying the director's a lock for Oscar and Golden Globe nominations."

"The *director* is a sadistic *bastard!*" Lucy hiccuped, feeling a stray tear drip off her chin and into the neckline of her shirt. "Why do I have to sit through an epic love story rooting for a couple I've become emotionally invested in, only to have one of the characters killed off in the last fifteen minutes?"

"To drive home the classic 'gather ye rosebuds' philosophy? To show that love itself lives on, regardless? Didn't you see *Titanic?*"

"I was asking a rhetorical question." She shot him a watery glare. "And I hated *Titanic*."

"I really am sorry, darlin'. Next time I pick the movie, I'll find someone who's seen it first to ask if the ending meets Lucy standards." Meaning that no children or animals were grievously injured, and the major characters lived to triumph another day.

"Next time? You're forbidden to pick movies from now on. What do you have against comedies? And the Three Stooges don't count," she added.

That drew a brief chuckle from him. "I really do apologize. If I'd known . . ." He stared at the yellow bits of shredded napkin that clung to her shirt, shaking his head ruefully. "Can I make it up to you? Let me take you to the Cheesecake Factory."

Yum. The trendy place got a little crowded for a simple dessert stop, but it was hard to say no to their decadent menu. "And maybe a back rub later?" she bargained with one last, exaggerated sniffle.

He laughed. "Milking this for all it's worth, are you?"

"Hell, yes. You deserve what you get for putting me through that emotional torture. Even if it was well acted and well written." Which, she admitted grudgingly, had definitely been the case.

Michael drove them out of the parking lot, slanting her an inscrutable glance as he turned onto the main road.

"What?" She resisted the urge to pull down the visor and check her appearance in the makeup mirror, knowing that after her tears she probably looked scarier than any special effects in a horror movie.

"I just don't want you to think I'm an unfeeling beast because I view movies like that differently," he admitted. "Dealing with fictional tragedy can be cathartic. And comforting."

Her eyebrows shot up. "Which part of the lovers being tragically separated by death was comforting, husband of mine to be?"

"Because at the end of the movie, you knew everything would be all right, eventually. Not today or tomorrow or ever the same, but all right. People cope."

She swallowed, moved as much by his tone as his words. His displays of emotion would never be as obvious as hers, but he was a sensitive man. Lucy was well aware that people usually adapted when it became necessary. She just hated like hell that it was necessary so often.

Even though the entrance hall was thickly carpeted and Asia was wearing soft-soled canvas shoes with her designer jeans and turtleneck, the MCG building was so quiet that she swore she could hear her own footsteps. All employees who were high enough on the company ladder to have their own offices had access keys, but few people chose to come in on the weekends. If overtime was required, it was often as easy to do it from home using a laptop or company-issued cell phone.

Asia would rather be here. The very building made her feel more connected to the job. *Here* she felt empowered. She'd built a career, made people money, earned the respect of her peers. So even though she'd rationalized that there were some files in her office she could use, maybe this little trip in today was more about ego.

I can live with that.

Strolling down a side corridor—which was dim but for the natural illumination filtering through vertical blinds—she was surprised to see light spilling out of Brandon's office. She paused outside his half-closed door, tapping on the wall beneath his gold-and-black nameplate to get his attention.

He looked up from his laptop, the long-sleeved Braves pullover he wore giving him a boyish air. His hair was different today, too, she realized. Normally he must use a smidge of styling gel to tame it; now it was affably rumpled, if not long enough to be shaggy.

"Hey, Asia."

She grinned at the picture he made, thinking that if she'd seen him like this early on, she wouldn't have considered him a threat all those times he'd been her main competition for a plum client. Her smile faded as she realized that most of her clients had become his anyway. *Only temporarily.* When she came back from her latest medical challenges stronger than ever, she'd give Brandon a run for his money—no matter how unexpectedly cute he was on a Sunday afternoon.

"I didn't think anyone came in on the weekends anymore," she admitted, her own presence notwithstanding.

"Sometimes I work from home, but here's better." He flashed a smile. "Here there's no big-screen TV with the game on. I've got some catching up to do, so the fewer distractions, the better."

She'd selfishly thought in terms of how his taking on her key customers had affected *her,* but his workload had to have increased exponentially. "I won't keep you; just thought I'd say hi."

"Glad you did. This place is a little creepy when there's no one here. Like the silence in a university library."

Feeling a moment of pleasant nostalgia, she leaned against the doorjamb. "I loved studying in the college libraries. Not in the main sitting areas, where half the freshman class met to work on group projects, but way back in the stacks, where you could be completely alone with hundreds of years' worth of knowledge."

"Actually, I think it was that completely-alone part that creeped me out," Brandon admitted. "I did most of my studying at the frat house, scarfing down pizza and trying to figure out how to get a hot girl to be my lab partner."

"Sounds like you," Asia said with an eye roll.

"Well, in my defense, I always tipped the pizza guy well and made sure I pulled my weight with the lab reports."

That sounded like him, too. As she headed down the hall, she pondered whether Brandon was better at balancing than she was. For all his success at work and competitive spirit, he still managed to have fun.

I have fun. No examples sprang to mind, but so what? She'd been preoccupied.

She'd fit fun into her schedule later; right now, she had a lot of work to do. She unlocked her office door and flipped the switch. Maybe Brandon didn't have quite the social life she imagined. After all, his fraternity days were well behind him, and here he was in the office on a beautiful Sunday, same as she.

Once she was settled in at her desk, she was delighted to find herself in the zone, where her thoughts were coming lightning-fast yet making perfect sense. She jotted notes to herself about calls she wanted to make during the week and suggestions she had for clients. Either she would phone them or give the notes to Brandon so that he could follow up on her brainstorms. She'd been pleasantly surprised that he was so receptive to her ideas.

The afternoon flew by, and when Brandon's voice jarred her from an e-mail she was composing, she was surprised to notice that outside her window, it was already growing dark.

"Maybe I shouldn't have interrupted," he said ruefully. "You looked pretty lost in thought."

"I don't mind." Now that she'd been pulled out of her trancelike state, she realized her body was sore. Some yoga stretches were in order, but not while she had an audience. "In fact, I hadn't realized it was so late."

He nodded. "I probably would have kept going if it weren't for my stomach growling. I was thinking of grabbing dinner at a sports bar somewhere. Just because I missed the game doesn't mean I can't catch the scores."

She wondered if he was referring to football or the post-season baseball play-offs. Though she'd given more than one customer tickets to a sporting event or even attended with potential customers, she didn't follow many team sports. Loved the Olympics, though.

"You're welcome to join me, if you'd like," Brandon added.

"What?"

"For food. I'm headed out for a bite to eat, so I thought if you were hungry, too . . ."

"Oh." She didn't know why the invitation startled her; she had business lunches and dinners all the time. If she'd had on one of her power suits, the offer wouldn't even have given her pause. Today she was without her armor. Maybe it was stupid to put stock in what she was wearing, but after all the physical changes that had been inflicted upon her, she used whatever she could to keep from feeling . . . *exposed,* her mind supplied, although it wasn't the word she would have consciously chosen. "Thanks, but I have dinner plans."

Since Brandon looked politely skeptical, she elaborated. "My mother's prayer group at church likes to be helpful. I've had two casseroles delivered to my apartment this week, and my freezer isn't all that big. If this continues, I'll be up to my eyeballs in pasta dishes that don't fit in the fridge."

He laughed. "Too much free home-cooked food. Now there's a problem most bachelors wouldn't mind having."

"I can bring you leftovers for lunch tomorrow."

"No argument here," he answered as he turned to go. "I'll be the guy with a fork and a rapturous expression."

Brandon didn't realize he was doing *her* the favor, she thought as she heard the elevator ding, the doors opening to let him in. When Southern women felt helpless in the face of bad news or tragedy, they cooked. And apparently cooking individual portions was next to impossible. None of the ladies who had brought her baked goods and entire prepared meals after her surgery seemed to realize it was just her and Al, who required only plant food. At least she'd always had plenty to share when Lucy or her parents visited. Actually, considering how many friends, colleagues, and former classmates she knew after living in the same city for over thirty years, it was sort of amazing there hadn't been more people to share with, but she'd deliberately limited the number of people who saw her at her worst. She'd been too tired to be any kind of hostess,

and she'd wanted to spare others the discomfort of not knowing what to say and the impulse to tell her she was looking
good when that was an obvious lie.

Sound logic, she thought now, reflecting on how few people
she'd let in during her last bout with illness. But . . . why hadn't
she seized the opportunity to have more guests over once she
was healthy again? Well, she'd just add it to her to-do list, after beating cancer, being the best maid of honor she possibly
could, and scheduling some spontaneous fun into her life. No
problem at all for a superheroine like Asia Jane.

"Of course, for the reception, we would open up both halves of
the room," explained Mr. French, the extremely tall manager.
At the moment, the hotel ballroom was divided by a partition,
with some kind of meeting in progress on the other side.

As Mr. French rehashed their pricing options with her parents, Lucy wandered farther into the room, her pumps clicking
on the laminate flooring that resembled wood. Mr. French had
turned the lights all the way up, but she had an active imagination.
It was easy to envision the chandeliers dimmed, the deejay Cam
had recommended set up in the far corner, her friends and family
chatting with Michael's along the buffet, while Lucy laughingly
insisted that, as the groom, Michael was obligated to dance with
her. He wasn't fond of dancing in public, but he compromised by
pulling her into his arms whenever they were at her house or his
condo and a song she liked came on the radio. Well, more often
at his condo than her house, since at her place they were likely to
trip over a basket of laundry or reports she'd stacked next to the
couch to read.

Her cell phone chirped and she grabbed it, knowing who it was before she saw the caller ID. "Hey, I was just thinking about you."

Michael's chuckle was self-deprecating. "Because you were mentally cursing me for being late? Again." They'd planned to meet earlier in the week to put together their registry and have a late dinner, but he'd been running behind even before the hour he spent in traffic.

"It's okay. I know how important these mediations are to you."

"Not just me. An entire company." The excitement in his tone grew, his words coming faster. "I feel like I made a real difference, Luce, that we're helping improve policy for— sorry. First I stand you up. Then I can't shut up about work."

She grinned. "You're forgiven, Counselor."

"You're entitled to more than an over-the-phone apology. I would stop and buy roses," he said, knowing how much she loved flowers, "but then I'd only be later than I already am. Go ahead and make the decision without me. I trust you and your parents. Are they annoyed I'm not there?"

"No." She glanced over her shoulder. "Dad's excited that I'm marrying a good provider, and Mom's busy drawing upon generations of frugal instincts to negotiate the catering menu and contract. The manager refuses to lower the price on the ballroom, but he offered us a major discount if we want to stay in their honeymoon suite after the reception. You should see it—Jacuzzi-style tub big enough to throw a party in, huge, heavenly bed. Gives a girl ideas. Like how you can make it up to me for being late." The tub at her place might not be as fancy as the one upstairs, but with some well-placed candles and bubble bath, it could still provide a sensual setting.

"Be careful with that tone," Michael drawled in an equally husky timbre. "It makes me think of you naked. And I'm trying to drive."

Her laugh echoed in the ballroom, and she darted another look toward her parents and the manager, feeling delightfully naughty. "Well, concentrate on the road for now. We can talk about the naked part tonight."

"Tonight," he agreed, his voice a caress. "Wow. I'm late but instead of my fiancée yelling at me, I'm getting sex? I am the luckiest man in Georgia."

"You knew I wouldn't be mad," she said. "Just try to be on time when we meet the real estate agent."

"I'll be there five minutes early," he vowed. "There's nothing more important to me than the home we'll make together."

Statements like that were why she adored him. In school, guidance counselors had asked her about the Future—an ominously capitalized word that represented questions for which she had no answers. Now it stood for her and Michael and the many happy memories they'd make together. No longer a question mark but a fantastic journey.

"Lucy?" Marianne asked, as her daughter hung up the cell phone. "The paperwork is all in Mr. French's office. Are you ready?"

"Absolutely." *Future, here I come.*

Six

Asia slid between the sheets, so boneless with exhaustion that she didn't even change clothes first. Merely kicking off her shoes inside the front door had sapped her energy.

Not that she'd had much to begin with. When Brandon had stopped by her office today, something he found reasons to do with increasing frequency, he'd caught her staring into space.

"You okay, Swenson?"

"Fine." At least the rote answer didn't require any mental effort.

"Liar," he'd chided. But he'd respected her unwillingness to discuss it, instead asking her opinion about a merger that had been announced.

The truth was, if it weren't for her radiation appointment this afternoon, she would have considered leaving work early to come home for a nap. Now she was finally in bed. Though radiation wasn't nearly as physically taxing as some other cancer treatments, she felt achy. *Get some rest; tomorrow will be better.*

She heard Brandon's inflection in her head: *Liar.* Tomorrow would be another radiation appointment, another day of somebody, somewhere, asking how she was doing. *Then quit moping and talk to someone who will actually understand.*

Inhaling deeply, Asia pulled herself into a sitting position. She retrieved her laptop, carried it back to bed with her, and reached across cyberspace to find out if her long-neglected friends would still welcome her to their bosoms. No irony intended.

From: "Asia Swenson"
To: [BaldBitchinWarriorWomen@wwwgroups.com]
Subject: news
Hi, ladies, it's been a while since anyone posted to this group. I hope that's because everyone's doing spectacularly well and having a busy fall, especially those of you with kids back in school. Unfortunately, I've had a bit of bad news.

She stopped. A bit of bad news? *And global warming is just a couple of balmy afternoons.* Still, her relapse was what it was. E-mailed histrionics full of doom and gloom weren't going to help anything. What should she type? *The worst has happened, girls!*

Baloney. The news Dr. Klamm had given her could have been far more devastating. People who died suddenly or in accidents received no warning at all. Some who were sick never got the chance to fight.

With a sigh, she returned to her e-mail. Maybe seeing her situation in black and white would give her the perspective she needed. Or, barring that, piss her off enough to regain her fighting spirit.

Recent tests reveal that it's back. There's been some
spread into bone, but I've been undergoing radiation and
will start chemo again soon. I'm trying to stay hopeful.

Funny, she'd *meant* to type, *The doctors and I are hopeful.*

I hope this message doesn't depress or scare anyone, but
I needed to tell people who would understand.
Wish me luck!
Asia

The first response popped up about two minutes later, un-
surprisingly from Deborah, their spunky, fifty-something loop
moderator. Deb, the oldest among them, had been celebrating
becoming a grandmother the week her mammogram results
returned, and she'd resolved immediately that cancer was taking her nowhere, as she planned to spend many years spoiling
her new granddaughter. It was her honest blog posts that had
encouraged Asia to comment; it was Deb who'd eventually set
up and named their e-mail loop. Karin, a recently divorced
single mother, had been another blogger in the same community, and she'd mentioned the burgeoning e-group to Thayer,
a friend of a friend of a friend. Some people, upon learning
you had cancer, automatically tried to put you in touch with
anyone else they'd ever known with the disease. It was the
world's weirdest variation of blind dating.

Oh, you should have lunch with my husband's cousin's roommate.
She had ovarian cancer. You two have so much in common!

As with first dates, sometimes the initial encounters were
hellishly awkward and barely lasted until dessert, while other

introductions led to long talks that were so natural, participants quickly forgot they'd just met.

After Thayer joined the loop, she'd brought along the last addition, Liz, about Asia's age and the mother of a toddler. Liz described herself as "disgustingly fragile" after enduring an emergency C-section, months of postpartum depression, then a breast cancer diagnosis all in under two years. Thayer and Liz had met on a message board where patients frequently exchanged information and asked about one another's experiences with different treatments and medications.

Amazing how important these strangers had become to one another. Asia had been as happy for the other four women when they received cancer-free blood work as she had been for herself, and several months ago they'd thrown a teasing "cybershower" for Karin, e-mailing pictures of ridiculous gag gifts. The silver lining of Karin's disease had been that it brought her and her ex-husband closer than they'd been when they were actually married, prompting him to propose again and give their life together a second chance.

Who understood the value of a second chance more than a woman who'd faced down death—or at least the very tangible possibility of it?

From: "Deborah Gene"
To: [BaldBitchinWarriorWomen]
Subject: Re: news
Oh, sweetie, you hang in there and let us know if there's anything we can do!
D.

For no logical reason other than that Deborah had always had such an empowered attitude, seeing her name on the screen made Asia feel stronger. It was like floating adrift in space, with only your thoughts and the cold stars for company, and suddenly receiving a radio transmission that let you know you weren't alone in the universe. Asia gathered the willpower to heat some soup and was actually reading more online about the merger Brandon had mentioned when the second message pinged.

From: "Thayer R."
To: [BaldBitchinWarriorWomen]
Subject: Re: news
Asia,
I'm so sorry to hear this, but of course you should feel free to share this news! I can only imagine what you're going through. I had a scare about six weeks ago that turned out to be nothing, but the entire time I was waiting for test results, I was trying to come to grips with going through it all again. I know you can do this. You've always been so strong—and we're here for you on the days when you don't feel like you are!
Hugs,
Thayer

That evening brought two messages from Liz, sent within five minutes of each other, according to the time stamps.

From: "MommyLiz"
To: [BaldBitchinWarriorWomen]

Subject: Re: news
Asia, I am sorry to learn of this turn of events and will cer-
tainly say a prayer for you.
Liz

From: "MommyLiz"
To: [BaldBitchinWarriorWomen]
Subject: Leaving the group
I feel awful for typing this, but I wanted to at least be woman
enough to say it honestly and not slink off into the night.
Every day I've been given with Johnny and our baby girl is
a gift, and I know that. But it's a gift with strings, because
every day I wonder if and when the cancer's coming back.
Whenever I wake up with the slightest ache, I wonder if
that's a tumor pressing against something inside. I wonder
if it's all going to start again and if my Hannah will have
to grow up without her mother. So far the doctors assure
me the cancer is still gone. I wish they could take the fear
away, too. So, I'm sorry, Asia, I really am, but I can't be
here for this. I am more grateful than I could ever express
for the way you were there for me during the scariest time
of my life, which makes me selfish and hateful because
I can't return the favor. It's been an uphill battle, not just
physically but emotionally, and I've clawed myself up to
where I am today. I'm not strong enough to handle anything that could pull me back down. As much as I love
you guys, Hannah needs me more, and I can't risk being
that person again, crying so much she's scared to come
near me. I'll be unsubscribing myself from the e-mail loop
as soon as I send this, so you don't have to respond, but

please know you're all in my prayers. And in my heart, for
whatever it's worth.
Liz Bennett

To that, no one had any response. Asia thought about
e-mailing Liz privately to say it was okay, that she understood.
Even though the desertion stung more than she would have
expected, wasn't this the same reason Asia hadn't gone to the
support group after Char died? There was a fine line between
possibility and reality, hoping it didn't happen to you and
watching it happen to someone else.

While certain facts had to be accepted, there was a valid
time for denial, too. If avoiding Asia helped Liz on her own
road to recovery, Asia couldn't honestly fault her for that. *At
least I still have Deb and Thayer.* Karin Dawb never e-mailed.

A week later they found out why.

From: "Thayer R."
To: [BaldBitchinWarriorWomen]
Subject: Re: Karin
Girls, I'm afraid I'm writing with sad news tonight. After
Asia's post last week, I realized how long it's been since
I spoke to Karin, which I attributed to her being a newly-
wed and making up for lost time with Paul and their son,
Jess. But it nagged at me, that once I got my cancer-free
diagnosis I let my friendships with you all lapse, so I called
her. Paul returned my message yesterday. Karin's cancer
recurred, growing fast, with mets in her brain. He said it
happened so quickly she barely suffered. I know we all
cared about her and will feel her loss, but the way she

seized life remains an inspiration to me. Paul said that he and Jess will always be grateful for the way their family was reunited before the end, these precious happy months they've shared. We can be glad for that.

Thayer

Asia lowered the lid of her laptop with trembling hands and swallowed thickly. She took a minute to offer up a silent, wordless prayer for Karin. The first warrior down.

Seven

Lucy exchanged an exasperated glance with her sister, but the customer service rep on the phone in front of them remained oblivious. She'd been more or less ignoring their presence since the moment they'd stepped up to the registry desk. The most annoying part was that they didn't even need her help to fill out Lucy's information. They'd done that through a computer at an automated booth. They needed only a scan gun to capture UPCs for the registry.

Earlier, Lucy and Michael had wandered a pricey department store with a sleek-haired woman in a red suit taking notes on what dishes, fine stemware, and bedroom linens they'd chosen. But Lucy was also putting together a second registry at a more practical, less chic store. She'd driven Asia to her last radiation appointment of the week, and now the two women were going to tackle the aisles of bathroom throw rugs, blenders that were affordable yet sturdy enough to crush ice for primo daiquiris, and various other sundry household items. Because Michael was a bachelor who'd spent more time at work than home until he'd met Lucy, and because Lucy had had roommates for most of her adult life, pooling her belongings with others', there was actually quite a bit the two of them needed.

Wishing vindictively that she was here on an official mystery-shopper evaluation, Lucy cleared her throat.

The bespectacled redhead behind the counter shot them an annoyed look, punctuated by an upheld pointer finger in the universal You'll-have-to-wait-a-minute sign.

"I have news for her," Lucy muttered to her sister. "If she doesn't get off that phone in the next thirty seconds, we're taking this registry elsewhere."

Asia grinned. "Oooh, you're not turning into one of those high-maintenance bridezillas, are you? 'Cause I have to say, I'd be kind of impressed."

"Some days high-maintenance and demanding sound fun. Honestly, I could have registered in the time she's spent on that call. I could have been married by now."

"It's the job of the maid of honor to make the bride's life easier, right?" Asia took a step forward, approaching the woman. "Excuse me? Is your manager working this evening?"

The woman's lips thinned as she put the caller on hold. "Is there something I can help you with?"

Asia gave a pointed look at the registry sign. "Well, we were thinking we might *register*."

"Bridal, or"—the woman peered over her glasses at Lucy, trailing her gaze down over the loose-fitting tunic top she'd worn to work with slacks—"baby?"

"Bridal," Asia said. "Now, if you could just hand me a gun?"

Lucy smothered a laugh, thinking that only her big sister could make a bar-code scanner sound intimidating. But the woman deserved to be shot—with a high-powered water gun, at the very least—if she'd just implied that Lucy looked pregnant.

"I am doing something about my weight," she resolved as she and Asia strode toward the far left aisle. The plan was to start at one end and systematically work their way to the other. Lucy had a tentative list, but she was sure there were goodies she and Michael had overlooked.

"Doing what?" Asia asked.

"Trying to lose it."

Asia shook her head with a half smile. "I inferred that part, Blondie. But how? Diet, exercise, gym membership? Please tell me you're not taking some weird pill that promises ten pounds gone in three days."

"I haven't worked out a comprehensive plan just yet, but I thought I'd buy a bathroom scale while we're here. We could price treadmills, too. And my supervisor's birthday was on Wednesday. A group of us took her to lunch, but I refused a piece of the cake." Yeah, with discipline like hers, she should waste away to a size two in practically no time.

"Gotta start somewhere," Asia said with a smile. She spun the scanner around her hand, Wild West style. "Speaking of which, see anything yet that screams gotta-have-me?"

Lucy wrinkled her nose. "Not so much." She hoped Michael approved of anything she chose; after a year together she had a handle on his tastes. He'd been more than willing to help her pick the big-ticket items, but as a guy, his threshold for shopping went only so far.

"We might as well walk up the rest of the aisle," Asia said. "Wouldn't want to miss anything. Besides, you can put it toward today's exercise quota."

Several aisles later, Asia had zapped a stainless-steel push-pedal trash can into the registry, and a couple of attractive soap dishes. Then she'd handed Lucy the scanner, unconsciously taking turns the way Marianne had admonished them to do their entire lives.

When they found themselves staring down a row of diapers, flat boxes of to-be-assembled cribs, and stroller accessories, Lucy chuckled nervously. "Don't need any of this stuff just yet."

"You sure?"

"What kind of question is that? of course I'm sure!" Damn, did *everyone* think she looked pregnant?

"Okay. You just seemed . . . as if maybe you had something you didn't know how to say."

"Don't be silly. I can tell you anything."

Asia stopped, gentle stubbornness evident in her expression and unmoving body. "So why the face when you saw all the baby stuff?"

"I don't know what face you mean."

"It was a lot like that painting *The Scream,* only without the hands pressed to your cheeks."

Lucy pointed the scan gun at her sister, making *pshu-pshu* sound effects. "Maybe I looked the tiniest bit anxious, but it wasn't *that* bad."

"Anxious about children? Michael's not pushing you to start thinking about a family immediately, is he?"

"Oh, nothing like that. I know he wants kids—we both do—but he's not the pushy sort."

"Good." Asia's stance relaxed a little, and Lucy wondered if her protective older sister had even realized she'd tensed. "Because you're not even thirty! You guys have plenty of time."

Time enough to grow up?

Some days Lucy didn't feel adult enough to be responsible for herself, much less another living being. Oh, she got to work on time and was in a monogamous, committed relationship . . . but there was a part of her that still wanted to spend Saturdays in her pajamas. Or say, "Screw cooking" and just open a package of Oreos for dinner. She must be some strange genetic glitch in her family; Asia had been mature since toddlerhood. Possibly Marianne could be persuaded to consider an Oreo dinner, as long as it was set out on china plates and they poured milk from one of her pretty glass pitchers.

"I'm not sure I'll be a good mother," Lucy admitted. It would be so like her to lock her keys in the car while her daughter was still strapped in the baby seat, or accidentally drop a red sock into a load of light blue rompers, turning half her son's wardrobe a particularly girlie shade of lavender.

Asia's dark eyebrows shot upward. "Are you kidding? You're a warm, loving person. I've always thought you'd make a great mother."

"Really? Thanks. You know, not long ago Mom was saying the same thing about you."

Lucy wasn't sure why she felt compelled to respond that way, when parenthood was probably the last thing on Asia's

mind these days, except that praise always ruffled her. Returning compliments was often the most comfortable deflection.

"I don't know." Asia ran her fingers over a fleecy blanket of
the palest yellow. "I tend to be something of a perfectionist."

"One of the reasons I've always looked up to you."

"But *you're* not afraid to make a fool of yourself."

Lucy frowned, sensing both insult and admiration in the
statement. "Am I going to have to shoot you with the scanner
again?"

"Kids need adults to be silly with them sometimes. They
need to know it's okay to make mistakes. Luce, do you think
I'm too . . . stiff?"

"With all that yoga? You're the most flexible person I
know."

"Lucy."

"Sorry." Lucy was at a loss, because the question had caught
her off guard. Asia was always so purposeful, so sure of herself.
"There's nothing wrong with you. Everyone, myself included,
adores you. Your doctors and nurses rave about what a great
patient you are. Half the people in our lives—parents, teachers—have always wished I were more like you."

"See, this is why you're going to be a good mom—because
you could have been resentful, but you have a bigger heart
than that."

Lucy grinned broadly. "Who said I don't resent you? I resent the hell out of you, you overachieving freak."

Asia chortled, the sound musical in Lucy's ears, since it
meant the topsy-turvy moment had passed.

"Let's get off this aisle," Lucy said, suddenly in a hurry
to be away from the tiny spoons and rubber nipples before

the conversation got even more surreal and she found herself tearfully offering to be a surrogate mother for her sister's baby.

Okay, no more weepy Lifetime movies for me right before bed.

On their way to small kitchen appliances, Lucy stopped in front of a novelty shower curtain, creamy orange printed with the cartoon of an old woman wrapping herself in one "corner" of the curtain and screeching in the dialogue bubble over her sudsy head, DON'T YOU KNOW TO KNOCK FIRST?

"Yech. Surely you're not thinking about registering for *that!*"

Lucy grinned. Something in the woman's exaggeratedly cantankerous expression amused her. "Maybe."

"I hope you're kidding." Asia peered at the wrinkled figure. "How exactly is an eyesore like that necessary?"

"It's fun," Lucy protested, even though her husband would probably have grounds for annulment if she started filling their new house with décor like this. It would make pictures of dogs playing poker seem classy in comparison. "Weren't you worried a few minutes ago that you might need to loosen up?"

Asia pursed her lips, considering. "You've shown me the error of my ways. I think it's more important for me to retain good taste. Besides, some things are so deeply ingrained in a person, there's probably no realistic way to change them."

By mid-October, Asia's life seemed like a movie captured on warped videotape, speeding up without warning in some places and slowing to a near stop in others. The days when she felt good flew by—a blur of working, consulting with Dr. Klamm, helping Lucy look for her as-yet-undiscovered perfect dress, taking Fern to lunch on her birthday, giving an opinion on wedding invitations, and going in for the suggested prechemo dental appointment. Other days lagged unbearably, even the simplest tasks beyond her abilities, depression a seductive misery that sometimes lured her into its tentacles despite her better intentions. Though she was still putting in something loosely resembling regular work hours—if not *her* regular hours—she normally went to bed soon after getting home and heating herself a piece of casserole du jour.

Then there was the strange push-pull she'd felt regarding the start of her chemotherapy treatments. Knowing what the experience had been like the last time around, she'd dreaded going through it again. But chemo was the next weapon in her war against cancer, the next altitude marker on her personal climb. Today—Thursday—had been the first of her new weekly cycle.

She'd hoped for Fridays, but she'd been one of dozens of patients to have the idea of having treatment on Friday and using the weekend to recover, so the clinic hadn't been able to fit her in. Much as it galled her to admit it, this other arrangement would probably work better, since the more chemo she had, the longer it took her to bounce back. She could work from home on Fridays, then get the rest she needed over the weekend and return to the office Monday in peak form.

In the future, Marianne would accompany her to most visits, so Lucy wouldn't miss as much work, but Asia's sister had insisted on being there today. Lucy had spent the afternoon in a chair next to Asia's mauve recliner, joking with nurses and other patients, and flipping through bridal magazines in search of ideas. They'd concluded that Lucy would use silk flowers for her ceremony, rather than real ones.

"With one of the ladies from church helping me do the arrangements, silk is cheaper and gives me more options," Lucy had said, adding with an almost shy smile, "Plus, that way I get to keep my bouquet forever."

Best of all, in Asia's grateful opinion, there wouldn't be the overpoweringly sweet perfume of fresh flowers.

"You all right?" Lucy asked, flicking a concerned gaze toward the passenger seat as she drove Asia home.

"I'm fine. I told you, I don't get sick immediately. With the meds they gave me, maybe I won't get sick at all." If she did, she prayed the medicine would mask the worst of it.

"Okay, just checking. You're awful quiet. Tired?"

"No. I ran out of things to say." She appreciated that Lucy had been trying to keep her spirits up with an animated running dialogue all day, but Asia craved some peace. "Actually, maybe I am more tired than I realized. I'll just close my eyes and catch a catnap."

"Absolutely!" Lucy took the hint. "I'll be as quiet as a mouse and let you rest."

Thank God. Now, if only Asia could bring her mind to a rest. Instead it was careening all over the place, bumping drunkenly into sharp corners before staggering off in another direction.

Brandon had been away from the office for the last few days, sent to Texas to try to sign a high-dollar client. He'd been due back today, and she wondered how it had gone. Halloween was coming up soon; would she look ghoulish enough by then

not to need a costume? Her appetite had been decreasing over
the last couple of weeks, even though radiation didn't make
her nauseous. Still, she'd forced herself to eat, knowing how
critical nutrition was right now; she didn't want a lecture from
Dr. Klamm.

"Asia?"

She started, surprised to find the car stopped in front of her
condo building. "I'm awake now."

"You looked so peaceful I thought about just driving in circles," Lucy said. Then she grinned sheepishly. "But you know
me—always waiting until the last minute to refill the gas tank.
I'm not sure I have enough fuel left for pointless circling."

"No, better for the environment this way, not to mention
I'd probably be more comfortable in my bed."

Lucy's hand hovered over the gearshift. "Want me to come
in with you? I'm happy to, but I thought . . . you might be a
little tired of my company by now."

A shaft of guilt pierced Asia for wanting her sister to shut
up earlier. "Was I being snappish?"

"No, nothing like that. I just wanted you to know that I'm
willing to stay, but my feelings won't be hurt if you'd rather
have the time alone."

"Thanks, Luce. I probably don't deserve you for a sister."

"Then it works out karmically, because I'm sure I don't deserve Michael for a husband."

"Baloney. You're perfect for each other."

Lucy shot her a tight smile. "Let's hope his parents think so."

The O'Malleys would arrive in town tomorrow night.
They had a full weekend planned, starting with the Georgia
Aquarium and Stone Mountain, then, the following morning,

a tour of the Margaret Mitchell House. Michael's mother had reportedly read *Gone With the Wind* so many times the pages had started to fall out of the binding, yet she refused to throw away her original copy, even when her children got her a replacement one Mother's Day. Sunday afternoon, Marianne and George were hosting a late lunch for Lucy's future in-laws.

"You can't be nervous," Asia said. "I thought they liked you fine when you met them before?"

"That was one dinner. We weren't serious enough last holiday season for me to go home with him. There's a difference between getting along with your son's date over a meal and approving of her as the person he'll be spending the rest of his life with."

"You're psyching yourself out. To dislike someone as sweet as you are, they'd have to be puppy-kicking evildoers. Since they raised a great guy like Michael, I think it's safe to assume they're not."

"You're right. You're always right. I'm just nervous." Lucy let out her breath. "See you Sunday?"

"Wouldn't miss it." Asia opened the car door, hoping that seventy-two hours from now didn't find her bent over a plastic bucket and regretting that promise.

By noon the next day, she still felt passably decent. Lethargic and sore, but not much worse than she'd experienced during really bad bouts of PMS. She'd only recently started having regular periods about a month before her relapse; cancer protocols could trigger faux menopause, although women as young as she was usually bounced back once they completed treatment. Funny, she didn't feel very young today.

You can get through this, she told herself, opening her refrigerator and bypassing a half gallon of reduced-acid orange juice in favor of bottled water. *You* will *get through this.* She had before and she would again, as many times as necessary. As pep talks went, hers fell flat. The thought of indefinite chemotherapy wasn't all that . . . peppy.

The kitchen phone ringing provided a welcome distraction. Brandon's cell phone number popped up on caller ID. She grinned, happier to hear his voice than she would have expected. After she'd followed through on her offer a few weeks ago to take him leftovers, they'd fallen into a semiregular habit of having lunch at the office together, microwaving the best casseroles Southern housewives could devise and talking client strategy.

"Hey, Peters," she said into the phone. "Let me guess. You're lost without my guidance and called to ask advice about something."

"Don't you sound plucky for a woman who didn't even bother coming in today." The smile in his voice supplied her mind with an instant visual.

" 'Plucky'? You're being deliberately annoying again."

"Too bad you're not here or you could give me the patented Asia Swenson glare in person."

"Patent pending," she corrected tartly. "Yesterday was a chemo day."

"So you took yesterday off *and* today? Slacker."

"You know, cell phone reception is notoriously unreliable. We may become disconnected," she bluffed. If she couldn't physically be at the office, being on the phone with him was the next best thing.

"All right, but then you won't find out how it went in Dallas, and we both know you're dying to hear if MCG signed Howzer."

"Like I don't know already? You're calling to gloat. If you'd failed to nab them, you'd be avoiding me."

"This isn't gloating; it's sharing the victory with a fellow teammate. You've gotta start following more sports, Swenson."

She snorted. "I'll add it to my to-do list."

"What else do you have on that list for today?"

"I have some calls to make." And if she got seriously ambitious, she might change out of the comfy terry-cloth robe and put on real-people clothes. Oh, the high-stakes drama!

"I'll stop tying up your line, then. But I wondered if there was room in your schedule for a celebratory dinner? I'd ask you to lunch, but I'm actually on my way to a meeting now."

Dinner? It was the second time he'd issued such an invitation. "I don't think so." She enjoyed their lunches together, but that was at the office. Not so . . . *Social? Personal? Threatening?*

The answering silence made her feel as if she owed him more of an explanation, which she instantly resented. If he'd meant dinner in terms of a date, a flattering but probably ridiculous theory, then it should be self-explanatory why she would refuse. The more relevant problem was that she might be suffering more negative chemo side effects by this evening.

But her pride hesitated to admit that. "I . . ."

"It's no problem," he assured her, his jovial tone unchanged. If he was disappointed or offended that she'd turned him down, he didn't sound it. Maybe he'd even experienced a twinge of relief that he wasn't using up his Friday night with her.

That possibility rankled. She scowled until she realized just how moody and irrational she was being. A wry chuckle escaped. Christ help her, she was a mess: thirty moods in thirty seconds.

"Asia? You laughing at me?"

"Not exactly." *Just having a nervous breakdown; don't mind me.* "Congratulations on getting the client on board."

"You can celebrate with me by bringing in more food on Monday. Damn, those ladies in your mama's prayer circle can cook."

"I'll tell them you said so. Maybe without the 'damn.' Have a great weekend, Brandon."

"You, too."

As she hung up, she acknowledged her weekend was off to a brighter start than it had been before he called.

"It's true what they say about Georgia hospitality. This has been a lovely weekend," Bridget O'Malley said, sitting next to Lucy in the backseat of Michael's modest sedan. The car dated to the previous decade, but it was paid off, and Michael took excellent care of it, never missing an oil change or tuneup and using only the highest-quality gasoline.

They were leaving the Margaret Mitchell House now, en route to Lucy's parents'.

Bridget leaned forward between the front seats. "You boys were nice to humor me by taking me to the Dump." The Dump, as the docent had explained to them, had been Margaret Mitchell's pet name for her residence. Bridget had soaked up every detail of the tour like a sponge. A sponge with an enormous crush on Rhett Butler.

Lucy grinned at Bridget's use of *boys*. Shaun O'Malley was older than his petite wife by several years, and Michael, though not remarkably tall, dwarfed his mother, who admitted to being five-foot-two in her bare feet.

"I tried to make my family watch *Gone With the Wind* with me at least once a year, but they usually found excuses to get out of it," Bridget said.

"That's because we hated seeing you cry," Michael told his mother. "You're always sobbing by the end."

Shaun grunted his agreement. "Aye, the waterworks."

Bridget sniffed. "It's just so sad. Bonnie, then poor Mellie . . . oh, dear, does anyone have a tissue?"

Lucy ducked her head, hiding a smile as she rooted through her purse. She may have found a kindred spirit in softhearted Bridget O'Malley. "Sorry, no. But I know something that might cheer you up. . . ." She trailed off, meeting Michael's gaze in the rearview mirror, her expression hopeful.

He raised his eyebrows.

She angled her head toward the exit sign they were passing.

"We haven't heard yet," he said.

True. They'd filed an official offer with their agent Friday night on the house they wanted, but they'd yet to get a response from the sellers. *Michael doesn't want to jinx our chances by saying something premature.* Though few people would guess it about the sharp-minded attorney, Lucy knew he could be endearingly superstitious. While he never *called* it his lucky tie, she'd noticed he always wore the same striped blue silk on

the rare days he was in court. He'd mentioned that if their offer was accepted this weekend, they could take the O'Malleys
by the vacant house.

Still, Lucy hated to miss this opportunity when the house
was so close and Michael's parents were so rarely in Atlanta.
Or, to take an opposing superstitious stance, maybe the more
you talked about something, the more likely it was to come
true. Power of positive thinking.

"We are right there," Lucy cajoled.

"Right where?" Bridget asked.

Michael sighed. "Near the house Lucy and I are considering buying. Nothing's official."

"Yet," Lucy added cheerfully.

He shook his head, but Lucy could see his smile in the
mirror. Moments later he was pulling up in front of a modest
split-level. If they got the place, she'd have to carry groceries from the garage up a set of stairs into the kitchen, but she
could use the exercise. She tried to see the small home from
the O'Malleys' perspective. Would they understand how she'd
fallen in love with the rosebushes that crowded the steps leading up to the front door? Or her exuberance for the many ways
she and Michael could transform all the interior white walls
into rooms that were uniquely theirs?

As she and Bridget climbed out on opposite sides of the car,
delicate-looking yellow leaves blew over a neighbor's backyard
fence and scattered across the driveway in a way that made Lucy
imagine someone strewing their path with flower petals. Fanci-
ful, she knew, but everything about this home brought out the
best in her imagination. Like the room directly across the main
suite that was almost too small to be a guest room. A nice office,

though... or nursery. She couldn't stand in that room, peering through the window that overlooked a charming backyard, without picturing herself holding Michael's baby.

She swallowed.

"Dear?" Bridget studied her face, questions evident in her voice and raised brows.

Lucy smiled. "I really want this house."

Shaun turned toward them with a teasing half smile. "Michael, don't let this one handle the negotiations. She'll bankrupt you."

Michael waited for her at the front of the car, taking her hand. "It's true Lucy isn't known for her poker face, but she has many other fine qualities."

They took their time going up the walk, Michael's parents asking about the house's age and condition. The sellers had been transferred through a company move, so had left the home empty. No one was home to let them in, but they weren't disturbing anyone by peeking through the glass panes on either side of the front door.

"I know it's hard to tell from out here," Lucy said, "but the living room is huge." There was no dining room or front "sitting" parlor—an omission Marianne might fuss over—but the extra square footage went into a spacious kitchen and a wide, warm living room with a high ceiling and romantic fireplace. When Lucy had first mentioned to Michael cuddling with him in front of a crackling winter fire, he'd reminded her that December temperatures in Georgia were as likely to be in the seventies as the thirties.

She'd mock-reprimanded him: "It's in your best cuddling interests to pretend otherwise."

"One entire wall of the living room," he was telling his parents now, "is a built-in bookcase that runs the length of the room."

"Perfect for housing all your tomes on employment law," Lucy said.

He nudged her with his shoulder. "And your romance novels."

They tromped to the back of the house.

"Such a nice yard for kids," Bridget said. "Fenced in, safe, just enough room to let them run wild out here so they aren't driving you crazy in the house, Lucy."

Lucy grinned, glad someone else shared her happy visions. This was *definitely* their house. She could see it. Not hearing from the seller yet was merely a technicality soon to be remedied.

But maybe standing here staring at the windows was the real estate equivalent of watching a pot and waiting for it to boil. Besides, her parents were expecting them. So when Michael caught her eye and looked pointedly at his watch, she nodded.

"We should be going. But thank you for stopping here first," she told him, reaching up to kiss his jaw.

"Thanks for prompting me." He looked around. "It's nice to know that I still love the place as much as I thought and that it wasn't a temporary infatuation."

As Shaun congratulated them on finding a nice investment and offered his advice for haggling over contract clauses, they got back in Michael's car and headed for the Swenson home. In the backseat, Bridget made conversation by asking about Lucy's family.

"And your sister's name is . . . Asia?" Bridget confirmed.

"That's right. She's my older sister by six years."

"Unusual name," Shaun mused.

"This from a man who wanted to call his daughter Fion-nuala," Michael teased.

Lucy thought Fionnuala had a lyrical ring to it. But as a kindergartner learning to spell her name, Michael's sister had probably been better off with Gail.

Bridget cleared her throat, "Michael told us about your sister's illness, dear. We're so sorry."

Lucy's smile froze on her face. She'd wondered if this subject would come up. She hadn't found a comfortable place to mention it in conversation, but it was best Michael's parents were forewarned in case Asia was having an off day after her chemo this week. Lucy should have known that Michael would be thoughtful enough to have told Bridget and Shaun instead of putting her through it. Besides, the more people who knew, the more good vibes, right?

"Thank you," Lucy managed. "I appreciate all good thoughts and prayers."

"Of course, of course," Bridget murmured.

As it turned out, Lucy's worries about Asia being too sick to enjoy the lunch were unfounded. They found her at the kitchen island, slicing hard-boiled eggs for the spinach-and-bacon salad their mother would serve with Vidalia onion dressing. Michael made the introductions, and George immediately won Shaun over when he offered him a bottled ale. During lunch, the mothers bonded by sharing anecdotes of their children's mishaps.

The main difference between the women's stories was that

Bridget had five children who'd been in various scrapes, while Marianne had only two. And of those two children, it wasn't *Asia's* name and peccadilloes that came up repeatedly over their lunch of fried chicken, corn-bread stuffing, and three-bean salad.

"It's a shame you have to be going back so soon," Marianne told Bridget. "We have another shopping expedition planned to find Lucy's dress. It would be such fun if you could join us."

"Cross your fingers and send us good thoughts from Kentucky," Lucy said wryly. "Our previous searches have been exercises in futility."

Marianne clucked her tongue. "Well, it's so important to find something flattering for your big day, and some women are just a harder fit than others."

Lucy's gaze dropped and she realized for the first time that a splotch of salad dressing had fallen on her chest. *Lordy.* She wanted to make a good impression on Michael's parents, and here she was spilling food on herself like a child. The worst part was that being, er, endowed as she was, the stains were always stopped in midair before they could fall harmlessly to the napkin in her lap.

Well, she'd always be generously endowed, but she still hoped to drop a few pounds before the wedding. She'd been trying to walk around her neighborhood before work in the morning, except when it was windy or cold or she'd had funky dreams the night before that left her too creeped out to be roaming the streets before the sun was fully risen. She'd tried a couple of low-fat dessert substitutes and generally got halfway through one before she deemed it entirely unsatisfying, chucked it in the nearest trash can, and found herself the genuine, whole-fat article. All in all, since her original resolution to trim her waist before the wedding, she'd gained two pounds.

And eight ounces—damn her decision to buy a scale with digital readout.

"So, did y'all enjoy the Margaret Mitchell House?" Asia asked. She'd been slender her entire life, but was still more sensitive to Lucy's feelings than Marianne—she of the two hundred deep-fried recipes.

"It was fascinating," Bridget said, launching into a recap of her favorite parts of the tour.

Once she'd finished, George joked, "You're lucky Michael was driving, or you never would have made it. Our Lucy's lived here her entire life and still gets lost whenever she goes downtown."

"Not every time," Lucy protested with a laugh. "Just most of them. It's those darn one-way roads. I know *where* I want to go, but I have trouble finding the turns that get me there. And is it really necessary to have so many streets with Peachtree in the name? It's as if sadistic city planners are trying to confuse people."

"It was originally a ploy to stimulate the economy," Asia deadpanned. "Tourists came, couldn't find their way out of town, and were forced to set up shop around Atlanta."

As good an explanation as any Lucy had ever heard.

"Well, Mrs. Swenson," Shaun began, patting his stomach in contentment.

"Oh, call me Marianne, please, both of you."

He inclined his head. "You're every bit the cook Lucy boasted."

"Thank you. I hope you saved room for dessert!"

Agreement came from all around the table, and Lucy thought again of the dress hunt scheduled for this weekend. "Actually, I think I'll pass."

"Don't be silly; I made one of your favorites," Marianne said. She brightened, turning to their guests. "That reminds me of the funniest story, when Lucy entered a pie-eating contest at this charity fair our church hosted."

Lucy's cheeks heated in anticipation of the story's conclusion. "You know what, Mama? I'll just go ahead and clear the table so everyone's ready for dessert." She stood, stacking Asia's plate atop her own.

As she walked around the table, she realized Michael had barely said a word during lunch. Was he feeling all right? Thinking about work? Was he sorry his parents had to go so soon? Lucy loved being close to her family and often wondered if it was difficult for him to have relatives scattered throughout the States, as well as a few still in Ireland.

She leaned close to him as she reached for his dishes, asking in a low tone, "Everything okay, sweetie?"

"Fine." His terse, monosyllabic response, so unlike him, wasn't convincing, but she wasn't going to push something he didn't want to discuss in a dining room full of people.

If it was serious, surely he'd tell her later.

✑

"Okay, ladies, this is it." Asia opened the door to a small but reputable bridal boutique tucked away in Kennesaw. The three very different gowns worn by mannequins in the window display were lovely, further raising her spirits.

She'd wondered if she would be up for dress shopping after this week's chemo session, but she felt surprisingly good. It was similar to how Fern had described morning sickness during her pregnancy; the nausea and exhaustion were definitely there, but if she pushed through them and even had a small, bland bite to eat, most times she could get beyond the worst of it. With the cool midmorning temperature and fresh air adding to her general sense of well-being, Asia was glad she hadn't canceled and left helping Lucy to her mom and Cam. Talking about wedding plans with the O'Malleys last weekend had made Asia aware of how little she'd done so far as maid of honor.

Cam echoed Asia's optimism as the four women stepped inside. "Today's the day. The Day of the Perfect Dress."

"It had better be," Lucy muttered. "We'll run out of weekends at this rate. And I'm already missing work here and there for other . . ." She followed this gripe with a guilty flush, and Asia knew that the days Lucy missed on Asia's behalf could add up quickly.

I've got to ask Mom more and rely on Lucy less. Marianne, who'd held various part-time positions during her marriage but was now officially retired, was more available, but she hovered in a way that Lucy didn't. And she rarely cracked jokes.

Shame coiled low in Asia's belly as she stole a glance at her mom's profile. She had no right getting so exasperated with Marianne. How difficult must it be to watch your child suffer a serious illness you were powerless to stop? A special kind of hell for any parent.

Something to keep in mind for next Thursday, when a nurse would once again hook Asia up to the IV full of toxic drugs. She wasn't just fighting for herself, but for her entire family.

"May I help you ladies?" A pretty, round-faced woman in a pastel pantsuit appeared in response to the soft jingle of tiny wind chimes above the door. Since it was still early in the day, they were currently the only customers.

"Yes, please." Lucy stepped forward. "I'm getting married in January and still haven't found exactly the right dress."

"January? Well, then, there's not a moment to waste, is there?" The woman stepped forward, tucking a curlicue of blond hair behind one ear and leaving a faint scent of patchouli in her wake.

The lush, pale-champagne carpet swallowed their footfalls as they passed a rack of bagged dresses marked with bright yellow RESERVED labels, a clearance area with dresses that had been discontinued, and a section of adorable lacy flower girl gowns in yellow, ivory, and pink.

The saleswoman stood Lucy in front of a three-way mirror and looked her up and down. "Why don't you step into the fitting room while I get my tape measure? Some of these dresses depend on rather exact sizing."

Asia could tell by the flush that stole across her sister's cheeks that Lucy wasn't looking forward to getting measured, but at least the woman assisting them had curves similar to Lucy's. It had to be tough to ask a size two to bring you a fourteen gown. Asia's problems fell at the other end of the spectrum. She'd already lost a couple of pounds in this newest round of treatment, and if the weight loss kept up, she could be a skeleton for Halloween without a costume.

The saleswoman hustled Lucy into a private room and

tugged the curtain shut. The sounds of material swishing and the *whsssht* of a zipper followed.

"I think I know exactly the right dress for you, hon," the woman said.

Asia exchanged glances with her mother; they'd heard that promise before, to no avail. But what the hell, there was a first for everything. Besides, Lucy had called earlier that week shrieking her delight that her and Michael's house offer had been accepted. Surely it was less difficult to find a dress than the perfect place to live.

The saleswoman dashed past them and was back in mere seconds. She caught Asia's assessing glance and smiled. "Wait until you see this one on her. It's such a lovely dress. We had a customer earlier this week who fell in love with it, but ... well, she didn't have the, um, necessary assets to do it justice."

"It's not low-cut, is it?" Asia asked. "Lucy's not looking to flash a lot of cleavage."

"Trust me," the woman said as she disappeared back into the fitting room.

"Cross your fingers," Lucy called out to them.

There was muttering inside the fitting room, followed by the saleswoman asking, "So? Was I right, or was I right?" Then silence.

A long silence. Asia fidgeted, starting to get nervous on her sister's behalf.

Lucy whisked the curtain back, her voice thick with happiness. "We did it. We found my dress. Why didn't I come here *weeks* ago?" She flashed a grateful smile to the attendant. "I'd hug you, but I don't want to do anything to muss this gown."

It was lovely on her, flattering her curves rather than

hugging them so tightly as to be obscene. The skirt flared out in a youthful, joyous bell shape without bringing to mind the petticoats and hoop skirts of a bygone era. The fabric appeared to be some kind of matte, as white as any Southern mama could want her daughter to wear, without the blinding sheen of some satin gowns.

"Oh, you're gorgeous," Cam said.

That was it, Asia thought, realizing Lucy's friend had put her finger on the essential difference. With all of the previous dresses they'd noticed the dress. With this one they simply saw Lucy, radiant and happy, exactly the way a bride should look. Asia knew the dress was just right, but if someone asked her to describe it, she'd be hard-pressed to give them the details of the hem or beading or sleeves. Instead, what she would remember was the smile on her sister's face.

The attendant led Lucy to a set of carpeted steps and a dais that ran the length of the mirrored wall. "You should see the back, too."

The material pooled into a modest length of lacy detail that would glide behind her as she walked down the aisle.

"It's perfect," Asia pronounced, meeting her sister's glistening gaze in the mirror.

With the question of the wedding dress answered, Lucy had a better idea of the look she wanted, and asked the salesperson to suggest gowns for the bridesmaids. But the woman pointed out that the bridal party shouldn't resemble clones, so they didn't need bridesmaid's dresses that in some way mimicked the wedding gown. That made Cam flinch, since all of her bridesmaids had worn tea-length dresses with cap sleeves and sweetheart necklines, the same as hers.

"Let's ind something you guys love," Lucy told them. "Michael's sister seems to be between the two of you in height and build, and she has red hair. If a dress looks great on Cam, it should be reasonably flattering on Gail, too. Reva and Rae will just have to go along with the majority."

Marianne sighed. "Those two girls would look fabulous in anything."

Asia and Lucy exchanged a commiserative eye roll. Reva and Rae really *did* look fabulous in anything . . . and had a way of not letting anyone forget it.

Marianne and Asia consulted with the saleswoman while Lucy considered different colors and fabrics. Finally Cam and Asia found deep green column dresses that came up high on the throat and laced behind the neck, perfect for covering some of Asia's scars and markings without making it look as if she were hiding beneath yards of material. The two women took their finds into adjacent fitting rooms. Hearing the chimes over the front door, the attending employee excused herself but promised to return momentarily with the shawls meant to be worn with the dresses in cooler weather.

Asia slipped into the dress and studied her reflection. Although she wasn't entirely happy with the way her body looked right now, the dress was still attractive. There wasn't much she could do about the sunken appearance of her eyes, but she reached in her purse for some lightly colored balm to moisten her lips. Then she smoothed her fingers over her somewhat crazier than normal curls.

When she pulled her hand away, dark strands came with it—the strands she'd been unconsciously bracing herself for every time she brushed her hair. Her knees trembled, and a piercing, tingling shaft of dizziness went straight to her head, throwing the small room into a weird moment of vertigo. After two deep breaths, she'd managed to quell the physical reaction. It wasn't as if her hair would all fall out today. And it wasn't as though this aspect of treatment came as a surprise.

"*Well?*" Lucy prodded from where she and Marianne waited, cheerful impatience in her voice. "Are you guys going to come out so I can see the dresses for myself?"

"Just a minute." Asia glanced at her hand to make sure it wasn't shaking before she reached for the curtain. "I'm ready."

"Perfect timing. Here she comes with those shawls," Lucy said. "If you guys both like the dress, we'll start looking at accessories."

Good idea, Asia thought. Maybe she'd ask the boutique employee if hats were in fashion this season.

Eight

Feeling stupid about sitting in the parked car apparently wasn't enough motivation for Asia to get *out* of the car. She stared sightlessly across the private deck, which was mostly devoid of vehicles this early in the morning. God, she was so tired. Last night she'd been restless, kicking the sheets into a tangle until she'd eventually pounded the pillow in exasperation.

Come on, she goaded herself. *This is your last real workday this week, and you have a lot to accomplish.*

Thursdays she lost to chemo, and Fridays she worked from home, her health allowing. The last two Fridays hadn't been too terrible, but by this past Saturday, serious nausea had kicked in, prompting the BRAT diet on Sunday. But she'd survived it. She was coping.

She was gargling baking soda to help with the mouth sores and had received a special toothbrush and a bottle of fluoride from her dentist so that she could continue to take care of her teeth without cutting her gums. Yesterday afternoon she'd taken a proactive step in light of the clumps of hair that were impossible to ignore after each shower—showers that were brief and lukewarm in order to keep from drying out her skin, which she faithfully moisturized.

Running a hand over the result of yesterday's trip to the salon, Asia wondered if the new style, not much longer than a man's crew cut, was the reason she hesitated to go inside this morning. She'd need a wig before Lucy's wedding— would probably want one before the weather turned seriously cold—but that was an outing she'd put off. Instead, on a whim, she'd decided this radical cut would help her with the transition before she went completely bald. The stylist had assured her she had a "shapely skull." And Asia had finally thought of some female examples of women who made practically no hair work for them: Sigourney Weaver in that sequel where she kicked alien butt, Demi Moore in that nineties military movie. Strong, attractive women.

Honestly, there was no one thing Asia couldn't handle. The nausea, the hair, the dryness. She should be on top of it—*was* on top of it. Her vision blurred, and she cursed, having no patience for this woman who couldn't even muster up the energy to get the hell out of her car. *You have stuff to do today.* Some data to compile for Brandon, bridal shower invitations she planned to personalize on her computer, quarts and quarts of water to drink before tomorrow's chemo.

A band of dread tightened across her midsection, and she had a sudden understanding of how a seat belt would feel if she were in a head-on collision, the very thing that was supposed to protect her cutting into her with sharp, unforgiving rigidity. The chemo was to help her, but the thought of going again tomorrow ... *Dammit.* Her throat burned with the impending moisture of tears she'd managed not to shed since September.

No, there was no one detail she couldn't handle. It was the whole fucking thing. It was cancer. It was being sick. It was feeling ugly. It was feeling like she needed a nap every day at noon like some fresh-faced kindergartner. It was having to congratulate her colleagues on high-dollar payoffs while she'd been relegated to the minor leagues. It was that she kept forgetting it was November now, October having been a blur, time she wanted back. It was staring at the blank new-message window in her e-mail program and wondering who the hell she'd planned to send it to, not that it would matter if she couldn't remember what she'd meant to type. It was not being able to shave her armpits because of the risk of nicking herself and getting an infection, not that *that* should matter, as she continued to lose hair in various and sundry places all over her body. She felt like a shaky, quivering, bug-eyed Chihuahua.

She felt weak.

A horrible, scratchy noise filled the car, the hoarse sob signaling a torrent of warm tears that slicked her face with salty moisture that was probably hell on her skin. She tried twice to suck in a deep breath and stop crying, but both times ended up choking on her own air. Drained of the energy to fight for composure, she simply leaned back against the headrest and went with it, balling one tight fist and pounding it against the steering wheel.

The resulting blare of the car horn scared her so badly she jumped, nearly banging her recently buzzed head on the ceiling. Startled out of her crying jag, she managed a hysterical laugh, then sat in sniffly, uneven silence until someone knocked on the passenger-side window and made her jump all over again.

Brandon Peters peered through the glass, apprehension evident in his expression. *Well, sure.* He was more experienced with handling dips in the market than psychotic episodes in the parking garage.

She heaved a deep breath, turning the key in the ignition so that she could lower the electronically powered window. "H-h-hey."

"Hey. Are ..."

She watched his face, mentally awarding him points for backing away from the obvious, "Are you okay?" The answer to that question was equally obvious. She wasn't even in the same hemisphere as okay. What she *was* was embarrassed. And thirsty. And currently backed up with snot, with nothing to blow her nose on. She didn't remember when she'd emptied the tissue box Velcroed to her glove compartment, but apparently she'd neglected to restock it.

"Can I get in?" he asked.

She hit the automatic locks. Despite her humiliation, his company wasn't entirely unwelcome. With an audience there was added impetus for her to get it together, which she hadn't been achieving very well on her own. Still, she wasn't sure she had the wherewithal to carry on a conversation. Disassociated words formed in her brain, but verbalizing even those fragments seemed a Herculean task.

Brandon slid in, and as she watched him fold his long legs, she noted distantly that he was taller than she'd thought when she first met him. Or maybe her perspective of the world was skewed today. He returned her assessing gaze, tilting his chin in her direction. "I like the new 'do."

And she thought men never noticed things like new shoes and haircuts. Her appreciative chuckle emerged as a croak.

His dark blue eyes remained uncharacteristically solemn. "If I give you a couple of minutes and maybe get you a glass of water, would you be all right to drive? It's my unsolicited opinion that you shouldn't be at work today."

"Giving medical advice now?" Her phlegmy, unsteady voice did nothing to disprove his theory.

"Okay, so I'm not a doctor; I just play one on TV. Or I could. Don't you think I'd look great as one of those prime-time medical drama stars, serious and sexy in scrubs on the cover of *TV Guide*?"

Inside, she smiled. Outside, her muscles weren't up to the challenge.

He dropped the joking tone. "You should go home."

"I know." It pained her to admit it, but she'd rather take the day off than risk having more of her respected colleagues see her in this state.

"You'll be okay to drive yourself?"

"Getting there doesn't worry me. It's *being* there I can't face." Frustration knotted in her chest. "Do you have any idea how morbid bedrest is?"

"So don't spend the day in bed. In fact, I have an idea. As the newest fake member of your health care team, I prescribe fresh air."

"You think I should rest on the balcony?" She'd need to slather on sunscreen first and pop open the umbrella she kept on her deck, but temperatures weren't expected to get very high today. Autumn had fully arrived, evidenced by sunsets that fell across the city earlier with each passing evening.

"No, my idea's better than that," he said.

"Of course. Well, don't keep me waiting, Doc; I'm eager to hear your diagnosis."

"It's a surprise." He crossed his arms across his broad chest. "Go home, conserve your energy, and be ready when I pick you up around one o'clock this afternoon."

"But . . . you have work to do." So did she, though they both knew she was in no shape to give it the concerted effort it deserved. It was one of those days when even if she stuck to filing, in six months a perplexed secretary would finally pull the missing Karlin folder from the N–P drawer.

"Hey, who's in charge here?" Brandon countered.

She lifted a brow.

"Okay, it is your car," he admitted. "And your health. But it's my prerogative to play hooky on a gorgeous fall afternoon." A slight dimple formed at the side of his mouth as he smiled again. "I'm the first to recognize my own importance, believe you me, but I'm reasonably certain MCG won't collapse if the company has to go a few hours without us."

Despite herself, she was intrigued. Whatever Brandon had in mind had to be more interesting than an afternoon of lying around her apartment with only an aloe vera plant and self-pity for company.

⟊

Marianne's car was waiting, parked but still running, when Lucy emerged from the main entrance for their lunch-hour errand.

She pulled open the car door. "Hi, Mom."

"You look nice today." Marianne smiled approvingly at the soft, pale sweater Lucy had paired with a floral skirt.

As happy as Lucy was that summer was behind them and the temperature was no longer hitting triple digits, she had to admit she wasn't really an autumn person. She liked spring, when everything was new and budding and the fragrance of flowers filled the air. Maybe grabbing this skirt out of the closet this morning had been her way to recapture that feeling.

She wondered if the shorter days and longer shadows were responsible for the smidge of depression she'd felt lately. Her wedding was just after the holidays, and she should be ebullient.

But she was starting to experience some nervousness about the house closing. With it still so many weeks away, she was half-afraid something would go wrong between now and then. *Maybe Michael isn't the only one harboring a superstitious streak.* Then, of course, there was Michael himself. He wasn't unaffectionate or argumentative, just not as ... connected as before. Could he be having cold feet? She wasn't brave enough to ask him. What if he thought she was neurotic for inquiring?

Worse, what if he admitted he *was* having second thoughts?

Today's trip to scout out silk flowers couldn't have come at a better time.

"We're meeting Enid there?" Lucy asked. At her mother's nod, she added, "It's so nice of her to do this for me."

Like the Swensons, widow Enid Norcott had been a long-time member of the Bueller congregation. Her husband, who'd started smoking back in the days when people claiming to be doctors were featured in cigarette ads, had died of lung cancer. Enid had once owned a thriving florist's shop, but when Stan got really sick, she'd sold it.

Lucy wondered if, after a few years alone, Enid ever wished she had the store back to occupy her time and mind. She'd picked up extra cash working as the floral consultant on several weddings in the community and had a gift for working with both fresh flowers and silk. Enid had offered to use her industry discount to help Lucy buy what she needed, and was willing to do the arrangements practically for free. Lucy suspected this was because of Asia. Everyone wanted to help, but often all they could do was pray and wait while she endured the necessary treatments. So they jumped at chances to assist the family in general.

"Do you want me to swing by a drive-through on the way?" Marianne asked. "It's not healthy to skip meals."

"I had a protein drink at my desk." *And an entire bag of salt-and-vinegar chips.* She concentrated better when things crunched. *So start packing celery sticks, or Michael's gonna need the Jaws of Life to get you out of your gown on the wedding night.*

Thinking of Michael and his indefinable distance, she sighed.

"Lucy? You okay?"

"Sorry. I'm not very good company. I haven't been myself lately."

"Getting married can do that to a woman."

"Thanks, Mama. I'm happy, honest. But it's like the happiness is this big, furry bear. One minute it feels all warm and fuzzy, and the next it goes into hibernation. It's still there somewhere. I just can't seem to wake it up."

Marianne laughed. "With your imagination, you could have written children's books."

Lucy blinked at the unexpected comment, not sure whether it was praise or a segue into one of the occasional spiels on what she could have done if only she'd applied herself.

"I never had to fuss at Asia for lying," Marianne went on, "but you told some interesting whoppers in your time, trying to get out of trouble, explaining how it wasn't really your fault. Some of your stories were so entertaining, I had to fight to keep from laughing and encouraging the bad habit." Marianne flashed her daughter a warm look. "But you never once tried to blame your sister, the only other potential suspect in the house."

"Well, who would have believed me? Asia was perfect."

"It's true that she rarely got in trouble, but you have a good heart, Lucy. I'm glad you managed to find a man who appreciates it."

"Me, too." She felt a bit better as her mom parked the car.

The place where they were meeting Enid was one of those huge, nondescript, concrete-floored warehouses filled to the exposed rafters with every possible decorative touch you could possibly need to make a place homey and special. Lucy followed her mother, ostensibly toward the flower section a mile back, although Lucy didn't know how Marianne could find anything in here without the aid of either a Global Positioning System or a Sherpa.

"Lily!" Enid Norcott's unmistakably gravelly voice echoed around them. "There's the beautiful bride."

Lucy fidgeted, resisting the urge to look behind her. "Um, actually, it's Lucy, ma'am."

"Of course, of course." The tiny woman patted Lucy's shoulder with gnarled fingers that remained deceptively nimble. "Guess I just have flowers on the brain. Let's look at what I've been thinking about for you, shall we?"

It was probably customary for consultants to ask the bride what *she'd* been envisioning, but Lucy was happy to get an expert opinion. What mattered most was a beautiful wedding, and as Enid quickly threw together sample bunches to illustrate what she had in mind, the woman's talent became evident. The bridal bouquet would center around creamy calla lilies, with red and white carnations and cranberry roses filling out the arrangement; there'd be an organza bow, seed pearls, and stephanotis. For the attendants, smaller clusters of roses and carnations, tied off with ribbon that matched their gowns.

Lucy was happily imagining how Michael would look in his tux and a calla lily boutonniere when Enid asked, "So your sister is actually going to be *in* the wedding and not just seated in the family pew?"

"Of course not," Lucy said. "I mean, of course she won't just be sitting. I want her up front with me."

"Sounds a little selfish, if you ask me," Enid said matter-of-factly, oblivious to the fact that no one *had* asked. "When my Stan was that sick, the last thing he would have wanted was to stand the whole time, especially in a room packed full of people who would see him get tired or sick or dizzy."

Selfish? What was it about aged Southern matrons that made them think they could say anything? Lucy cast a glance toward her mother, seeking assistance, but Marianne was standing just out of earshot, studying the colored netting they would use to decorate bottles of party-favor bubbles. "Mrs. Norcott, you probably mean well offering advice, but Asia isn't that sick."

Enid raised her penciled-in eyebrows.

"After all . . ." Well, Stan had *died,* though it seemed heartless to point that out. "The circumstances are just very different." Asia wasn't dying. She was only in her thirties. Treatments had advanced. She was going to get better.

"If you say so, dear."

"I do say so!" Lucy's voice sounded shrill even in her ears, and she must have increased her volume, because Marianne turned toward them. "My sister isn't that sick. She's getting better." *Or will, once she's finished the chemo.*

"That's what we thought about my Stan, too, but you just never can tell." Enid moved to pat Lucy on the shoulder, but Lucy sidestepped the crone's touch.

What the hell was wrong with the woman that she couldn't understand how inappropriate she was being? It was sad that she'd lost her husband, but that was no reason to be insensitive to other people's pain or ignore other people's medical successes. Lucy opened her mouth, not sure what she planned to say, except "quit comparing my big sister to your dead husband," but Marianne was suddenly at her side, speaking for both of them.

"Enid, you've been a peach, but I'd better get Lucy back to work. Call you later?"

When the two Swenson women were in the privacy of the car, Marianne asked, "Is there something I should know about? I thought her advice on the flowers was wonderful, but you seemed upset at the end."

Lucy bit the inside of her lip. If there was one thing her

mama hated, it was for her daughters to be ungrateful. Plus, Lucy wasn't sure what it would do to her mom's mood to bring up Asia's disease, to speculate on whether Asia would get healthy once and for all. "It's nothing. And you're right: The flowers will be lovely."

On the ride back to the office, Lucy tried to cheer herself up by visualizing the finished bouquets. But suddenly the only flowers she could think of were the wreaths and sprays that had filled the memorial room of a family-owned funeral home after Granpy Swenson had died. Those had been beautiful arrangements, too.

Brandon lounged casually in the doorway of Asia's apartment, as if he were in the habit of picking her up. "You ready to go?"

"How would I know?" She placed her hands on her hips. "You won't tell me where we're going."

He grinned down at her. "Don't you like surprises?"

"No."

"Because there have been too many bad ones?" he asked quietly.

She mulled this over. "Not really." Cancer was a nasty surprise, and having it back was like being forced to sit through the excruciating sequel to a movie she'd hated the first time. But other than being sick, she'd led a rather charmed life. Dates to proms with handsome high school boys, great grades in college, her first choice of jobs, a family who adored her and didn't suffer any real dysfunctions. "I just like to be—"

"In control?" The smile had returned, complete with dimple.

"I was going to say prepared." Her clients liked that about her. When you were investing other people's money, you had no business being a loose cannon. "So, am I? Prepared? Should I be wearing a skirt, packing an umbrella, carrying a crossbow?"

He gave her pima cotton top and khaki pants a lingering once-over, and she was shocked to feel warmth in her face. Maybe just the prelude of a hot flash brought on by chemically induced menopause. His blue eyes met hers. *Or maybe not.* Her stomach pitched in a slow, not unpleasant way.

"You're fine," he concluded. "Sensible shoes, nothing about your outfit that would get us thrown off the links."

"Links?"

"Yeah. I told Fern I would be out of the office this afternoon because I was golfing."

Which made it something of an excused absence, since so much business was done on the greens . . . by people other than Asia, anyway. "I've never been."

"You've never played golf?"

"Tennis was my game." *Is,* she told herself. Just because she didn't feel up to competitive athletics right now didn't mean she wouldn't again. Still, how could this man possibly think she was up for eighteen holes when she hadn't been able to get out of her own car earlier?

His expression softened at her hesitation, but the twinkle in his eyes remained mischievous. "Just trust me, Swenson."

Nine

Asia had never paid attention before to what Brandon drove, yet it seemed fitting that he owned a red sports car. She stopped at the curb, resisting the urge to roll her eyes. "A little predictable, isn't it?"

"Just get in," he said. "You'll forget your disdain when you see how it handles."

Fastening the seat belt across her lap, she retorted, "If you wanted me to really appreciate how it handles, you'd let *me* drive."

"But you don't know where we're going," he said. There were plenty of notable golf courses in Georgia, and she'd never set foot on any of them. "I can't believe you've never been golfing with any of the clients. Or any of our bosses, for that matter."

"I can't believe I've never done a lot of things," she muttered. It didn't bother her that she'd never golfed, but there were other activities she'd always meant to do, new skills she'd hoped to learn. . . .

"Hm?" Brandon turned toward her. "I didn't catch that."

She bit the inside of her lip, not sure how comfortable she was sharing her feelings. Then again, maybe opening up to more people was one of those things she could learn to do.

"It's just that life moves by so fast," she said. "I keep my eye on a goal and my head down, nose to the grindstone, so to speak. I meet the goals, so I should be happy, but then when I look up . . . College was a blur. I saw it as a stepping-stone, and it got me where I wanted to go, but it was over like that." She snapped her fingers. "I wonder if I should have gone to more parties or taken some obscure course that interested me just for fun instead of for résumé fodder."

"You could always enroll in some postgrad courses," he offered.

Asia smiled to herself, understanding now what Lucy was always saying about women just listening while men felt they had to offer concrete solutions to problems. "I know. I wasn't specifically talking about college, though. It was just an example." of years that had disappeared before she knew it. Maybe she should take this second round of her illness as a reminder to slow down, to enjoy her life and the people in it.

A few minutes down the road, Brandon asked, "So, what are some of the specific things you want to do? And no sensible goals, please, just a grandiose list with no reality-imposed limits."

She laughed. "Well, in that case, there's always Everest."

"As in, Mount Everest?"

"Yeah, but it's an inside joke. When Lucy was little, I used to read to her at night or to keep her occupied while Mom cooked dinner. Dr. Seuss was her favorite. So when she graduated from middle school, I got her this book, *Oh, the Places You'll Go!* It was typical Seuss, with the rhyming text and colorful illustrations, but it was more a motivational book about life than a story. It ended with the prompt to go find your mountain."

"I take it that's what you brainy types call a metaphor?"

"Yeah." Everyone had their own climb to make, with unique triumphs and obstacles; you could be there for others, but you couldn't take their journey for them. "Lucy was so nervous about starting high school she said she doubted she could even conquer a molehill, and I—" She broke off, self-conscious about revealing the silly details. Not everyone would get it, just as not everyone could make her giggle or brainstorm superhero names with her.

"You told her she could conquer Everest if she put her mind to it," he said. "I have an older sister myself."

"The one in Germany," she remembered.

He nodded, his expression thoughtful. "She convinced Dad to move there with them after Mom died. He can spend time with his grandchildren and see European golf courses. I didn't realize until you started talking how seldom I see them. Or how much I miss my big sister."

Unable to contemplate how much she and Lucy would miss each other if they were separated, Asia cleared her throat. "Everest would be on my silly, no-limits list. But seriously? I thought it would be great to see places. Isn't that supposed to be a benefit to making great money when you're young and single—the ability to travel? I hope your dad's enjoying those overseas golf courses. I've never been to another country. Hell, I've never even seen Hawaii, and *that* doesn't

require a passport! I've always heard Hawaii is lovely." Maybe
instead of giving the *Places* book to Lucy, she should have held
on to it herself.

"Well, we can't get you to another continent today, but
hopefully I'm taking you somewhere new. Ever been here?"

He turned into a parking lot, and she glanced at the sign-
post that towered above them.

"Miniature golf?" Her peal of laughter filled the car. "You're
blowing off work to play minigolf and you let the office assistant think it was business-related? You're awful."

"But I have a terrific swing." Brandon opened his door. "I
told you, fresh air will do you good."

No argument there, she thought as she walked with him
to an open-air cement-block building painted lime green.
A heavyset man was perched on a stool behind the counter,
reading a magazine at the register and periodically running
beefy fingers through thick, wavy hair that gave Asia a twinge
of envy.

Brandon cleared his throat.

"Can I help you"—the man looked up, his bland expression
curling into a smirk at the sight of Brandon, his button-down
charcoal shirt belted into a pair of slacks, and Asia—"*kids* with
something?"

"We'll need a couple of clubs, balls, the usual stuff necessary for a round of golf," Brandon said mildly.

Asia was half-afraid the only clubs behind the counter
would be so short she'd have to squat down to make a shot,
but apparently they got plenty of teens on dates and parents
out for a day with their kids. Once Brandon paid for eighteen
holes, they carried their full-size clubs down a path decorated

with plastic cobblestones and a brightly dressed lawn gnome waving hello.

"So have you at least played Putt-Putt before?" Brandon asked. "When you were a kid?"

"Maybe. I have vague recollections."

"Well, I'll go easy on you," he drawled. "Because I am a golf god. I've found it handy when it comes to closing deals."

"Really?" She arched a brow. "It's so sad that you had to rely on some macho display of gamesmanship. *I* always got ahead with my mad skills and admirable work ethic."

He gave her a mock glare. "You're just bitter because no one ever showed you how the game was played. Someday I'll teach you all the basics of hard-core golf. Woods, irons, stance, grip, the head, the shaft, the sweet spot—"

"Does Freud know about this game?" If she hadn't heard most of the terms before, she'd think Brandon was putting her on.

Pausing, he stifled a grin. "Anyway, I don't think today's game will call for that kind of precision."

She glanced at the first hole. "Not unless precision golf generally includes purple gorillas climbing mock skyscrapers." As far as she could tell, each hole included some cartoonist's take on an iconic movie scene, with a prop or sculpture that blocked the shot. So even if you could negotiate the curve of the green, managing the right angle and enough spin that the ball went toward the hole without so much speed that it simply bounced out, you were probably going to be thwarted by the Wicked Witch of the West swinging, pendulum-like, on her broom over the hole.

Brandon nodded toward the black rubber mat that served

as a tee, his body language radiating good-natured challenge. "You want to go first, or should I show you how it's done?"

"Just step aside before I hit you with the club."

"Okay, this hole is listed as a par three. If you hit it in four, that's a bogey. Two is a birdie."

"The only term I need to know is hole in one."

He smirked. "Have at it, Tiger."

She whacked the hell out of the ball, getting decent longevity . . . right into the "fairway" of hole number four. "I'm guessing that's considered out of bounds?"

"Brilliant deduction."

"I've always been a fast learner." She went to retrieve the bright red ball, glad the place was mostly deserted on a cool Wednesday afternoon. It wasn't that she didn't want anyone to witness her humiliation, just that she would have felt bad about knocking someone unconscious with her slice.

By hole number three, however, she'd fallen into a rhythm. It felt barbarically good to swing at something, focusing her entire body on a specific point of impact, while the controlling, calculating part of her warmed to the idea that she had to keep herself in check in order to reach her goals. She made the shot in two strokes.

Brandon putted in his own purple ball. "I'm impressed."

"You should be! I shot a bird."

He laughed. "Birdie. In golf, you shoot a birdie. In Atlanta traffic when someone cuts you off on I-75, you shoot the bird."

She grinned, already strolling toward the next hole, where players had to aim the ball through the gaping, toothy mouth of a great white shark head that made her want to quip, "We're gonna need a bigger club." As she bent to place the ball, some inner female radar told her she was being checked out. Stifling the impulse to straighten so fast she gave herself a head rush, she sneaked a glance behind her. Sure enough, Brandon had allowed his gaze to trail down over her, um, backside.

It's called an ass, Asia. When she felt herself blushing, she added, *And you're acting like one.* Okay, so Brandon had looked at her butt. *Big deal.* It had been a fleeting glimpse. Besides, what if she were wrong? Perhaps he was just gauging the course, mentally lining up the shot for his turn, and her butt had been in the way.

She was an intelligent, experienced thirty-four-year-old woman. So why did she suddenly have all the sophistication of a pimply high school freshman with her first crush? Maybe it was the juvenile ambience of the mini–golf course. Or maybe it had been a long damn time since anyone had made her feel like an honest-to-goodness woman. Face it, the only men she'd undressed for lately had all been wearing white lab coats and stethoscopes. It was too easy to forget that her body was something other than a battleground for health issues, more than a receptacle for Adriamycin.

Straightening to adjust her shot, she suddenly smiled, glad for the reminder that she was alive and vital, that her muscles were energized by the air and activity. Whether Brandon liked what he saw or not, she was grateful for the little tingles that brought to mind pleasant nights in her past and gave her hope for the future.

She hit the ball with confidence, this hole bringing her ahead of him in score. "No trying to switch the rules now and tell me the higher score wins," she told him. "I wasn't born yesterday."

"A few lucky shots and she gets cocky. This is a marathon, Swenson, not a sprint. I have plenty of time to catch up."

The Zen-like philosophy sounded utterly unlike the competitive man from the office. She suspected he'd be singing a different tune if he were the one with the better numbers. Or maybe she just didn't know him as well as she'd once assumed. After all, today had certainly been a surprise.

At the ninth hole, they paused to take advantage of a cold-drink vendor and sit at a wrought-iron, umbrella-shaded table. Asia had been tempted to order a blue raspberry slushee, remembering how she and Lucy used to get atrociously bright drinks, then stick their stained tongues out at each other. Instead she went with the more practical choice, water. Though it wasn't terribly hot today, her skin would still be chapped after this outing, and she was supposed to drink plenty of fluids in preparation for tomorrow.

As she twisted the cap back on her empty plastic bottle before tossing it expertly into the nearest trash can, she slanted a smile in Brandon's direction. "Thank you for bringing me here."

"Are you kidding? You think I'd rather be at my *desk* on an afternoon like this? I'm just out enjoying the air before the weather turns truly cold." He paused, the mask slipping. "But I'm glad I could help."

The concern in his voice brought that morning back with painful clarity, when she'd been a shuddery, tearful mess in her car. She hated that anyone—especially a colleague whose professional respect she wanted—had seen her like that. Worse, a good-looking colleague who only minutes ago had made her feel like an attractive woman. Lord, she needed to get over herself. If he had been staring, it was probably because he was watching like a hawk for any sign of impending breakdown.

She stood, ending further conversation by marching to the next tee. Her shot went wild, hardly improving her mood. By the twelfth hole she was trailing Brandon's impressive lead and barely responding to his occasional observations with more than a half smile.

At thirteen, they were supposed to aim around the top of a small-scale Statue of Liberty sticking up through the ground à la *Planet of the Apes*. Her shot bounced off the torch. After Brandon's turn she tried again, with no more luck the second time.

"I could help if you want," he offered.

Her hands clenched on the club. "I don't need help."

He waited as she screwed it up for a third time. "You need something."

By the next hole, an homage to *Yellow Submarine*, he'd apparently decided it was too painful to watch. She was in the process of rearing back for her first stroke when she felt first his body heat, so close it immobilized her, then his hands, one on her waist, another curling over her arm.

Her breath caught. "You shouldn't sneak up on me! I could have injured you."

"If I'd bothered asking, you would have declined assistance," he pointed out. The fact that he said it so reasonably made her hate him a little.

Was it so wrong to want to be able to do something by herself? Without needing someone to drive her or bring her a cold washcloth or sit next to her in her car as she bawled?

"I can do it alone." She wasn't even aware she'd snapped the words until she felt him stiffen. "Brandon, wait—"

"Forget it. I like winning anyway. I just normally prefer an opponent who gives me a better run for my money. Go ahead; take your shot."

Her vision blurred into a red haze as she choked the club. She almost swung in a fit of temper, but stopped at the last minute. Brandon didn't deserve her anger, and it certainly wasn't helping her any. She just wanted... Taking a deep breath, she stared at the green hill in front of her. At the top was a submarine. If the ball went through the right portal, it would roll through to the hole on the other side. She had to focus on that one small opening, put everything else out of her head. Take control of this one stupid thing, a window on a fake submarine that shouldn't mean anything, much less have her near tears of frustration at the thought of doing as badly as she had on the last hole.

She visualized sending the ball straight through that opening, down the incline into the waiting hole below, then coiled her entire body and swung as she exhaled. *I did it!* The ball actually went where it was supposed to, and she jogged a few steps upward to peer around the sub. Brandon joined her as they watched the ball roll down at the perfect angle, circle the cup once, and land with a soft thud. Her first ever hole in one!

She let out an exultant war whoop, then spun and gave him an impromptu hug.

"I stand corrected," he murmured. "You don't need me after all."

Breathing in his scent, a subtle cologne combined with the fresh, autumny outdoors, and swaying so close she could see the sun glinting in his eyes, she suddenly feared he was wrong. Maybe she did need him, or at least the way he made her feel in moments like this. Did it bother her? Should it?

She'd been so struck by her own reactions and rushing thoughts she'd forgotten to move, but Brandon wasn't complaining. Or letting go. Instead, he leaned almost imperceptibly toward her, and panic hurtled at her like a semi truck with failed brakes. Too sophisticated to flinch shrieking away like a girl scared of her first crush, Asia forced another smile—a habit she'd had too much practice with lately.

"If I still had hair and boobs and didn't know better," she said, deflecting the moment with wry humor, "I might've thought you were about to kiss me."

His arms dropped to his sides with audible slaps, his jaw rigid. "If you didn't have that chip on your shoulder, maybe I would have."

Chip? Who the *hell* did this guy think he was? "What I have is cancer."

He stared at her, measuring his words. "Which makes a tidy excuse for pushing people away, doesn't it?"

Fury surged through her. Cancer was not the equivalent of telling a guy you couldn't have dinner because you were washing your hair. How dared this arrogant jerk downplay the fear and pain of her situation? Asia was normally the type of woman who finished everything she started, but she'd be damned if she wouldn't call a cab before she spent another four holes with *him*.

"I think we're done here," she told him, stalking back in the direction they'd come. She realized almost immediately that the course was designed to be a loop back to the club stand and that it would have been quicker just to walk toward the eighteenth hole than retrace their steps. *Turn around. Don't be an idiot.* But her face was already flaming, her breath coming in short, jerky bursts, and nothing her mind had to say could force her legs to stop the course they'd started.

Brandon didn't make any response; nor did he follow. She got to the booth where the beefy man sat, his two bushy eyebrows beetled over his eyes as he glanced from her to where Brandon was already waiting for her. The few moments alone had tempered her fury to a sad, heart-heavy annoyance, but it was difficult to tell whether that was an improvement. Equally difficult to tell whom she was most annoyed with.

The ride from her place to the minigolf course had been quick and companionable. The ride home, stiff with awkwardness and hostility and unspoken accusations, took years. Asia had always thought you had to be in a relationship for months to achieve this kind of contemptuous silence, and she hadn't even been out to dinner with the guy.

Brandon could probably spend his time with any woman he wanted. Despite what he'd said about reveling in playing hooky this afternoon, she knew he lived for the job, for the thrill of investing other people's money and watching his choices net brilliant results. So why had he spent this afternoon with her? Why the little calls to see how she was and the lunches during which they strategized like two partners, after years of merely being civil acquaintances who tried not to get in each other's way?

Theory one: He felt guilty because he'd been handed her clients instead of legitimately beating her out for the accounts.

Theory two: He felt sorry for her, especially after her horrendous display that morning.

Well, he'd have to feel pity, wouldn't he? What human being could have watched another dissolve like that and not experienced sympathy? Certainly she would have felt terrible for anyone who was such a wreck, yet acknowledging what her own reaction would have been didn't make her any more forgiving about his.

What she'd really liked about Brandon in the last month was his nonchalance about her illness. He didn't flinch from any mention of her cancer, wasn't shy about asking how she was, but he didn't dwell on it either. Sometimes he even made jokes. Had all that casualness been an act, his attempt to make her feel like a normal person?

So how do you want *him to behave?*

Fawning in concern like her parents, like Fern? Or completely callous, so she could think he was a bastard and hate him instead of her own physical frailties?

She was too tired to be rational. By the time they reached her apartment, she found herself hoping he accepted some sort of sudden job transfer to the Yukon so she wouldn't ever have to see him again. She wasn't sure what exactly had happened today, why her emotions felt like they'd been stuck into that fancy blender Lucy had registered for, but she didn't care. She just wanted out.

With that tempting thought in mind, she grabbed the handle of the car door.

"Asia, wait."

She winced, wishing he'd stuck to "Swenson."

"It was nice of you to take time out of your schedule so I could get some fresh air," she said. She sounded pathetic. Like a dog that had needed to be walked. "But—"

"I wanted to be with you." His voice was far too serious and adult, and she wanted him to shut up. "I like being with you. Mostly. But you're not the easiest person to—"

"Do you mind? Maybe you didn't notice, Brandon, but I kind of have other things going on in my life. Like trying to stay alive. I don't have room for men's egos and these weird relationship talks, especially with people I'm not actually in a relationship *with*." She felt out of control, skidding over the line from harpy to full-fledged bitch. But she just wanted to escape.

"All right." He neither tried to stop her nor assist her as she lurched to the sidewalk. As she reached to shut the door, though, he said, "Asia? Promise me you'll remember something. The cancer . . . it's just something you have. It's not who you are."

*

"Can I come in?"

Lucy opened her mouth to tell her sister of course, but as Asia was already pushing past her and into the foyer, responding seemed like a moot point. Instead, Lucy just said, "Hello. I'm surprised to see you."

Asia spun on the heels of her canvas tennis shoes. "Because I rarely drive myself anywhere these days?"

"Because it's unlike you to show up out of the blue without a phone call," Lucy said. "On any day." Asia had many fantastic qualities; spontaneity wasn't one of them. Then again, her sister's thoughtful restraint meant that she never made mistakes like impulsively grabbing red hair dye at the grocery store, only to regret the bright orange result three hours later.

Speaking of which . . . "You cut your hair."

Asia nodded. "It looks okay?"

"Looks great. You really pull it off." On another woman it probably would have been too severe. Asia, strong but disarmingly feminine, was exotic enough to make it work.

No one else in the Swenson family was remotely exotic, not even Reva and Rae, who despite their identical beauty were really just garden-variety pretty blond Southern belles. Had their parents picked out Asia's distinctive name because they'd known that she'd be different, special? Or had Asia simply grown into their expectations?

"So, are you on your way home from work?" Lucy asked.

"No." Asia's lips twisted. "I'm not sure what I'm on my way to. Or from."

Okay, this was different. Asia seemed cryptic, testy . . . uncertain, even. Was it wrong that Lucy found less-than-composed Asia endearing? "Come in; take a load off. Can I get you something to drink?"

"Water, thanks. Room temperature, if you have any bottles in the pantry." Asia crossed the room to sit in a green velour love seat, leaning her head back to call after her sister, "Am I interrupting any dinner plans, or Michael coming over?"

"Uh-uh. I hadn't pinned down meal plans." Lucy had vowed on the way home to have another one of those protein drinks and call it supper, but she'd already caught herself thinking about the pecan pie in her freezer. She'd bought it for a night when she'd planned to cook dinner for Michael, but he'd ended up taking her out to a restaurant because she was so daft she'd forgotten two of the main recipe's key ingredients. The pie had been lying in wait behind the ice trays ever since.

She sighed, thinking it was a good thing she didn't have her mother's talent in the kitchen. Marianne made a chocolate bourbon pecan pie that was sin on a plate.

"I can't stop thinking about food," she admitted aloud.

Asia didn't seem to realize this was an ongoing problem and not simply a complaint of hunger. "Maybe we could order in. I don't suppose there's a place that delivers steak?"

"You want red meat?"

"Yeah." Asia sounded surprised herself. "I guess I actually worked up an appetite today, or my body is craving the iron. Why not? Got to keep up that hemoglobin."

"Well, I have some potatoes in the pantry. If you can wash those and pop them in the oven, I'll run out to grab a couple of steaks at the market around the corner. They won't take long on that little electric grill Dad got me for Christmas."

George was known for giving practical gifts like small home appliances, auto-club memberships, ten-pound flashlights that doubled as self-defense weapons, and once, on Lucy's birthday, a set of all-pink tools, made "just for her."

"Sounds perfect, Luce. Thanks for feeding me."

"Hey, it's what Southern women do." It wasn't until Lucy was halfway to the store that she realized she still had absolutely no idea why her sister had dropped in tonight. Not that Lucy minded the company, but she could tell by Asia's edgy demeanor that something was wrong. *Something besides the drugs and the side effects and going back in for more tomorrow?* Maybe chemo was all that was bothering Asia tonight. It was certainly enough to stress out even the most serene of women.

Intuition told Lucy there was more.

She was carrying in two plastic bags crinkling with steaks and bottled water when Asia informed her from the kitchen, "Michael phoned a minute ago. Said he was checking in but that you don't have to interrupt our girls' night by calling back."

"Oh." Lucy bit the inside of her cheek, wondering if Michael had noticed she was avoiding him. Actually, *avoiding* was too strong a word.

"Everything okay with you two?" Asia asked.

"Well, of *course.*" Lucy plugged in her indoor grill. "I mean, we're buying a house together, getting married. His parents like me. What could be better than all that?"

Asia paused, her mind obviously racing. She looked as if she were trying on and rejecting responses the way Lucy had wedding gowns.

Time for a subject change. "Any particular reason I'm being favored with a visit?"

"Besides that I love you and you're my very favorite sister?" When Lucy merely folded her arms across her chest, Asia sighed. "I had a very weird day. Maybe I need advice. Or just to vent."

"Really?" Lucy felt herself stand a little taller.

One afternoon during Lucy's freshman year of high school,

Asia had called from college. At first they'd exchanged idle chitchat. Eventually, the conversation had come around to the announcement that Asia had broken up with her boyfriend. She'd been the one to end the relationship, because he was getting more demanding and she hadn't wanted anything to disturb her studies, but she'd still been upset enough to want to talk to someone. Lucy had been honored that her worldly older sister had called *her*, instead of choosing one of her many equally sophisticated friends on campus.

"This isn't about a man, is it?" Lucy asked, spurred by the memory.

Asia hesitated, her cheeks flushing.

"It *is*? You're kidding!"

"Only tangentially, not in the . . . the romantic sense. I spent the afternoon with one of my coworkers." Asia slid the pepper grinder along the counter to Lucy, then watched her season the meat. "Brandon Peters. I've mentioned him before."

"Some." Once after Asia first met him and described him as "intelligent but arrogant," once after Asia admitted he'd made her laugh at the office holiday party with the kind of purposefully campy karaoke performance Asia could appreciate but would never participate in, then here recently when Brandon got most of Asia's best clients. Lucy had expected her sister to take that harder, but the next time she'd said Brandon's name in passing, it was only to tell Marianne that the man really liked Susannah Graham's white-cheddar macaroni soufflé. *Obviously if she's feeding the guy, she's not holding a grudge.*

"I spent the day with him," Asia said haltingly. "But not at the office. He . . . took the afternoon off to spend it with me."

"So it was personal, not work-related?" *Curiouser and curiouser.* Lucy cocked her hip against the counter.

"I don't know what the hell it was. All I . . . Do you know how many movies he ruined for me today? I don't ever want to see *King Kong* again."

Lucy didn't realize Asia had been a fan in the first place.

"Or *Wizard of Oz,* or *Star Wars,* or *Jaws,* or *Gone With the Wind*—"

"Where the heck did this guy take you? I thought they closed the Planet Hollywood downtown."

"We were golfing. 'Just something I have'? *Just?*" Asia stared into space, then shook her head. "I don't want to talk about it anymore."

"Okay. But do I need to toilet-paper his yard in retaliation?"

Asia grinned. "I'll get back to you on that. Enough about me. Didn't you and Mom go looking for flowers today? Tell me you found something absolutely perfect."

Calla lilies bloomed in Lucy's mind, followed by Enid Norcott's gnarled hands and her skeptical "if you say so." "I did. But I'm kind of burned out on the wedding right now. Let's not talk about that, either."

"This is going to be one chatty dinner."

"How about we watch a movie while we eat?" Lucy had a small table shoved against the wall in lieu of an actual dining room, but more often than not she served meals on the walnut-finished folding trays she stored behind the couch. She headed for the yellow cabinet she'd salvaged and thumbed through some DVDs.

She pulled out *While You Were Sleeping,* one of her classic comedy standbys, but when she opened the case she found *Breakfast at Tiffany's. Oops.* She had the absentminded habit of popping whatever disk she was taking out into the case of the one she was about to watch. Michael called it her potluck filing system.

"You in the mood to watch anything in particular?" Lucy asked over her shoulder.

"Anything but *Yellow Submarine*," Asia said, her dark tone bizarrely emphatic, considering Lucy didn't own the movie.

What the devil had Brandon Peters done, and what exactly did the man mean to Asia?

❧

Asia watched Marianne scurry toward the door, trying not to rush or look relieved that Asia had sent her to complete a short list of errands. If only Asia could admit to her mom that *she* was relieved as well, she'd alleviate her mother's guilt.

While Asia appreciated Marianne's providing transportation to and from chemo today, she knew from past experience that the woman got uncomfortable when she had to sit through the entire treatment. Once, in the early phases, Asia had been given a private room; Marianne had been able to sit and chat with Asia as if their outing were no more serious than a trip to the manicurist. But in the general room, surrounded by everyone else . . . Marianne didn't have Lucy's spunk; she wasn't able to cut up with Asia and make small talk with the nurses.

Instead, Marianne's eyes darted around the room, taking in all the sick people. Asia could almost hear her mother calculating odds, wondering which of the patients in the recliners would return to 100 percent healthiness and which ones . . . wouldn't. Because the current medical reality was that *someone* was going to relapse, *someone's* body wouldn't respond to the chemo; *someone* was going to die. You didn't wish anyone ill, but you hoped like hell that statistical someone wouldn't be your loved one. Or even yourself.

No, no, no. This wasn't a competition. Her getting better did not affect the odds of anyone else's struggle or vice versa.

Thinking otherwise was just cancer screwing with her brain. Cancer or the heavy-duty pharmaceuticals. Either way, she'd been borderline nutso and unfocused all week. She'd been bouncing across the spectrum of emotions like a spinning blue racquetball, never knowing where she would land or what was going to set her off again.

Well, wondering if a coworker was about to kiss her would definitely do it. Her mind inched toward yesterday's unexpected interlude with Brandon, but she quickly shoved the memory away. Maybe she'd been too hasty in sending Marianne for prescription refills. Now Asia didn't have her mother's conversation as a distraction.

Asia's gaze collided with another woman's, a petite lady, probably early thirties, bald under a pretty yellow-and-blue scarf. The last time Asia had glanced that way, there had been a man sitting with the woman. An attractive, clearly nervous man, fidgeting with his sunglasses and his keys, jingle-jangling his way through the afternoon.

"Sorry," Asia said. "I wasn't trying to stare. Just looking off into space."

"I know the feeling." The woman offered a tired smile.

"Don't worry. If I'd wanted privacy, I could have drawn the curtain. Having someone to talk to is nice. As long as that someone isn't driving you crazy." She said it with a half frown directed at the empty seat.

Asia laughed. "Friend or family member?"

"My husband. I've been doing this for months, and I swear, he's getting *less* comfortable with it. At the beginning he was all, I don't know, gung ho. 'We can do this, Steph. Blast the cancer and take no prisoners.' I'm not sure he was up for the reality."

Brandon's words, meant at the time about minigolf but certainly applicable here, shimmered in Asia's mind like a silvery heat wave over the asphalt: *This is a marathon, not a sprint.*

Since Asia was in no hurry to reflect on what was bothering her, she wedged a foot back into the closing door of conversation. "Nice scarf."

"Thanks." Steph grinned, tilting her chin toward the dark velvety fuzz on Asia's head. "Nice hair."

"Thank you. It'll be gone again soon, though." The interim haircut had been a temporarily balm to her ego. She'd ask Lucy about going with her to find a wig; she'd need her sister's objective opinion.

" 'Again'? This isn't your first go-round with chemo," the woman concluded.

"Nope." Asia avoided the grim details. She told herself it was because she didn't want to scare the other woman with stories of a recurrence, not because admitting she had metastatic cancer made her feel like a failure. "You?"

"First and hopefully last!" No sooner had Steph uttered the

statement than she cringed in apology. "I'm sorry; that wasn't very sensitive."

"Don't be silly. You won't hurt my feelings by not wanting to do this again. No one wants to go through it again. The Popsicles they feed us here aren't *that* good." Asia would be perfectly happy when it came time to permanently give up her seat at the cancer club.

"Have we met before?" Steph asked.

"Not formally. If we're both on the Thursday roster, our paths have probably crossed."

"You look familiar, so that's probably it. Or maybe I saw you at one of the support groups."

Asia shuddered involuntarily. "I don't attend one."

"Me, either. But I've stood outside several before chickening out and walking away."

"Why do you think you're afraid to go in?"

Steph swiveled in her seat, meeting Asia's eyes. "Because I'm not good at this. I'm not the woman who writes a book on finding the silver lining in her cancer cloud, then donates the royalties to the American Cancer Association. I'm not the person who decides to grab life by the balls and suddenly go skydiving."

"I doubt your doctor would approve that anyway."

"You know what I mean, don't you? I want to be one of those bright, determined spirits who goes to group and talks others through crisis. I'm afraid I would depress everyone because, mostly, I just think it's the pits. I have to tell my little boys that it'll be okay and that God has a plan, but I get tired. I *want* to be positive, yet there's this voice in my head, and all it says is, 'This sucks, sucks, sucks.'"

"Well." Asia craned her head to exchange solemn glances with her comrade. "At least we can be positive it sucks."

Steph's snort of laughter drew glances from across the room and smiles of approval from various nurses on the floor.

"I'm Asia Swenson, by the way."

"Stephanie." The woman cracked up again. "Steph Holland. We sound like we should form our own intercontinental coalition."

"Or at the very least our own nongroup group."

"So, if it's not too nosy to ask, why aren't you in one?"

"I have lousy people skills?" It was more a shot in the dark than an answer.

"You're being too hard on yourself," Steph said with all the wisdom of a virtual stranger. "You seem friendly enough to me."

Asia flashed a noncommittal smile, noticing that Steph's husband was on his way back to his wife's side.

It wasn't a matter of friendliness. She liked people, and you didn't grow up with Marianne as your mother and not learn how to be gracious to others. Asia just wasn't easy with those others sharing her space. Lucy had gone to college for only a few semesters, but at the beginning of each year there, she'd looked forward to seeing whom the university had assigned as her roommate, to meeting a new person and fitting that person into her life. Now one of those people, Cam, was about to be a bridesmaid at Lucy's wedding. Asia had barely spoken to any of her roommates since she'd been handed her diploma.

Postschool, Lucy had again found roomies, claiming Atlanta's rent was too steep to manage alone. Asia had compensated for her rent by picking up more overtime hours. Was it just the cancer making her feel isolated, or had she somehow become a person who pushed others away?

Brandon's angry eyes shone in her mind, icy-bright with hurt when she'd scoffed at the possibility of his kissing her. At that moment she hadn't known how else to react. Didn't he understand how long it had been since a man had *touched* her?

Lucy and Marianne had always been huggy people; Asia had not. But in the last year, she'd been grateful for their comforting embraces, which they'd never stopped offering, even as some of her other acquaintances had inched away. As if it weren't bad enough she'd had vomiting and fatigue and weird skin issues, did people have to make her feel more repulsive by not meeting her gaze or not letting their bodies come into contact with hers?

She'd discounted how much that bothered her. But even once her hair had grown back and her skin had taken on a glow from all the nutrition, water, and exercise, some part of her had continued to feel like a leprosy-ridden pariah. That was the part of her that had, rather ungracefully, freaked out when she let herself get close enough to touch Brandon Peters. She hadn't just inched away, rejecting him in the hundred subtle ways people had used around her; she'd tried to use her circumstances, her "deformities," to throw a steel wall between them. He'd responded by pointing out the chip on her shoulder, and the more she thought about it, the more she conceded his point. *Oh, crap, crap, crap.* Did that mean she owed him an apology?

No, he had no right to talk to you like that. Chip on her shoulder, indeed.

Then again . . . One of her favorite aspects of the friendship that had crept up on her was how he didn't pussyfoot around her because of her illness. So wouldn't it be hypocritical of her to demand he pull his verbal punches because she was sick?

Damn, she hated being wrong.

Ten

Asia stood at Fern's desk, nodding periodically to indicate that she was listening to the woman's stories about what cute things baby Tommy had done over the weekend. But Asia kept one ear focused on the hallway behind her, waiting for the ding of the elevators, the self-assured fall of footsteps as Brandon strode toward his office, greeting people along the way.

"Are you okay?" Fern asked.

"What? Yeah, I'm great." The worst of this weekend's nausea and exhaustion was behind her, and she'd awakened feeling almost well rested this morning. She should; she'd gone to bed last night around seven.

"You seem . . . antsy." Fern blushed. "Probably eager to get to your desk, huh? I swore I wasn't going to be one of those obnoxious parents who bored people silly with stories about how the kid rolled over or smiled for the camera."

"You're not obnoxious! I like hearing about Tommy." Asia liked seeing the pictures, too, although every time she peered at that chubby face and those wide, innocent eyes, she experienced a pang in her midsection. Would she ever look into the eyes of her own baby?

Since chemo and radiation could play merry hell with a woman's reproductive system, Asia had elected to have eggs frozen before she started treatment the first time. In vitro procedures aside, there was always adoption. Plus, she would be a kick-ass aunt for the cute nieces and nephews Michael and Lucy provided. Maybe cool aunt was even better; she could return the kids when they were hopped up on sugar and she needed peace and quiet.

Fern sighed, regarding her with a sympathetic head tilt that made it clear she'd followed Asia's train of thought. "You know, I'm not sure I've mentioned it, but the supershort hair looks really good. Makes your eyes pop. You have great eyes." Subtext: *I'm sorry your ovaries don't work anymore.*

"Thank you, Fern. I appreciate that." She did, too. Just because people weren't always sure what to say didn't mean they shouldn't get points for trying.

The low ping of the elevator arriving caused a slight flutter in her pulse, but Asia resisted the urge to swing her head around and see who was behind the doors. She didn't have to. A moment later she heard Brandon call out his good morning to the front-area receptionist. Asia took a breath to steady herself. It wasn't that the man himself made her nervous, she tried to tell herself; she'd simply been caught off guard by his eerily correct insights. Now that she'd had some time to regain her balance, she looked forward to smoothing the waters with him.

He approached them, preceded by the aroma of coffee, a

rich scent she'd once enjoyed that now, unfortunately, turned her stomach.

She inhaled, willing away the queasiness.

"Fern, is that a new picture of Tommy?" Brandon asked from behind them. He barely glanced at Asia as he sipped from his travel mug and leaned closer to get a better look at the photo Fern held out for inspection. "Good-looking kid, obviously takes after his mama. Just to let you know, I've got a phone conference this morning, so everyone else will be going to my voice mail for at least an hour. If it's important—or if the caller is impatient—I'm sure they'll buzz back to you."

"No problem," Fern said cheerfully.

"Asia." He deigned to notice her, nodding hello and, apparently, good-bye.

Like aloha, she thought as he walked away, *or ciao*. Now her name doubled as a greeting and a farewell. How very international.

She'd just catch him later. After all, she'd yet to figure out what to say. Even if she had, Fern's desk probably wasn't the appropriate place.

Taking advantage of her physical well-being, Asia threw herself into catching up on work. She had a highly productive morning, not even realizing how close it was to lunch until her phone rang and she noticed the crystal clock on her desk when she reached for the receiver.

"Asia Swenson."

"Hey, Asia, it's Cam. Just calling about the shower. I know you're über-organized, so you've probably got everything well under control, but do you need any extra help?"

"In addition to everything you've already agreed to do? Nothing I can think of, but I wouldn't be able to do this without you." Asia was having the event at her place a week from Sunday. Cam and Marianne were bringing the bulk of the food. In addition, Cam had promised to supply some pictures of Lucy from college, and she'd been the one to suggest a couple of games that had proven popular at her own bridal shower.

"I've heard from everyone on the invitation list," Asia said. "Twelve yes, five no, bringing us to a total of fourteen, counting Lucy and myself. I've picked up the tablecloths, napkins, plates, et cetera. Michael's sister is flying in for the shower, but she has to work Saturday, so Lucy will pick her up at the airport and bring her straight over on Sunday. I'm looking forward to meeting her."

"*I* can't wait to meet the infamous Reva and Rae. Are they really as pretty as Lucy says?"

"It hurts to look directly at them," Asia confirmed.

Beyond the interior window of her office, she noticed Brandon headed for the elevator. If she hurried, they could ride down together. "Cam, could I call you back later? There's someone I really need to grab before the day's over."

"Sure, no problem. If all else fails, I'll see you at the shower and we can talk more then."

Trying to walk quickly without looking as though she were rushing, Asia exited her office. She wasn't fast enough to catch up to Brandon before he pressed the down button, but she called out, hoping to stall him: "Brandon, wait!"

He showed no sign of hearing her as the elevator doors opened, and she wasn't about to yell. Still, she could have sworn their eyes met for a moment as the doors closed. Was he angrier than she'd realized when he dropped her off last week? Or just nervous about what to say? Or maybe just late for a lunch appointment, and she needed to get over herself.

But when he ducked into the men's room that afternoon as she was coming back with bottled water from a vending machine, she knew he was avoiding her. It ticked her off that she'd graciously concluded he'd had a point and now he wouldn't even let her apologize.

She sat at her desk, fuming in the general direction of her computer screen before punching her index finger down on the mouse and clicking the e-mail icon.

> From: "Asia Swenson"
> To: "Brandon Peters"
> Subject: Dodging me
> Stop it. I want to talk to you.

That pretty well summed it up. Hoping she wasn't being an idiot, she hit send. Then, because she was an adult living in the real world and not a seventh grader, she pushed it out of her mind and went back to work . . . occasionally checking the bottom of her screen to see if she'd received mail.

To his credit, he didn't make her wait long.

> From: "Brandon Peters"
> To: "Asia Swenson"
> Subject: Talk?
> Are you sure? You realize that requires interaction, the kind that could lead to people actually getting closer to you.

She ground her teeth as she typed.

I'm sure. Come by my office at your convenience. You'll
have to leave your high horse outside, though.

A second later her phone rang. "Asia Swenson."

"Did you want to *talk,* or exchange insults?" Despite his
words, there was a smile in his voice.

Her body loosened, making her belatedly aware of tension
she'd been carrying in her shoulders. "Is there a law saying we
can't do both?"

"You're an odd bird, Swenson."

"Duck, technically. In my family, the saying was always
'odd duck'. But before we get too far into calling each other
names—or waterfowl—I just wanted to say I'm sorry for the
way things turned out after our golf game." The admission was
easier than she'd expected, possibly because it was over the
phone and she didn't have to look into those azure eyes. If you
weren't used to making apologies, this was definitely the way
to ease into it. "Although, you have to admit, you were kind of
an ass."

He was quiet, probably wishing he'd stuck to avoidance.
"Yeah, I kind of was. I was mad. When you made that crack
about my kissing you if you still had hair and br— Well, you
know what you said. It made me feel shallow. I know I show
up at Christmas parties with pretty dates and drive a red car,
but . . ."

"I never thought you were shallow." Not since getting to
know him, anyway. "It wasn't about that. It wasn't about you."

"I know."

So they'd cleared the air. And now there was just this awkward silence hanging above them like a creaky antique light fixture that might crash to the floor at any moment and didn't even work, except to serve as a base for cobwebs. Yes, this was definitely progress.

"I should let you get back to work," she said.

"Right."

When neither of them hung up immediately, she thought of the way she'd felt in that recliner on Thursday, telling Steph she had no people skills and wondering when her active, successful life had become lonely. "Brandon? Do you want to come over this weekend? I was thinking of maybe a small get-together on Sunday. Not like a, um, party or anything. Just an early dinner, maybe some board games."

"That sounds fun. Thanks for inviting me."

She let out the breath she'd been holding and told him she'd get back to him with the details. Then she hung up so that they could each return to their jobs.

Board games? Did she even own any? She hadn't thought about that when she'd made the spontaneous gesture. For that matter, she hadn't been thinking about the timing. She normally still felt pretty puny on Sundays, following Thursday's chemo. They were having Lucy's shower on a Sunday only because it was best for everyone—the guest of honor included—to have it on a weekend. What was Asia doing, booking social engagements two Sundays in a row?

Sometimes, even when he was annoying her, Brandon had a way of temporarily making her forget she was sick. You kind of had to love that about the guy.

Lucy was absolutely thrilled when her big sister rang the door-bell. The way the evening was going, Lucy would have been thrilled if a vacuum-cleaner salesman showed up at her door.

Her mother and Michael had already arrived and were test-ing Lucy's patience. Michael, normally her knight in modern armor, was being . . . moody. Something was bothering him, al-though when pressed, he denied it. Was she about to join her life with someone who wasn't comfortable being honest about his emotions? The ironic part was that Michael was here to lend moral support.

Lucy and the other two Swenson women were addressing the invitations tonight. Since calligraphy hadn't been part of first-year law, Michael wouldn't be actively assisting. But he'd said he would have felt guilty about sitting at his place and watching a game while she continued doing all the work for their wedding, even though he had gone to look at tuxedoes and was in charge of finding a videographer. He'd said he could at least help fix dinner for the ladies, which had sounded nice when he volunteered. Now, however, she found herself wish-ing he were home with the game or bowling with her father instead.

Marianne Swenson had kicked off the calligraphy session with reminiscences about how bad Lucy's handwriting had been as a kid and crayon-wielding adventures from Lucy's early graffiti years. Lucy had just nodded and smiled, know-ing that if she seemed upset, her mother genuinely wouldn't understand why.

"But, honey, that was years ago," Marianne would protest. "You were so cute."

Cute. A rule breaker with failing penmanship, but cute.

Asia had never been cute. She had been pretty. She had mastered cursive by the third grade.

So what? Lucy asked herself as she opened the door. *You're going to pick now to start having spasms of sibling rivalry?* of course not. She had her failings—just ask Marianne—but Lucy wasn't petty. And why should she be jealous? She was getting married. Asia . . . was not.

At least, not yet. Lucy forced optimism into both her thoughts and her smile of greeting. "Hey, sis."

"Back atcha. I come bearing self-adhesive stamps."

"Then you're in the right place." Lucy swung the door wider, lowering her voice. "Throw me a lifeline, will you? Michael's being Mopey, the forgotten eighth dwarf, and Mom's being . . . Mom."

Asia flashed a grin, then glanced over her shoulder with faked worry. "You know, I may have forgotten something very important in my car."

"Abandon me, and I will change your maid of honor dress into something truly horrific. I'm talking lamé and polyester. They make sequins in neon pink, right?"

"Asia, is that you, honey?" Marianne called from the living room. They'd dragged Lucy's small dinette table into that room so they could have the combined space of that surface, plus the coffee table. Also, Marianne had tutted that Asia would be more comfortable on the padded love seat than in one of the straight-backed chairs. Asia rarely complained, but her combined treatments could cause serious joint pain, to say nothing of general soreness. "Lucy, get her in out of the cold. And close the door, for pity's sake. You're letting in moths."

Asia wiggled her eyebrows, in perfect imitation of the expression she used to make when they were young and Lucy was getting fussed at for something. Lucy's response was the same as it had always been—to choke back a laugh she'd have to explain to their mother. The silent moment of mischief, a secret between the two sisters, proved that Lucy wasn't the only one who experienced blips of rebellion.

Lucy tried to keep the chuckle out of her voice, glaring her sister into good behavior. "Yes, ma'am. We were just coming."

When they made it to the living room, however, there must have been telltale gleams of guilty merriment in their gazes.

Marianne sat back in her chair, folding her arms across her chest. "What?"

"Nothing," they chorused, like a couple of teenage boys about to boost a car.

"Sometimes I just don't know." Their mother pinched the bridge of her nose, talking over Michael's halfhearted hello from the kitchen, where he was assembling dinner. "I wonder if I went wrong somewhere with you girls. Very wrong."

"Not at all," Asia said smoothly. "You were an excellent mother, with two successful daughters to show for it and a soon-to-be son-in-law. Now, why don't you guys show me where you are with these invitations, and let's get cracking?"

It wasn't until they'd declared a break and adjourned to a dinner of chicken, zucchini, and pasta that Lucy realized her sister was trying to catch her eye. They hadn't talked much

during the calligraphy work because Lucy had a bad habit
of inserting random words from conversation into street addresses.

Everything okay? she mouthed at Asia, absently passing her
mother the salt.

When her sister nodded, relief flared in Lucy's chest, painfully sharp. Whatever it was her sister wanted to talk about, it
wasn't another major medical announcement.

Asia cleared her throat. "Luce, Michael, are you guys, um,
busy on Sunday night?"

Lucy exchanged a quizzical glance with Michael, then answered for both of them. "Not as far as I know. Something you
need?"

"I'm having . . . a couple of people over. I'd really, really like
it if you guys could come."

"Sure," Lucy said. "I mean, if that's okay with you, sweetie?"

"Sure," he echoed.

"What people?" Marianne asked.

"Just friends. Like from work. And chemo, maybe."

"Is this some kind of support exercise?" Lucy asked tentatively.

"No, nothing like that," Asia rushed to assure them, looking
horrified even at the suggestion. "This is just a social thing."

Not "just." Lucy knew something more important was going on. She also knew Asia would beat her senseless if she continued to pry in front of their mother.

"We'll be there."

When Michael stood to clear the table, Lucy laid her hand
over his arm. "I'll get it, sweetie. You cooked. I'll clean. Asia,

want to keep me company in the kitchen? Enid e-mailed me pictures of sample bouquets. They're on the counter."

As soon as they were alone, Lucy rounded on her sister. "Spill. What's the deal with Sunday?"

"No deal. Thought we'd have a casual dinner, maybe play some games. You have board games of some sort, don't you? Can I borrow one?"

"Who's 'we'?"

"Well, with any luck, this woman named Stephanie I met at chemo and her husband. I'll bet they could use a low-key night out, if she can get a sitter. And you and Michael, of course. And Brandon."

"Peters?" Lucy squeaked. "Last I heard, he was an ass who'd singlehandedly ruined the history of film for you. What happened with you two?"

"Nothing. He's trying to be a friend, which I appreciate. I, um, could use friends." Asia ducked her gaze. "I'm not popular like you."

The admission shocked Lucy speechless. Popular? Her polished and confident sister, who even managed to make losing her hair look chic, thought Lucy was popular? "Clearly you're forgetting you had to threaten my bullies when we were kids."

Asia waved a hand. "That was then. People love you. All those temp jobs you did? Everyone wanted you to stay permanently. You make people laugh."

That's me, court jester. "Asia, I had all those temp jobs because I couldn't figure out what the heck I wanted to be when I grew up. I never had a plan."

"Maybe plans are overrated. You're in management and about to get married, so you obviously did something right."

Lucy blinked. "We got off topic. You were going to tell me more about Brandon."

Asia smiled. "You sure about that?"

"If you want access to my closetful of board games, you're gonna have to give me something. And I have quality, gather-the-party-round-the-television interactive DVD trivia games, too."

"There isn't more to tell, honest. I overreacted the day he took me to play minigolf, and I offended him. He's let it go since then, and I apologized. We're back to normal."

"And normal includes a triple date?"

Asia shot a glance toward the living room, as if worried their mother had heard *date* through the wall. "It's not like that. It's just six people getting together for some food and a few laughs."

Well, that *wouldn't* be a date, then. Because until Michael, many of Lucy's dates had included being too anxious to eat, stressing about whether he'd get her jokes or think she was trying too hard, then worrying about the kiss that may or may not mark the end of the evening. Good times.

But even Lucy had managed to find her prince eventually, and Lord knew Asia deserved a happy distraction in her life. Lucy couldn't *wait* to meet Brandon Peters.

At the knock on the door, Lucy popped out of her seat like one of those automated gophers they used to bonk with mallets at arcades. Lucy had never done very well at that game, always hesitating a second too late over bashing a cute little animal on the head.

"Want me to get it for you, Asia?"

Nice try, sis. "Thanks, but I am the hostess." Asia stood, resisting the urge to fidget with the bandanna she was wearing. Earlier in the evening she'd tried a prettier, silky scarf, but the damn thing just slid around on her bald head, making her paranoid about anything staying in place. She and Lucy were meeting after work one day this week to visit two reputedly top-quality wig shops.

Michael took Lucy's hand, gently pulling her back down onto the sofa. In a stage whisper he told Asia, "She's eager to meet this Brandon."

Asia exchanged smiles with him. "No kidding." The younger Swenson's first words of greeting had been, "He isn't here yet, is he?"

"But we're an hour early," Michael had said before Asia could answer. "Why on earth would he be here already?"

He wasn't here now, either. When Asia opened her front door, it was to find Rob and Stephanie Holland standing close together. Casual observers might assume they were simply an affectionate couple—which, as far as Asia could tell, was true—but a prolonged glance showed that Steph was sagging against her husband for physical support.

"I am so glad you were able to make it," Asia said, welcoming them both but smiling particularly at Steph. Though pale, the woman looked spirited. Determined. "Come on in, and let's find you a place to sit."

"Thank you. And thanks again for inviting us," Stephanie added.

When Asia made a point of looking for her at the chemo center on Thursday and issuing the invitation, Steph had laughed. "I thought you had no people skills. So what are you doing arranging a party?"

Asia had explained this wasn't a party, just a chance for some casual fun.

Steph's expression had turned wistful. "Fun. I seem to remember having that once. Let me see if Rob's sister would be willing to babysit. Again. I swear, the poor woman spends more time at my house than hers these days. Can we bring anything?"

"Absolutely not," Asia had said. "Just promise me that if, come Sunday, you're not quite up to it, you won't apologize." As far as she was concerned, cancer patients were entitled to crappy off-days without having to feel bad about feeling bad.

But it looked as if Asia and Steph had both survived the worst the weekend had to throw at them. Asia had made it through yesterday on bland foods, a pharmaceutical cocktail from the assorted pills residing in her kitchen cabinet, and sheer willpower. Still, she was weak today, and grateful her sister had come early, bearing sandwich trays that awaited Asia's guests in the refrigerator. There had been a time when Asia's go-to dinner for a group was a pan of lasagna that could bake while she got ready; now her stomach would tolerate neither the acidic tomato sauce nor flavorful garlic.

"Stephanie, Rob, this is my sister Lucy and her fiancé, Michael

O'Malley. Guys, meet Rob and Stephanie Holland." She turned to Steph. "Brandon isn't here yet, and Al's in the kitchen."

"Al?" Rob asked.

"Her aloe vera plant," Stephanie said. "And you were so right about that, Asia. I'd been using the stuff that came in a tube, but the sap from my own mature plant works so much better."

A lot of processed aloe vera had some alcohol in it, which could further dry their skin.

"Glad I could help," Asia said, thinking briefly of the late friend who had given her the plant.

Rob was helping his wife sit down when the next knock sounded. Asia turned toward the door, half expecting Lucy to beat her there. *Michael must have restrained her.*

Was it Asia's imagination, or had her pulse accelerated the tiniest bit? There was no reason for that, really. She and Brandon were friends, like her and Steph.

Okay, not exactly like that.

Her breath caught when Brandon smiled in greeting. Between that and noticing how much his navy shirt deepened the color of his eyes, there was a split-second delay before she registered the huge bag he was carrying.

"What's in there?" she blurted, mentally kicking herself. Had she even said hello yet? Marianne would disown her.

He laughed. "I suddenly got a whole new image of you. Before, I would have said you were the type of person who unwrapped a present carefully and saved the bows. Now I'm wondering if you shred the paper in a fit of impatient curiosity."

Her skin flushed with warmth. "I didn't mean to be rude. I'm not usually impatient."

"No apology necessary. Glad I piqued your curiosity." His grin widened, exposing the dimple. "Let me in, and I might even tell you what's in the bag."

She really was failing Hostess 101. "Of course you should come in."

As he stepped over the threshold and toward the living room just behind her, he paused at the O'Keeffe print, shooting her another surprised look. "Not what I would have expected. I've been here a minute and a half, and I'm already learning lots of new things about you."

"Actually, that was a gift from Lucy." She nodded toward Michael and Lucy. "My sister and her fiancé, Michael."

Brandon set the bag next to the sectional couch and shook hands with them. "Pleased to meet you. And congratulations."

When he turned to meet Steph and her husband, Lucy mouthed, *Wow,* behind his back. Asia rolled her eyes, trying to downplay the budding romance she knew Lucy would be hoping for, but secretly, she had to agree with her sister's assessment. Brandon rated pretty high on the *wow* scale. Why had it taken her so long to notice?

Introductions were barely completed before Lucy said, "So what's with the bag? I'm naturally curious and have regrettably little impulse control."

Brandon laughed. "Then maybe I can enlist you to plead my case, if I tick off our hostess. I was passing this party supply store and went in on impulse, but by the time I got here, it occurred to me that it might be rude to hijack another person's social function."

Lucy's eyes lit up. "Asia won't mind that you were being thoughtful and brought a few things over."

"A few?" Asia asked. "You could fit a whole keg in that bag."

Brandon pulled out a handful of plastic garlands. Leis, Asia realized. He gave two of them to Lucy and was placing one around Steph's neck.

"I hear the tradition in the islands includes a kiss hello," Brandon told Asia's friend. "But in light of the big guy sitting next to you, I'll forgo that part."

"Good decision," Rob joked.

Brandon approached Asia with a pink lei sporting fake purple orchids. *She* didn't have a significant other sitting next to her. Brandon's eyes met hers, and she knew he was considering that kiss. It would be platonic, she was sure, just a peck on the cheek, but he simply placed the circle over her head and backed away. Who could blame him after the last time he'd considered kissing her?

He glanced at the bag. "I also have those tiny paper umbrellas for drinks, a bamboo table torch with a votive candle, and an Elvis *Blue Hawaii* CD. It was either that or Don Ho. Besides," he added, curling his upper lip and pitching his voice lower, "I do a mean Elvis impression."

When he swiveled his hips in demonstration, Lucy laughed and said to no one in particular, "I like him."

Steph was smiling, a wistful expression on her face. "Rob and I spent our honeymoon in Hawaii. Thanks, Brandon. I didn't know I was getting a tropical vacation when we left the house tonight."

"You're welcome." He turned to Asia. "So is it okay that I turned this evening into a luau without your permission? I just thought, What the hell? We'd bring a little bit of warm Hawaii into downtown Atlanta."

She swallowed hard at his unexpected gesture. He'd remembered her offhand comment the other day, her panicky regret that she should be doing more with her life. That she might not get the chance. "You are full of surprises, Peters."

He ducked his head. "And you don't like surprises."

"I could learn to," she said.

"Really?" He shot her a smile that was half pleasure and half mischief. "Then wait until you see what else I have."

She groaned. "I'm afraid to ask."

"Steph, did you guys pick up any hula steps while you were in Hawaii? Maybe I don't need the DVD after all." He'd pulled a long raffia grass skirt and a DVD—instructional, Asia assumed—out of the bag.

Steph laughed. "A few, but I was under the influence of rum. I'm definitely not qualified to teach someone else."

Brandon raised an eyebrow in Asia's direction. "You'll try a few moves with me, won't you? You have to get the whole island experience."

Lucy was beaming. "If you can get her to put on a grass skirt, you are so invited to my wedding."

"Lucy!" Asia scolded, but since she was trying not to laugh, no one took her seriously. "Brandon, feel free to put in the hula DVD. We'll watch."

Lucy sighed. "She has this thing about being silly in front of other people."

Brandon's eyes went serious for a moment as they met hers. "Maybe *that* should be on your list."

She thought about the suggestion, about the qualities she'd always admired in her sister and about how good it felt to smile like this. *Maybe it should.*

Eleven

L ucy flipped through the radio stations in Michael's car, trying to find something soft and slow that matched her dreamy mood. The sky outside was unbelievably clear, a bejeweled stretch of black velvet. After an evening of laughing and cutting up, she was relaxed and anticipated being alone and intimate with the man next to her.

"I had such a good time tonight," she said.

"Me, too. That was fun. Although our attempts at hula dancing probably dishonored decades of Hawaiian cultural tradition."

She laughed. In actuality, they'd tried that for only a few moments before moving on to the comparatively tame board games, but everyone had pulled grass skirts on over their clothes and made the effort. Even Asia, though protesting that she looked idiotic, had swayed her arms and hips a couple of times. Brandon seemed good for her and therefore automatically earned Lucy's seal of approval.

But Lucy was preoccupied with her own date for the evening. She squeezed Michael's hand. "It's nice to see you in such a good mood. I've been . . . worried about you."

His gaze flitted to her for a moment before returning to the dark road. "I told you not to."

Let it go.

She should. They were having a great evening, so why argue? It was unlike her to be confrontational. She'd given him the space he'd obviously needed to work out whatever was wrong, and they could move on from here.

But she heard herself saying, "There's a difference between telling me not to worry, which is vaguely condescending, and honestly telling me there's nothing to worry *about*. We both know something's been bothering you."

His jaw had tightened as soon as she'd said *condescending*. Bad sign. Then again, perhaps it had been a bad word choice.

"Shouldn't the truth be a cornerstone of marriage?" she prompted. He'd have to agree with that.

"You know I wouldn't lie to you about anything important, Lucy."

"Anything *important*? You get to prioritize what truths are worth sharing with me?"

"There are some truths you don't want to hear," he snapped.

She drew back, not sure if she was more surprised by the anger in his tone or the hostility she could feel surging through her in response to being patronized. What can of worms had she opened?

"You're emotional." He lobbed the accusation like a grenade. "You cry at the drop of a hat. Which is a valid part of your personality, and you know I love you, but it's difficult to share certain things if I'm worried you'll fall apart—"

"Fall apart? Just because I can get weepy about something doesn't mean I'm a weak person."

He hesitated. "That's not what I said."

"The hell it isn't! You made me sound like some little kid you have to protect from the big, bad world." She had an uncomfortable memory of the way she'd sobbed in his arms the night they'd learned Asia's cancer was back. *Screw that.* If the man couldn't be there for her when her sister was critically ill, then—

"Lucy, maybe we should table this discussion until I can figure out a better way to put this."

"You mean until you can find a way to spare my delicate little feelings?" The venomous voice was unfamiliar in her own ears, but the anger was dangerously liberating. "What are these 'things'?"

"Excuse me?"

" 'It's difficult to share certain things,' " she mimicked like a bailiff reading back pertinent testimony. "Which things?" One minute she'd been half of a happy couple, and now there were *things.*

He ground out an exasperated breath. "Your family. The way you are with them."

She didn't know what she'd been expecting, but that hadn't been it. "What?" She and her family were close, always had been. Unlike many of her friends, it had never occurred to her to go away for college. She couldn't imagine not having her mother's phone number being a local call or not being able to grab lunch with Asia and catch up while they window-shopped at malls Lucy couldn't afford.

Or was that Michael's point, that she should be more independent, like him?

"My brothers and I—hell, even Gail—we're confident by nature. Cocky at times. I'm not advocating arrogance, but to see you put yourself down, watch you *let* your family put you down . . ." He sounded disgusted.

This was how Michael saw her? Her anger had been like a balloon, quickly inflated and now suddenly popped, leaving a whooshing, sucking wound in her side. Pain rushed in to fill the vacuum.

"They don't put me down. Every family has its . . . Don't you and these confident, cocky brothers of yours rag on each other? Tease each other about past events and have in-jokes?"

"Yeah, we do, Luce, but it's not one-sided. With you, it's like—God, you're going to take this the wrong way—it's like you're the butt of every joke. And you allow it."

Butt of every joke.

Was there a *right* way to take that description? She bit her lower lip, driving her teeth into the skin as if to distract herself with a less brutal hurt than what the man she loved was inflicting. "You don't know what you're talking about."

His silence spoke volumes.

"Asia and I tease each other," she added.

"Even when your parents are in earshot? It's like there's this family pecking order, and you—"

"Yes, you've made it very clear where you think I rate." Tears stung her eyes, but she'd be damned if she'd shed one in front of him. It would only prove his theory that she fell apart at the drop of a hat. *Bastard.*

"It's not what I think at all," he said softly. "I think you're amazing. Which is why I asked you to marry me, Lucy. But *you* need to think you're amazing. Did you hear your mother the other night? I swear, you couldn't even address an envelope without her suggesting a better way to do it!"

"That's how moms are with their daughters," Lucy said, thinking of how Cam had considered eloping before her marriage because her own mother was driving her nuts. Even Steph had said tonight that part of the reason they'd chosen Hawaii was because, after the chaos of wedding preparations, escaping the continental United States for a few days seemed like a good idea.

Michael was quick with a rebuttal. "Your mom's not that way with Asia."

This was awful. If Lucy had had a secret, unspoken insecurity as an adolescent, it had been that her parents might love Asia more than they loved her. She'd outgrown that, was comfortable with the Swenson family dynamic. But now the man who was supposed to know her better than anyone else in the world was making it sound as if maybe, maybe . . . maybe that thing that had been too painful ever to say out loud, that thing it had been disloyal even to think . . . might be true.

"You come from a family of five," she said, her voice remarkably calm. "When there are only two kids, it naturally invites comparison."

"And you have to wind up on the bottom in every single comparison?"

It wasn't enough that he'd exposed the wound; now he had to poke at it with a sharp stick. She wanted to tell him to shut up, but she was afraid that if she did, he might remind her that she was the one who'd pressed for this conversation. Lucy didn't think she'd be able to forgive him that smugness on top of everything else.

"They love you, Lucy, I know they do. But you should stand up for yourself."

"And do what? Pick a fight with my mother over something that bothers you, not me? Tell Asia that I resent her because I was a bigger screwup when we were kids?" The anger was flooding back, and she welcomed its warmth, drawing it around her in a protective cloak. "In case you hadn't noticed, Michael, my family has bigger concerns. My *sister* has *cancer.* My mother and father are *terrified.* And I am not so petty that I'm going to bitch about a few isn't-Lucy-silly anecdotes if it takes people's minds off bigger problems. Frankly, I have done a lot of silly things, and I'm beginning to wonder if agreeing to marry *you* wasn't one of them!"

Her exclamation reverberated silently, echoing between them psychically if not audibly. *Shitshitshit.* This was exactly the kind of impulsive mistake that fueled all those Lucy-is-silly stories. What she wouldn't give to take it back.

Even in the dark she saw his hands tighten on the steering wheel. "You don't mean that."

"No. I didn't." She kept her words on a tight leash, not trusting herself. "Honestly, I don't even know where it came from."

"Years of repressed anger?" he suggested, his voice dark with grim humor.

"You're off base about this. You're entitled to your own feelings about the situation, but that doesn't make them right."

"Can we at least agree that you're not objective? Try being in my shoes, an outsider listening to everything. It wouldn't bother me if I really believed it didn't bother you. But you let it seep in until you doubt whether you deserved your promotion, and question whether you need to drop a few pounds." He turned the car onto her street. "I just want you to stand up for yourself, darlin'. I want you to be happy."

"*I* get to decide what makes me happy. Maybe I should stand up to my family more, but that's my decision. Maybe I should also stand up to you."

He recoiled. "I don't put you down."

Hadn't he done exactly that numerous times in this conversation? "You try to make decisions for me. I tell you I want to lose a few pounds; you end up suggesting we go for ice cream. How is that supporting my choices? You know I like romantic comedies, but convince me that dark, densely plotted movies that border on the pretentious will be good for me. You take it upon yourself to censor your own feelings about me, concluding that it's better to lie and tell me nothing's wrong than to treat me like an equal! When you're working late and I cut you some slack, it's all, 'You're the best, darlin'.' But when I'm laid-back and cut my family slack, I'm a wimp? I don't think it works both ways."

"Lucy—"

"No." She yanked off her seat belt, determined to make it across the driveway and to her front door before any bitter tears came. "Good night, Michael. I'll call you in a few days when we've both had time to think."

She shut the door with a precise click and marched toward her house without glancing back. Not bad for an overly sentimental and spineless woman.

⚘

The last leftovers had been cellophane-wrapped, and Asia's counters had been rubbed down with disinfecting wipes. She'd been glad Brandon had lingered behind, volunteering to help her tidy up and making it clear to Lucy she didn't have to stay. Still, now that the place was clean, Asia experienced a flutter of nerves, like the first time she'd gone off the high dive. She'd argued with her parents that she was ready, and staring down at that blue water, she'd known how much she wanted to do it. But that didn't mean jumping came easily.

"Dime for your thoughts," Brandon said. "I adjusted for inflation."

She leaned against a counter. "I had fun tonight. You make me laugh almost as much as Lucy, and that's saying something."

"She's terrific," Brandon said. "Anyone could tell just by looking at you two that you're sisters."

"Really?" They'd never resembled each other in the slightest.

"Your eyes. I know they aren't the same color or anything, but there's the same spark. Must be a Swenson thing."

"Must be." She grinned, thinking of her family and how much they meant to her despite their idiosyncrasies. After all, *they* put up with *her* quirks. "Brandon, thanks again for coming tonight. . . ."

"But it's time I got the hell out and left you alone?" he asked cheerfully.

"Probably," she admitted. By Atlanta nightlife standards, it wasn't late, but her energy had been flagging for the past half hour. "I don't know if you've noticed, but I tend to wear out easily."

"I noticed."

She followed his gaze to her refrigerator, where several magnets bore the names, addresses, and phone numbers of medical facilities. She'd posted a drug fact sheet an oncology nurse had given her, as well as a typed copy of her medical history, which she could take with her to fill out the nine thousand forms she must have been handed since her first diagnosis. On days when she was suffering chemo brain, it could be difficult to remember the related medical histories of everyone in her immediate family or whether she had any known allergies.

On days chemo brain *really* kicked in, it was difficult to remember her full name.

"I'll leave," he promised. "Get some rest, and I'll see you at work tomorrow."

True, but she'd never see him the same way. "About what you did tonight..."

"Shanghaiing your party and forcing you to wear a grass skirt?"

She put a hand over his, stopping the self-deprecation. "You know what I mean."

"If you really want to go to Hawaii, you'll get there someday. This was just to hold you over in the meantime," he said with a tender half smile.

She thought about what he'd asked her the afternoon he'd taken her to the Putt-Putt golf course, about what specific things she wanted to do. Things she might regret not doing. Suddenly she knew what was at the top of her list. She took a step closer to him.

Oh, he smells good.

His eyes widened at her nearness, then dropped to her mouth before returning to capture her gaze.

Her mind raced, thinking about things like bad breath and mouth sores and dry lips... and how nice it would be to be touched for no other reason than because someone really *wanted* to. The man had taken her to Hawaii for the evening. The least he deserved was an aloha kiss farewell.

She stretched up to brush her lips across his. He immediately dipped his head, kissing her back. Not aggressively, but confidently and with definite feeling. There was restraint in the way his mouth sampled hers, as if he didn't want to deepen the kiss without her permission. Part of her wanted to give it, and the rest of her was startled by what she'd already done. Jumping off the high dive was enough for now; learning how to do a reverse somersault all in one night might be a bit much. She pulled away slowly, coming back one last time to nip at his bottom lip.

He rested his forehead against hers. "I wasn't expecting that."

She grinned. "Hey, I have surprises, too."

"I can't wait to discover more of them." He straightened, studying her face. "I know that what with the minigolf and tiki torches, I can seem like a guy who doesn't take anything seriously."

She lowered her gaze, abashed. She'd thought that about him before she got to know him better.

"But I'm not oblivious. I know you're sick. It just doesn't change how I feel."

"Which is?" She couldn't believe she'd been brave enough to press for clarification. What would she say if he turned the question on her?

"I like spending time with you and want to spend more. You're an intriguing woman. You're sharp. Attractive."

She winced, glad his first impressions of her had been

formed when she had long hair and her own figure, but wondering how she stood up to that memory now.

"When we were playing golf and you made that crack about not having hair and boobs—"

She winced again. Maybe Brandon wasn't as suave as she'd thought, because he was making her feel more self-conscious than flattered.

"—I reacted badly. I wanted to be the noble guy who didn't notice superficial shit like that. But after I had time to think about it, I realized I was being dismissive. I shouldn't have treated the subject like it was unimportant. of course it's important. But you *are* attractive. You have the most gorgeous eyes I've ever seen."

The way he was staring into them now made it easy to believe him. A flush spread across her skin, a warm tingle that reminded her that not every physical reaction was an irritating side effect. Her body could be a source of pleasure, too.

"Walk me to the door?" he asked. "I know I should go, I'm just having trouble saying good-bye."

Somewhere between the kitchen and her door, his fingers laced with hers.

As he stepped into the hallway, he told her, "Just so you know, I get how important the job is. I wouldn't ever say or do anything at the office that would make you feel unprofessional."

She almost laughed at that, because he'd often been a flirt at work. Harmless, sure, but not above making an outrageous statement or flashing that smile of his. If he turned into a stuffed shirt overnight, people would probably assume they were sleeping together. The thought made her light-headed.

"I don't think you have to change anything about your behavior at work," she told him, wondering if he noticed that she sounded slightly breathless.

His smile told her he had. "Sweet dreams, Swenson." He punctuated it with one last kiss before he turned.

The perfect ending to the evening, and the perfect beginning to something new and sweet and unexpected.

Twelve

"Thanks again for meeting me," Lucy said, feeling guilty that Cam had treated her to lunch and Lucy had barely touched the food. The waiter had looked offended that she hadn't at least wanted a to-go box for her shrimp and grits entrée.

"That's what friends are for," Cam said. "You were there for me to vent when *I* was the one getting married. I have to tell you, most of the couples I know go through this. It's like God's test or something. Surviving the wedding preparation gets you in better shape to deal with the trials of marriage itself."

"If you say so." Lucy fiddled with the straw in her sweet tea. She'd thought that the prewedding fights would be about stuff like who got to sleep on which side of the bed for the rest of their lives, or deejay versus band for the reception. But Michael opining that she was her family's whipping girl? "I know he loves me, Cam. I don't think he was deliberately being cruel. But it still hurts."

"Well, sure it does, honey."

"And I'm still pissed." Anger was an atypical emotion for her, and she wasn't sure what to do with it. It rattled around inside like a sharp gasket that had come loose and was poking her in soft, vulnerable spots.

Cam averted her gaze.

"What?"

"Nothing."

"Something." Lucy straightened in her chair. "Unless you truly find that empty table in the corner fascinating. Cam, look at me."

Her friend did, apology and guilt on her pretty face. "I want to support you. I'm here for you, Luce."

"But?"

"No, that's it. That's all I was going to say. Did I, um, tell you I started a new painting?"

Which was a relief, since Cam's brief flirtation with sculpting had been an unqualified disaster, but not the point. At least this time when Lucy dragged the truth out of someone who cared about her, she wouldn't be as blindsided as she'd been with Michael last night. "What *aren't* you saying?"

"Well, part of me—tiny, you understand, minuscule—kind of, sort of, gets where he was coming from. But he was still wrong to tell you everything was okay, then dump it all out when you guys were having a perfectly good evening," Cam finished in a rush of solidarity.

"You think I'm a wuss, too?" Lucy sighed. A boyfriend's pomposity was just one person's opinion; her best friend's seconding the opinion dangerously resembled a consensus.

"Of course not. But maybe your family doesn't . . . take you as seriously as they do Asia."

"She does have more serious things going on than I do," Lucy pointed out.

"No." Cam was adamant. "More *critical* maybe, but more important? Done right, marriage is a once-in-a-lifetime event! These plans you're making aren't just seating charts and nosegays. They're your future."

Lucy changed tacks. "Asia and I are so different. Our parents recognize that. It would be weird for them to treat us exactly the same."

"Fair enough." Cam signaled for the check, looking dissatisfied with the conversation's resolution.

"Asia is really wonderful," Lucy felt compelled to add. "She's never been superior or smug with me. She's happy about my promotion and my engagement, no matter what's going on in her life."

"Agreed." After rooting around in her purse for a moment, Cam fished out her credit card. "You know I think the world of her."

"So what exactly is it that you and Michael want me to do?" Lucy asked in frustration. "Make some declarative statement to my parents about how they have to be as proud of me as they are of her? Maybe I could figure out a way to use it as a wedding toast."

"I'm not advocating that you *do* anything. It's your family, babe. I was just saying I can see Michael's point."

"Kind of, sort of," Lucy said dryly.

"Exactly. Was it disloyal even to say that much? I can call him an insensitive fart-blossom if it'll make you feel better."

Lucy laughed. "Thanks, but I can live without that description of the love of my life."

"Okay. I promise next time you call, I'll do better. You and Michael never fight, so I was off my game. Although, as a former bride, I should have warned you about this eventuality."

Lucy wouldn't have believed her anyway. As her friend said, she and Michael never fought.

At the beginning, she hadn't wanted to rock the boat by complaining about insignificant things. Later she'd taken their lack of discord as proof that they were a compatible couple. Now she just wondered if she was a coward. She'd been angry at Michael for keeping his true feelings to himself, but did she do the same thing? Did she swallow concerns that were easier to ignore than put into words?

Cam signed her credit card slip with a flourish, then flashed a quick smile. "You're getting married, Luce. This is one of the happiest times of your life. It will all be worth it once the wedding's behind you and you've popped the cork on the bubbly."

Happiest time of her life? *Yeah.* And she was a happy person by nature. And all Michael wanted was for her to be happy. It felt too ungrateful to admit that despite all this freaking *happiness,* sometimes she just wanted to scream. So instead of voicing the admission, she swallowed it back, too, and told herself that eventually the feeling would pass.

Asia's week was fantastic. Through Tuesday, anyway. For two days she'd arrived at work with a renewed sense of energy, tackling her job with zeal and feeling like her old self as she laughed in the elevator with Brandon and took a colleague out to lunch. Maybe too *much* like her old self, refusing to recognize her limits. Both nights she came home with plans to call Lucy and tell her about how things were developing with Brandon, but both nights she fell asleep not long after walking in the door.

She awoke Wednesday with a headache that escalated until she finally had to concede defeat and leave work while she could still drive safely. Brandon offered to come check on her that evening, bring her something for dinner, but she told him that if she managed to fall asleep through the pain, she didn't want to risk anything waking her up. She left Lucy a message canceling their wig hunt, then unplugged her phone.

Her finger-stick test on Thursday proclaimed her well enough to have the day's chemo, but she didn't see Stephanie, which left her worried. Friday she was so tired she barely had the energy to swallow water, and Saturday was the worst day she'd had so far. She twisted into one nearly bearable position on the couch and tried to maintain it without moving a muscle, hoping that if she stayed perfectly still the nausea swimming and flipping in her stomach like vicious tadpoles would eventually cease. How would she ever be well enough to host Lucy's shower tomorrow?

Because she felt too sick even to sleep, she spent a lot of time just staring at the Georgia O'Keeffe painting Lucy had given her. Maybe she would ask Cam to paint her a canvas to hang. Something soothing, in light blues and greens. For one half second, she actually thought about calling Cam and begging her to contact all the attendees and tell them Cam was now hosting Lucy's shower at Cam's house.

But thoughts like that pissed Asia off just enough to put some color back in her cheeks. Cancer was part of her particular mountain, but one day she'd have it conquered and would stand victorious, her hair whipping in the wind. of course, she could wish for a little less altitude sickness along the way.

Her mother called Saturday evening to say Reva, Rae, and Aunt Ginny had arrived in town, and ask if Asia would like to join them for dinner. Asia refused instantly but tried to sound upbeat about seeing them all the next day.

When her alarm went off on Sunday morning, she opened her eyes cautiously, waiting to see if the room spun. She didn't dare push herself into a sitting position, but she lifted her head a fraction from the pillow. Though her stomach tightened, it didn't seize in immediate rebellion. The worst had passed.

Her lips felt thick and dry, her throat scratchy, and she decided that staying hydrated was her first order of business. Then she should think about getting dressed and preparing for the shower. She was so relieved Marianne and Cam were both arriving early. Even the thought of setting out napkins and brewing sweet tea sounded intimidating right now.

By the time her mother got there, Asia had put on a loose-fitting blue dress and fuzzy Christmas socks over a pair of regular gym socks because she couldn't seem to get her feet warm.

Marianne frowned over the top of the two stacked casserole dishes she carried. "Are you going to be all right?"

"Of course." But her mother continued to give her that worried, let-me-feel-your-forehead look. "I'm fine, Mama. Some of the books say that while rest is crucial, too much lying around can actually make the fatigue worse. Once I'm moving and having fun, I won't think so much about how I feel."

At least, she hoped that was the case, because currently she felt like dog shit.

"You *really* don't look good, sweetheart. Do you want some help with makeup?"

They'd attended a seminar together during Asia's early treatment that specialized in cosmetics for women with cancer, those with sensitive-skin issues and no eyebrows. Marianne might not remember a medical term from one doctor's appointment to the next, but she could help her daughter maintain her dignity by adding splashes of beauty. She'd also made Asia two warm caps to keep her body from losing so much heat from the top of her head. They were much appreciated, especially on cold November nights.

"Thanks, Mom, but I'm moving at the speed of a snail on Valium, and we have more important things to take care of before guests start showing up."

"The most important thing you have to take care of," Marianne said firmly, "is yourself. You go rest on the couch. I'll get things under control in the kitchen."

On another day Asia would have protested. Today she was just grateful for the order. She must have dozed, because a knock jolted her from a dream she hadn't realized she was having. She'd imagined she was hanging Lucy's shower banner by the front door, but that every time she got one end even, the other side fell.

"I'm here to help," Cam chirped as Marianne let her in. "I have extra folding chairs in the trunk of my SUV if you think we need them. And before I forget, here are the pictures." She set a folder on the coffee table.

They'd decided to do a takeoff of the old television show

This Is Your Life. On the back of the front door, they were hanging the ugly shower curtain Lucy had liked when they'd filled out the bridal registry. Marianne shook her head whenever she looked at it, but Asia assured her Lucy would think it was funny. On the wall next to the curtain was taped a computer-generated banner that read, LUCY SWENSON THIS IS YOUR SHOWER. Pictures of Lucy throughout her life were being displayed all over the living room, along with pictures of her and Michael together.

Cute couple, Asia thought absently, standing near her television set and wondering what she'd been about to do.

Cam came into the living room with a roll of tape. "What are you doing up? I thought we agreed you'd stay off your feet, since you don't have to officially hostess yet."

Right. She should sit. Sofa . . . very far away.

"Asia?" Cam's voice came from a great distance, taking on an edge of hysteria. "You okay, sweetie? You don't look so good."

Should've taken Mom up on that makeup assistance.

She was dimly aware of Cam helping her to the couch and of voices a few minutes later. Guests were starting to arrive. Maybe they should open the balcony doors. It seemed warm, and would only get more so once the living room was full of people.

"Here."

Asia accepted the cold glass that was being pressed into her hand and blinked. "Lucy? When did you get here?"

"Just a second ago. Gail's flight came in a few minutes early, which made a nice change from my always being late to everything. Cam took her in the kitchen to meet Mom. She thought you might need a second."

Asia sipped the cool water, forcibly clearing her head. "No. I'm a little foggy—tired, I guess—but once I wake up, I'll be fine."

Lucy gestured toward the pictures around the room and the shower curtain. "Your idea?"

"If you like it, yeah. If you hate it, it was all Cam's doing."

Lucy laughed. "So you really are okay? You had me worried there for a minute."

"I told you, I'll be fine. By the way, you get to keep that ugly shower curtain when this is all over. I certainly don't want to get stuck with the eyesore." She lowered her voice. "This is the first time you've met Gail, right? How'd it go on the ride over?"

"Great. She's as nice as his parents. His *family's* terrific."

"Luce?" Was it Asia's diminished mental capacity, or did her sister sound sarcastic?

Lucy shook her head. "Nothing."

Another knock temporarily halted their conversation, and Asia pushed herself to her feet. A good hostess should answer the door. Several of Lucy's coworkers arrived in a convivial clump, Aunt Ginny following on their heels, accompanied by Reva and Rae. The gorgeous blondes wore dresses identical except for the fabric's hue. Among the pastels and autumn colors, their jewel-tone green and purple stood out so clearly they might have worn sandwich-board signs that said, LOOK AT ME.

Well, why not? Asia thought with detached amusement. If she had those curves and flowing gold locks, she'd be inclined to work them, too.

Soon the living room was crowded with women of different heights, colors, and fashion sensibilities. Asia knew she'd never be able to remember the names of those she hadn't met before today, and was relieved when Cam passed around adhesive name tags and a dark pink marker. Asia made it a point, however, to sit next to Gail for a few seconds and tell her how much the Swensons all loved Michael.

When all but two of the guests had arrived, Asia called for everyone's attention. "Thank you guys for coming today to help Lucy celebrate her upcoming marriage to Michael O'Malley. I hope you'll all pile your plates high with food and get to know one another. The plan is to eat now, then embarrass the bride with lots of fun games before we let her have gifts and dessert."

This agenda got good-natured cheers.

Confident that things were going well, Asia excused herself to the kitchen. People would assume she was checking on food or bringing out more ice, and she could try to refocus her thoughts without worrying anyone. She hadn't missed a Monday of work since chemo started, but maybe she'd call in sick tomorrow. After an extra day of rest, she'd be right as rain.

"Anything I can do for you?" Cam asked, sticking her head around the corner.

"What?" Asia almost jumped, looking around for her excuse to be in here so that Cam wouldn't worry. Or worse, tell Lucy.

But as Cam stepped closer, she looked too preoccupied to notice that Asia wasn't actually doing anything. She dropped her voice to just above a whisper. "I can't put Lucy on the spot by asking her at her own shower, but did everything get all straightened out with her and Michael? After our lunch on

Monday, I assumed they'd returned to their habitual state of bliss, but something in her eyes . . ."

There'd been a nonblissful state and Lucy hadn't mentioned it? "Straightened what out?"

"Their fight. From this weekend." Cam's face paled. "You didn't know? Oh, no! Me and my big mouth."

"It's okay," Asia insisted, not feeling her words. "You know Lucy and I talk about everything. We probably would have discussed it except, this week was just so chaotic and she's been giving me time to rest."

"Right." Cam lowered her gaze, conveying that there might be other reasons Lucy hadn't mentioned the fight.

The feverish sensation Asia had been experiencing was compounded by the dizzying surprise that Lucy and Michael were having problems. They'd seemed to get along fine when they were here on Sunday, but Cam had said *lunch on Monday*. Had they fought after leaving her apartment? Asia glanced at Cam's guilty expression.

Had she somehow been *responsible* for their fight?

Cam cleared her throat. "We should get back to the guests."

"Of course." Asia preceded her into the living room, where the aromatic mixture of floral body sprays, citrus shampoos, and musky perfumes hit her in the midsection like an unrelenting wave. Nausea knocked her off balance, almost literally, as she reached out blindly to steady herself.

"Asia?" Lucy's concern sliced through the laughing buzz of conversation.

"I'm fine," Asia maintained as all eyes turned toward her.

She nodded once for emphasis. Then the room darkened, and the floor rushed toward her.

≈

Lucy waited with her mother in an area of the hospital with special rooms for immunocompromised patients, holding Marianne's hand and explaining again what the doctor had already said. On the ride there, Lucy had called Michael on her cell phone. George had taken him bowling that afternoon. The two men were on their way, but construction on 285 had delayed their arrival.

"Neutropenic," Marianne repeated like an elementary schoolchild learning a new vocabulary word.

"Her white cell count is too low, Mama, damaged by the chemo." Lucy scooted closer to her mom on the uncomfortable bench seat.

"Don't they give her something to prevent that?"

"Yes, but her immune system is weak right now, so she got sick. They just need to make sure it doesn't get any worse. They have to get her all better before they do more chemo or any other treatment."

Marianne looked up with unshed tears glistening in her eyes, so like Lucy's. Although Marianne had a slighter build, the two of them were clearly related. Physically, Marianne had nothing in common with Asia except a flat chest. "Got sick? She's already *sick*. The doctors don't know if she'll ever get better, do they?"

It was true that many women with metastatic cancer were never cured, but some of them were able to beat the cancer back enough to live seemingly normal and healthy lives for significant stretches of time. Every day offered a new possibility for improvement, advances, cures. *Miracles.*

Lucy hugged her mom, but Marianne glanced up with an expectant expression, as if she hoped for more. As if she needed her daughter to say something. Like what, other than that this entire day was ironic as hell?

It had started with her nervously meeting Gail at the airport. Though Lucy and Michael had technically put their argument behind them earlier this week, his words hadn't quite yet turned to numb scar tissue. His doubts about her lay just below the surface, waiting for Gail to find fault with her. But Gail was delightful and seemed enchanted that Lucy would be her sister-in-law in a few short months.

Then there'd been the shower, which the guest of honor was no longer attending. Most people had gone home, of course, but Aunt Ginny had stayed with her girls. That had been Lucy's compromise, since they'd wanted to come to the hospital. Cam had promised to keep them fed and reasonably entertained until Lucy could call with an update. So Cam and a few others waited in a room of glossy photos and unopened gifts while the bride-to-be sat in a waiting room with outdated reading material.

The most painful irony was that her robust older sister, the person Lucy had once seen as her protector, could be laid low by the common cold. Viruses that *toddlers* caught and generally recovered from with little more than extra sleep and juice could potentially kill her sister.

"You're right, Mom, it's unfair. All we can do is pray and hope for the best."

"That's not enough," Marianne balked.

Do you have a better idea?

Lucy bit back the retort, her habit of not talking back to her parents coming in handy. She'd lashed out at Michael earlier in the week, and the possible repercussions of that exchange still haunted her. After insinuating that it had been a mistake to accept his proposal, she felt lucky he hadn't broken the engagement. Just *regular* lucky, not that dewy-eyed, I'm-not-worthy worshipful attitude she'd had earlier in their relationship. Did that mean the bloom was off the rose?

She'd called him on Tuesday, with mixed feelings about the fact that he'd waited for her to do so. On the one hand, she'd pretty much told him not to contact her. But what woman didn't want to feel like her man would fight for her? Not that he'd ever had to; he was gorgeous and compassionate and successful. Lucy was . . . Lucy.

While she didn't think she'd been pathetic or needy in their relationship, there had been times when she felt she didn't deserve him. So maybe he wasn't entirely wrong when he'd cited her low self-esteem.

During her phone call, she'd been composed and mature. "While I don't agree with everything you said, thank you for finally respecting me enough to say it."

"I do respect you, Lucy. I love you."

"I know. And I'm not really angry anymore, but I have a lot to think about. Us, the house closing next month, the wedding, my sister. Even work, scheduling an influx of requests and upcoming shops around customers' holiday hours and our own people's vacation days. I may be a little out-of-pocket, and I didn't want you to get the wrong idea and think that I was"— sulking?—"holding a grudge."

"Of course not," he'd said. "That's not like you."

So he only thought her self-abasing, not vindictive. Nifty.

Boy, she was certainly turning bitter as fall rolled into winter. Maybe while she was in a building full of health professionals, she should ask someone about seasonal affective disorder. Or maybe this was just garden-variety depression over one of the most important people in her life being critically ill.

At the sound of footsteps, Lucy straightened, peering around the corner to see if Michael and her father had arrived, or if this was someone like her, stranded in the halls, waiting for news of a loved one, feeling impotent because there wasn't anything tangible they could do. She had a sudden yen to visit the maternity ward. That wing probably had the only joy-filled waiting rooms.

The person in the hall turned out to be the doctor who'd first spoken to them after Asia was admitted to a room.

"She's awake, but exhausted," he said after his initial greeting.

"Is she all right?" Marianne asked.

"Her condition hasn't changed much since we spoke before, but she's on an IV of antibiotics that should help. Right now we want her to rest and to limit her chances of exposure to germs. We ask that no flowers be allowed in the room, and visitors are to be kept to an absolute minimum. She is, however, asking to speak to her sister." He turned to Lucy. "You'll need to wear a mask over your mouth and nose."

Marianne pressed a hand to her chest, looking puzzled. "She didn't ask for her mama?"

Lucy patted her mother's shoulder. "You know Asia. You raised her to be so considerate, she probably wants to apologize for interrupting the shower."

"You're probably right." Marianne shook her head, the ghost of a rueful smile playing about her lips. "But surely she realizes the shower's unimportant next to this."

"Still." Lucy stood, following the doctor, uncharitably eager to be away from her mother.

Asia was in a room with special airflow to reduce the chances of infection. She was pale and looked smaller in her hospital gown, gloves, and knit cap than she had in the dress she'd worn earlier. The medical monitors and rolling IV stand on either side of her might have been her bodyguards. Or her captors.

"Hey," Lucy said. "I understand I have you to thank for getting me out of that waiting room with Mom. She's pretty worried about you." It was easier than saying, *I'm worried about you. You're my big sister, and you are not allowed to die on me.*

"Least I could do," Asia said in a weak voice that probably meant her throat was hurting. "Since I'm the reason you had to be in the waiting room in the first place."

"Yeah. Well." She moved closer to her sister's side. "Where else would I be?"

"Dumb question, Blondie. Your shower, maybe, having a great afternoon with people who care about you?" Her voice was raspy, but she pushed on, obviously hell-bent on speaking her mind. "It's not just the being sick I hate, you know. Like if I knew I was going to throw up five times a day at certain hours,

I'd schedule around it. What pisses me off is how the cancer screws up all the other parts of my life. And now yours."

Lucy swallowed, tempted to protest that stuff like this built character. But it would be insincere. She didn't want more character. She wanted her sister healthy, and she wanted her damn bridal shower with friends and family who'd come to town specifically to spend the day with her.

For a moment on the drive to the hospital she'd flash-forwarded to her wedding. What about that day? Would Asia feel well enough to stand at the front of the church? Maybe Enid Norcott had been right when she'd said Lucy was selfish for putting her there.

What if Asia collapsed that day, too, from all the activity and the crowd, and Lucy had to postpone her nuptials to stand in another room like this one, wasting the gorgeous gown it had taken them so many trips to find?

I'm going to hell. Was she honestly worrying about how her sister's cancer would affect her wedding?

Well, dammit, it was her wedding day. Little girls all over the world tottered on their mother's high-heeled sandals and stuck lace doilies on their heads and pretended they were getting married. Every woman in love should be entitled to the dream, entitled to want that one moment in the spotlight without her happiness being eclipsed by . . .

Guilt shoved back at Lucy, reminding her that in a perfect world women also had the right to be healthy.

Mothers, like Stephanie, should never have to lie in beds like this one wondering what their children would do without them, asking themselves if their husbands knew which bed-time stories brought the most comfort and which video games played too close to bedtime caused nightmares. Women like Asia shouldn't have to be here, wondering if they'd live long enough to fall in love or get the chance to become a mother.

"You have got to get healthy," Lucy said fiercely. "You've always, always come through for me if I asked for something. So I'm asking you for this."

"Lucy—"

"We've got a big day in January," Lucy said on top of her, trying to ignore the fact that Asia's hazel eyes shimmered with tears. "I asked you to be my maid of honor, and you said yes. So you're just going to have to get better. Your chemo is scheduled to finish before then. Your counts will be good. You look smashing in the dress, and we will find a fantastic wig. Brandon won't know what hit him. You *do* plan on taking him to the wedding, don't you?"

Asia hiccuped. "Yeah. I was meaning to mention that."

"See, you have a lot to look forward to," Lucy said, desperation making her optimism sound manic. And *she'd* been impatient with Marianne for not handling today's crisis better. *Hypocrite!* It had taken Lucy less than ten minutes to make her sister cry. *I'm supposed to cheer people up.* Now she was failing even at that.

"Meaning to ask you something, too," Asia said. "Everything okay with you and Michael?"

Lucy froze, not a good enough liar for an immediate and convincing denial. How did Asia know about the fight? The last time she'd seen them together had been at her place, when things had been good. *Cam.*

Asia sighed. "Why didn't you tell me?"

"When I asked you at the shower if you were feeling all

right, why didn't *you* tell *me* the truth?" Lucy didn't believe her sister had gone from feeling peachy to needing an ambulance within the space of an hour.

"When you're undergoing treatment, sometimes feeling crappy becomes the norm, so you don't think much of it." But that was only half the truth, and they both knew it.

They'd been trying to protect each other. Because that was what family did.

"I shouldn't stay long," Lucy said. "When I came in here Mom was still alone, and the doc said you need your rest."

"Okay. But, Lucy? I will be at that wedding, and I will walk down that aisle in the processional, if I have to drag a damn IV stand with me to do it."

"In that case, I'll get each of the bridesmaids one so your accessories are properly coordinated."

"Deal."

Thirteen

Lucy hadn't been able to sleep, so as soon as Michael's headlights cut across the curtains, she padded toward the front door. He had a key, but she'd absently latched the security chain earlier, knowing deep down she would be awake.

She'd chased him off at the hospital earlier, telling him he should take his sister to dinner before Gail had to get back to the airport. Poor girl, she'd flown in for one day to attend a shower that had ended before Lucy could even open the be-ribboned bag Gail had carried on the plane with her. Michael had promised he'd come check on Lucy after dropping his sister off at Hartsfield.

"If that's all right with you," he'd added almost shyly, as if worried Lucy wouldn't want to see him.

As she opened the door for him, she wanted nothing more. Well, *most* of all she wanted some doctor with a whole roomful of degrees to look her in the eye and swear Asia would never be ill again. But next to that, what Lucy desired was to be wrapped in Michael's arms.

He folded her into him, standing there in the foyer for a moment before backing her in a clunky, slow dance to the love seat. He took in her flannel plaid pajama bottoms and green sweatshirt, one he'd left there after the third time she'd borrowed it out of his closet. "Did I wake you when I drove up?"

"No. I've just been sitting here."

He smoothed her hair behind her ears. "You should have put in a movie for company, darlin'."

"Didn't want any." She checked herself, glancing up to meet his gaze. "But that doesn't extend to you. I know this week's been . . . well, awful between us. Let's never fight again. But even fighting, I want you with me when things are bad."

He squeezed her tighter. "Same for me. *And* when things are good. I want you with me for always. I've been a real lout."

"Oh?" She tucked her legs under her and leaned against him.

"Gail and I were reminiscing about the first time a boyfriend broke up with her. She couldn't tell our parents why she was so down in the mouth, because they didn't know she'd had a boyfriend to begin with, but my brothers and I knew. She told Colin, and he can't keep a secret. Anyway, when I saw Gail crying, I wanted to kill whoever had hurt her. I know I don't talk to my family nearly as often as you do, but I love them. And I couldn't imagine if . . . I don't tell you nearly enough how brave and compassionate you are, being there for your mom and patiently waiting for the doctors to finish this cycle of medicine."

Lucy sniffed. "Thank you."

"Also, Gail says you're fantastic and I'd better not do anything boneheaded to mess it up."

"I like Gail."

"Is there anything I can do?" he asked. "Take over some part of the wedding planning so you have one less thing to worry about? Let Asia borrow my lucky tie?"

Lucy laughed. "I *knew* you were superstitious about that tie. Were you wearing it the first time you worked on a winning case?"

He drew back, studying her. "No. I was wearing it when I met you. Luckiest damn night of my life."

"Oh." Her throat clogged with tears, and she blinked rapidly, trying to clear her vision. After a moment of not being able to speak, she had an idea. "Michael, there might be something you can do."

"Name it."

"Find reasons to spend time with my dad. Like bowling today. And the two of you have been talking about patching up that one section of fence in the backyard. Mom has me, but Dad has never discussed his feelings with me or Asia. I assume he and Mom talk, but he's always the stoic comforter. I doubt he'll confide in you, and you don't need to pry; I just want him to feel like someone's . . . there. I think it will be easier for him if it's a guy. And whatever you do, don't let him know I put you up to it."

"You're a good daughter, Lucy Swenson." They sat silently for a few minutes. "You think you could sleep now? Because if you're not tired, I have an idea of what might cheer you up."

She raised her eyebrows, feeling far too drained to want sex. "Oh, really?"

"Want to drive over and look at our house?"

She laughed, surprised by the suggestion. "We'd probably look like burglars casing the neighborhood in the dark."

"So that's a no?"

"I don't have the energy tonight to get falsely arrested and try to explain to our future neighbors that we're not nuts."

Tonight, all she wanted was to sleep in his arms and hope that tomorrow brought better circumstances for all of them.

Well, there were some perks to being sick . . . sort of. Though her white count was in a healthy enough range for the doctors to release Asia from the hospital by Wednesday morning, they didn't think her body was up to more chemo just yet. So she had a reprieve. Instead of sitting in her regular recliner this Thursday afternoon, she was shopping with Lucy. Asia was supposed to avoid major crowds and their potential germs, so the mall was out. But she didn't think she was running a risk by being in the specialty women's boutique.

Along one wall were breast prosthetics and post-mastectomy lingerie, but at least half of the small, upscale store was devoted to wigs, scarves, and hats, ranging from novelty items to sophisticated evening wear. One pink baseball cap proclaimed DOWN WITH CANCER in glittery rhinestones. *Hear, hear.*

Asia smiled at her sister over the head of a platinum-haired mannequin. "What do you think, Luce? Is it true blondes really have more fun?"

Lucy laughed, turning away from a layered auburn wig. "Blond? That would certainly surprise Brandon when he shows up tonight."

He'd offered to come by with popcorn and a movie if Asia was feeling up to company after her shopping expedition; he'd bring soup and an expedient good-bye if she wasn't. Tonight would be the first time she'd seen him since he visited her in the hospital, and she was feeling vulnerable. The night she'd kissed him, he'd assured her he wasn't blind to the realities of her illness. He'd been sincere, she knew. Still, those realities had probably looked different in her apartment after a playful evening than they had in a hospital room, when she was plugged into machines and monitors and he had to wear a mask because she was so fragile that even the air he exhaled could harm her.

She and Lucy might not find the right wig for her today, or they might find one but have to order it. If at all possible, though, she wanted to wear one tonight. She wanted to look like the healthy woman she'd been when Brandon first met her.

A subtly elegant salesclerk wearing artful makeup but no perfume that Asia could discern—a welcome omission when Asia's senses were so easily overwhelmed—stepped out from a curtained back room. "Good afternoon, ladies! Can I help you?"

"I hope so." Asia reached inside her purse for the picture they'd brought. The girls on her loop had said it would help to give the saleswoman a specific image of what she wanted. At this point Asia would feel silly with long hair, but she had a photo of her and Lucy from this summer, laughing at a Fourth of July parade. Asia's short hair was dark and curly and some-how sassy. She could use a little of her sass back.

The woman glanced up from the candid shot and met Asia's eyes, smiling in a way that let Asia know she understood exactly how she was feeling. "I think we can find you just the thing, dear."

And it was amazing how much finding the right thing boosted her spirits, Asia reflected later, after Lucy had dropped her off. She'd noticed her sister slanting her glances throughout the ride.

"It looks so natural," Lucy had commented.

"Almost feels it, too."

"I'll walk you up and then skedaddle so you can get ready for your date," Lucy had promised. But she'd frowned as they were stepping into the elevator. "You okay? You've been doing that all afternoon."

Following her sister's gaze, Asia looked down to where she was rubbing the right side of her abdomen. "It aches. Everything aches. Sometimes I hardly even notice. Don't worry. The doctors said I was okay to come home, remember?"

After a few days in the hospital, it seemed even more important to highlight the hominess of her condo. She lowered the overhead lights in the living room, thankful to whoever had invented the dimmer switch, and lit a grapefruit-and-petitgrain wellness candle that Thayer had mailed her. She was in the kitchen pouring herself a glass of water when she heard a knock.

It seemed too soon for Brandon to be here already. But he was. She smiled as she let him in. "You're early."

"I left because . . . Hey, you look nice."

"You left because I look nice?" she teased, enjoying his reaction.

"I wanted to see you. I didn't want to risk getting tied up in traffic, so I ducked out a few minutes early." He moved to kiss her hello, then stopped. "I suppose I shouldn't?"

"On the cheek might be okay." Although it was a poor substitute for what she wanted. Trying to make the most of their evening together, she asked brightly, "So, what movie did you bring?"

"A classic." He held up the DVD case and a bag of microwave popcorn. *"Casablanca."*

"Hm." She shook her head in mock sorrow. "This is seriously going to damage your standing with Lucy."

"How could anyone not love *Casablanca?* Bergman, Bogart, great lines, great song, great story."

"She has this thing about happy endings."

"It has a happy ending. Rick does the right thing, lets the girl go, and is a better person for having loved her. He's optimistic by the end; he has Sam and Louis. 'This is the beginning of a beautiful friendship,'" Brandon intoned out the side of his mouth.

A burst of laughter escaped her. "Yikes—that was your Bogart?"

He quirked an eyebrow at her. "I do a great Bogey."

"Um . . . Better stick to Elvis."

"Everyone's a critic. Fine, let's hear your Bogart impression," he challenged as he followed her into the kitchen.

"I don't *have* a Bogart impression. Much like you, apparently."

"And this is the thanks I get for offering to come over and cook you dinner," he said with a wounded expression.

She sat at the table. "If I recall, you offered to preheat the oven and pop in one of the casseroles from Mom's church friends while we watch the movie. Hardly a four-course meal made from scratch."

"Heartless woman. For all you know, I had a really tough day at work, and now you're abusing me."

She propped her cheek on the back of her hand. "Did you have a bad day?"

"Not really, no. Before I forget, I'm supposed to give you this. After Fern and I crossed paths at the hospital Tuesday, I, uh, think the cat's out of the bag about our seeing each other. I didn't confirm or deny, but . . ." He looked so sheepish as he handed her the get-well card that her heart melted.

"It's all right. It's not like the company has an official no-dating policy, and I have plenty of other things to worry about than what Morris thinks of my having dinner with you." She opened the envelope and read the card, gazed at all the signatures scrawled in blue and black ink. The names were of people she hadn't entirely realized had come to mean so much to her while she'd been doing her job. She missed being in the office, and she missed her colleagues, too. Chatting in the kitchenette, seeing Fern's new pictures of Tommy . . .

"You okay?" he asked. "You seem upset."

"Not about people realizing we're seeing each other," she hastened to assure him. "And not even really upset. Homesick, maybe? I miss being there."

They selected a casserole for the evening, and as it cooked, he told her all about work. Knowing what was going on there didn't make her miss it less, but at least she no longer felt out of the loop. The oven timer dinged, and she suggested they go ahead and eat in the kitchen.

"Then we can curl up on the couch and watch the movie," she said.

"I'll hold you to that."

She grinned. "That was the idea."

Though she appreciated his help with dinner and knew

that vitamins were essential to her battered immune system, she wasn't very hungry. While he ate, she picked at her food and let her mind wander. Unfortunately, it circled back to something she'd been thinking in the hospital.

"Brandon? Can I . . . ask you something?"

"Of course." He waited for her to continue. When she didn't, he set down his fork and held her gaze. "Is something wrong?"

"I wanted to know something, but I understand that it might be very personal, possibly even painful for you."

He stilled. "Well. Now that you've warned me, go ahead."

"You mentioned that your mother passed away. How did she die?"

"Heart failure. She'd had a weak heart all her life. Not that she was actively sick or that it slowed her down much, just that we were aware of the condition. The doctors were really worried when she was pregnant with my sister, then even more worried when she was pregnant with me, because she was a few years older by then. But she did fine for as long as I can remember. Until one day, she didn't."

"So it was sudden."

He nodded. "Yeah. The doctors liked to monitor her on a regular basis, as they would any patient, but even they didn't expect her to just drop—"

"I'm sorry. I shouldn't have pried."

"No." He covered her hands with both of his as though he could physically prevent her from pulling away emotionally. "I'm glad you asked. It isn't fun to talk about, obviously, but I don't try to pretend it never happened. It's okay."

She believed him, but she still suspected that when he

stood a moment later to clear away the dishes it was because he needed a minute to regain his composure.

The possibility that whatever had happened to his mother had been drawn out had bothered her. Asia was still hopeful about her own condition, but if he'd already endured a prolonged illness with the most important woman in his life, it seemed cruel to ask him to experience it again. She was glad if Mrs. Peters hadn't suffered.

Feeling guilty for the pall she'd cast over the evening, Asia tried to make up for it while Brandon put in the DVD. "All right, I think I've got it," she said from the couch.

"Got what?"

"My Bogey impression. Want to hear?"

He stopped what he was doing and grinned over his shoulder. "Dazzle me."

She dropped her voice several octaves and tried to speak as if around a mouthful of marbles. "'Here's looking at you, kid.'"

Laughing, he grabbed the remote. "That was pretty good. Disturbingly good, actually."

"Better than yours, right?"

He put an arm around her. "Shut up and watch the movie."

Fourteen

Not to be hypercritical about hospital food, Asia thought two weeks later, but she couldn't get all that enthused about the block of orange, stringy substance that was euphemistically billed as yams.

Of all the places to spend Thanksgiving. Having to go back into the hospital would have been depressing at *any* time, but right before the holiday sucked the big one.

Unfortunately, not to be outdone by her white blood cells, her red count had rebelled, sending her in last week for a blood transfusion. A series of complications and gastrointestinal unpleasantness had conspired to keep her here. *Congratulations, you have cancer. Kiss your dignity good-bye and plan on lots of fun conversations about bowel movements.*

All of which was why, instead of holding out one of her mother's Wedgwood plates for a drumstick, Asia was here, alone in a semiprivate hospital room.

It was bound to be worse for the nurses and attending physicians. They were *healthy* and still stuck here. When Lucy had called earlier to say she was bringing over a plate of their mother's home cooking later, Asia had wished her sister could bring full plates for each of the staff. But not even Marianne made that much food.

There was a rap against the door she couldn't see from around the curtain, and a male "Hello?"

Brandon.

Asia's emotions about seeing him were mixed, just like all the medical results she'd received this week—*Your red count is up; unfortunately so are your tumor markers. Your bone scans showed nothing new, but we need to take a look at your liver.*

"I'm in here," she called back.

He rounded the divider, looking so healthy, so damnably attractive, she wished the situation could be equalized somehow. Maybe new hospital regs should require handsome men to visit only when *they* were wearing backless cotton sacks, so she wouldn't feel so disproportionately exposed. Besides, she'd love to sneak a peek at his tush.

"Happy Thanksgiving," he told her. "I know better than to bring flowers, so . . . here."

He handed her an oblong cardboard box with a crooked bow smashed down on top.

"You didn't have to bring a present." She reached for it automatically. "But thank you."

Unable to stop himself, he was already smirking by the time she retrieved the contents.

Client files! "You're dumping work on me when I'm supposed to be *resting*? You ass," she said affectionately. *Thank God.* She'd been going out of her mind with boredom.

"I made some notes and wanted to get your thoughts about

some opportunities after the holiday," he admitted. "In a slightly less self-seeking gift, I also got you a one-year subscription to a DVD rental service. You type in the movies you want online; they mail them to you. I was a little surprised you didn't have anything like that already."

"Until recently, I didn't have to. Lucy has such an extensive DVD library I just borrowed hers, but with the downtime I've had lately, I think I've seen everything she owns twice. Thank you."

He placed a silver rectangle on her bedside table. "Figured with all the DVDs and the time you keep racking up here in your home-away-from-home day spa, you'd need a portable player, too."

"Brandon . . . that's too much. You shouldn't have."

"One day, when you're feeling better and so inclined, we'll talk about the various lewd ways you can make it up to me," he drawled.

She laughed, but wondered if he knew how close to home his joke hit. The evening they'd spent nestled close and watching *Casablanca*, she'd experienced pangs of longing. Still, having the fantasy and having the bravery or drive to follow through . . . One day, she hoped.

Today wasn't that day.

"I appreciate the visit," she told him, "but it's Thanksgiving." Though his father and sister were in Germany, Brandon had extended family in South Carolina, within reasonable driving distance. She hoped she hadn't kept him here. "You should be with loved ones."

"What makes you think I'm not?" He cocked his head, his gaze pointed and unflinching.

Love? Dammit. She hadn't seen that coming.

In fact, she had done her best not to define her own feelings ... which wasn't difficult when your brain was medically addled half the time. Her vision misted and blurred as she thought of the big and small ways in which he'd been there for her since that first afternoon when Morris explained she would no longer be able to handle her full workload; the ways in which Brandon had surprised her, supported her, made her laugh, helped her surprise *herself.* Then she juxtaposed that with the new tests the doctors wanted to run, evaluating bilirubin and taking ultrasounds of her liver—tests that didn't bode well for her.

Or for those emotionally invested in her.

Everyone was raising stakes that were already out of her control—Brandon with his subtle declaration, the doctors with their new concerns—and all she really wanted right this minute were some of her mom's mashed potatoes. She wanted that feeling of stuffed contentment and serenity she'd had as a kid at the Thanksgiving table. It was hard to imagine anything too terrible when there was food as far as you could see and you were sandwiched among a mother who adored you, a sturdy father with shoulders you could lean on, and an admiring little sister who made you feel like the coolest person on the planet.

God, she missed that sense of security.

"Brandon."

"It's the holidays. You say anything negative and pessimistic, and I am siccing the ornery nurse of Thanksgiving past on your butt."

"Brandon. Sit. Listen to me."

He dragged the wide, padded visitor's chair, meant to pull into a poor man's futon for overnight guests, closer to her bed.

"I wasn't . . . looking for any kind of relationship," she said. Which hadn't stopped her from kissing him or wanting to spend as much time with him as she could. "I care about you so much." That sounded lame in comparison to what he'd intimated. But what did she have to offer anyone at the moment?

She looked away. "I'm a bad risk, Peters. Don't invest more in me."

It had been three weeks since she'd been strong enough to have her regular chemo, and the problems she'd been having could no longer be blamed solely on the drug regimen. Some of what was happening now involved more lasting damage. And if her liver scans discovered spreading cancer . . . No one had said anything final—she suspected she still had time—but she also suspected that there would never truly be a cancer-free future for her. Her oncologist had suggested she look at her condition as a chronic disease, one some women treated and lived with for years. For the rest of her life, there would probably be medical challenges, unexpected hospital trips at the worst possible times. She could deal with that, especially given the alternative, but Brandon didn't have to.

"Asia, didn't anyone explain risk-reward ratio to you?" he asked. "Sometimes the highest risks yield the best payoffs."

"There are other opportunities you can gamble on," she said stubbornly. "Ones that don't include breast cancer."

He lifted her chin with his fingers. "I've said before, cancer is not who you are. And it doesn't define how I feel about you. It doesn't make me regret anything. It doesn't make me feel sorry for you, it doesn't make me admire you. Your wit and your heart and your determination and an enviable Bogey impression—those are the things that I admire. Those are a handful of the reasons I'm falling for you."

Her heart squeezed. Despite the good sense she'd been trying to show, he wasn't the only one falling.

Normally on Thanksgiving, the Swenson house was warm with laughter and the nutmeg scent of pumpkin pies in the oven.

Right now the house smelled like charred biscuits. Lucy couldn't remember the last time her mother had burned anything. *I should have noticed the smell before it was too late.* Lucy was only one room over, but her mind kept shutting down, leaving little blanks in her awareness. Which explained why next to the good silver box on the table lay five sets of utensils. Five knives, five salad forks, five regular forks, five teaspoons. *Idiot.* There were only four of them today.

She was so used to setting that extra place. The thought turned horribly morbid, making her wonder how many holidays it took for a person to lose a habit like that. She snapped the box shut. This was just *one* Thanksgiving Asia was missing—one out of thirty-four. Lucy wasn't helping anyone by overreacting.

According to Asia's doctors, early lab tests suggested that despite treatments, her cancer might be spreading. Still, she was stable for now, and they wouldn't know more until they took additional tests after the holiday.

Holiday. Stupid word. Cancer didn't take holidays.

With the table set, Lucy joined her mom in the kitchen. George and Michael were watching pregame football coverage one room over. Once, Michael had raised his eyebrows in Lucy's direction, silently asking if he should help her or stick with his post. She'd thought that considering how jittery Marianne had been all morning, staying out from underfoot was probably Michael's best course of action.

"What else can I do?" Lucy asked now. She thought about simply hugging her mom, but was afraid that might make the other woman cry. One or two bungled recipes notwithstanding, Marianne was holding it together; Lucy didn't want to be the reason she fell apart.

"Not much left to do in here, I guess." Marianne surveyed the various containers of food on the counters, as if she couldn't quite recall how they had all gotten there. "The sweet-potato casserole is more done than I would have liked. Reckon maybe the stove's off a little?"

"That could be," Lucy agreed, throwing her mother a lifeline.

"I'll ask your father to take a look next week. He's always been good at fixing everything."

Once they had the dishes on the table, Marianne asked softly, "You'll take her a plate?"

"Right after the meal, if you want." They'd decided to visit Asia in shifts. That way the room wouldn't get too cramped, and they could help her stretch out her Thanksgiving instead of spending huge chunks of time alone.

As all four of them took their seats, Marianne looked to her husband. "Will you say the blessing, George?" She asked the question every year, the traditional opening ceremonies.

Blessing the food and carving the turkey were his official duties. He cleared his throat, and they all bowed their heads.

"Heavenly Father, we thank You for this day," he began in

his familiar rough baritone. "We thank You for this feast before us, the loved ones ar-around this table and the l-loved ones who . . . who could not be with us right now. We ask, God, that You . . . we ask . . ."

He fell silent for so long that Lucy actually raised her head and looked in his direction in time to see him lurch to his feet. He muttered a rushed, "Excuse me," before leaving the room.

Her heart pounding and her eyes damp, she glanced across the table at her mother.

"We ask," Marianne finished in a surprisingly clear voice, "that You hold those loved ones in the palm of Your hand and make them well and whole. Amen. Eat, you two, before it gets cold." Rather than take her own advice, she stood and went into the kitchen.

Lucy could see her father gripping the counter, his back to them, his shoulders shaking. *Oh, Daddy.* Her heart broke.

Marianne came to stand behind him, resting one cheek against his shirt, and Lucy had to turn away. Watching was too painful, too intimate. This was their grief to share, as parents, as spouses, and she had no right to it. When they returned to the table, no one mentioned what had happened. Lucy did notice that her parents held hands throughout the meal. It must have made cutting and eating and pouring difficult, but they managed.

Without moving in an obvious rush, after the meal was over she helped clear the table and signaled to Michael that they should go. She'd never in her life wanted so badly to get away from her home. Besides, her parents might prefer to be alone.

On the drive to the hospital, Michael spoke only once. "Are you all right?"

No. "Yeah." To say anything else seemed petulant. She, after all, was as healthy as a horse.

They found a parking space pretty easily. Lucy had always heard that hospitals got more crowded around the holidays, but maybe that was just emergency rooms. Michael walked her inside, and she tried to lean against him in the way that had once felt natural. She'd become so stiff in the last couple of weeks that she felt like a stranger in her own skin. It was from bracing herself each time they got a new piece of information about Asia's condition.

"I could carry some of that," Michael offered.

On her arm hung a small bag with utensils, condiments, and paper napkins printed with wild-eyed turkeys wearing pilgrim hats. In her hands, she'd balanced a small Tupperware container of pie on top of a foil-covered platter of food. Marianne had wanted to make sure Asia had a small portion of everything being served so she could pick and choose what appealed to her, and so much food couldn't fit on a regular plate. Lucy was using a party tray. One of the ones her mother had specifically purchased for the bridal shower, actually.

Lucy should let Michael hold something, knowing her own history with coordination and balance. Yet she couldn't relinquish any of it.

"Thank you, but I've got it." Southern women brought food. If that was all she could do for Asia today, then by God she would do it. She probably had enough to feed an entire nurses' station, much less her sister, who'd lost almost fifteen pounds in the last few months.

As the rabbit warrens of the hospital led them to the cancer ward, she glanced up and noticed that someone had painted large blue-and-lime-green butterflies on sporadic ceiling tiles. Occasionally the winged creatures were depicted alighting on yellow flowers. Meant to be cheerful, no doubt, for patients being wheeled through on gurneys, looking toward heaven and wondering what their fate would be.

But to Lucy, the out-of-season butterflies were toxic and depressing. They didn't belong trapped inside, weighed down by the fumes of industrial-strength disinfectant, flying past doors marked BIOHAZARD: SPECIAL PERSONNEL ONLY and rooms emitting the Darth Vader–esque sounds of patients on breathing machines.

Lucy was lost in these thoughts when Michael stopped her.

"Three twenty-one, right? I think that's her room on the corner."

She turned, already pasting on a smile. "Hello?"

"I smell food," Asia responded gamely.

They pushed aside the curtain and found her sitting up in bed, looking as though she wasn't in as much abdominal pain as she had been earlier that week.

"Happy Thanksgiving," Lucy said, feeling truly stupid. How could Asia be having a happy day?

"You too, Blondie. I watched the Macy's Thanksgiving Day Parade this morning and thought about you, guessing which were your favorite floats. You guys just missed Brandon."

Lucy was warmed by the knowledge that he'd visited. "So, have you mentioned this male friend of yours to Mom and Dad yet? They're coming later, by the way."

"They've heard me talk about him as a coworker and

friend." Asia steepled her fingers together. "I don't know if I've specifically mentioned that he's seen me at the hospital, but then, I don't detail every time Stephanie or Fern drops by, either."

"Uh-huh," Lucy said with a deliberate roll of her eyes. Asia could tell—or *not* tell—their parents whatever she was comfortable with, but Lucy knew full well that Brandon and Asia were more than friends.

She busied herself setting up food on one of the bedside tables. "Mom and I weren't sure what you could tolerate or would want today, so there's a little of everything. It won't hurt her feelings if you haven't eaten much of it by the time she comes."

"Right now, I could just use something to drink. Michael, if you can find a nurse outside, would you see if someone could bring me more juice as soon as it's convenient?"

He nodded. "Will do."

Once he was gone, Asia patted the side of the hospital bed, indicating that Lucy should sit with her. It was a tight but cozy squeeze. When Lucy had been four or five and storms terrified her, they'd both crammed into Asia's twin bed. Asia had read Dr. Seuss to her until she fell asleep or the storm passed. She'd loved Dr. Seuss. There'd been one book Lucy hadn't liked, though, because the shadowed drawings had seemed threatening.

She'd sneaked downstairs one night and thrown the book in the trash, covering it with some junk mail so no one would see what she'd done. Her act of rebellion and success in ridding the house of the dreaded book had made her feel invincible for the next couple of days. She wished she could summon that invincibility now, transfuse it into her sister as easily as the doctors did blood.

> *I would cure your cancer if I could.*
> *I'd make it leave, oh, yes, I would.*
> *High, I'd search for medicines, then low.*
> *Grape-flavored miracles to make your hair grow.*
> *You would not have cancer, sis of mine.*
> *Never, ever. Not one single time.*

"How are you doing?" Asia asked.

Lucy laughed grimly. "I should be asking you that."

"If you ask, I might have to tell you." Asia affected a shudder. "You don't want to know."

"I'm all right," Lucy said. "Almost everything's taken care of for the wedding, except we still need a marriage license and have some standard prenuptial counseling at the church with Pastor Bob. You're going to have to tell Mom sooner or later about Brandon, because he's going to be on the reception seating chart."

Asia sighed. "I told him today he should cut his losses."

"What?" Asia had finally found a great guy, and she was trying to run him off? Would the nurses object to Lucy beating the patient over the head with a pillow?

"I don't want to be pessimistic, Lucy, but . . . that scan Dr. Klamm is doing next week might . . . not be good news."

Lucy took a deep breath, knowing her sister could be right but praying she wasn't. "Your friends Rob and Stephanie? You wouldn't expect him to walk away from her, would you, even if she took a sudden and unexpected turn for the worse?"

"That's different. They took vows to stay together in sickness and health. They had a chance to really get to know each other and fall in love before the cancer interfered. That's not the case with me and Brandon."

"Maybe he's been secretly in love with you the entire time and you're only just now letting him into your life."

Asia snorted. "I saw one of his last girlfriends. I don't think he was pining for me while dating *her.*"

Lucy had a sudden flash of insight that she wanted Asia and Brandon to become more seriously involved; she wanted people to love Asia, not just the family, but others, like Stephanie and Fern. Addressing all those wedding invitations had made Lucy think about the way the people in her life defined her, where she'd come from, who she was. The more people who crowded around Asia, loving her the way Lucy did, the more she would be kept alive in their collective memories when—

If. Lucy blinked furiously. *If.*

"You shouldn't be here," Asia said quietly. "It's depressing."

"Maybe I'll go to the maternity ward before we leave," Lucy blurted. "Looking at all the babies wrapped up like burritos in their pink and blue blankets sounds cheerful."

Asia's smile was bittersweet. "I've been thinking about babies. Yours and Michael's. Do you think you'll start trying to have a family right away?"

"I'm not sure." Lucy experienced another pinch of foreboding sadness, hoping she had a little girl one day who shared Asia's intelligence and gold-green eyes. And hoping Asia was there to give the girl advice on the subjects Lucy herself didn't know much about.

"Promise me something?" Asia squeezed her hand. Lucy

couldn't help notice how cold her fingers were. "If you have a daughter—"

"Asia." The word was imploring. Lucy didn't know where the conversation was headed, but it felt like tearful territory. Territory better left ignored and uncharted, for there were undoubtedly dragons.

"*If* you have a daughter, you have to promise me . . ." Now Lucy wasn't sure the difficulty her sister had with the words was due simply to throat pain. "Promise me you won't name her Asia."

"Well, of course not," Lucy said, a hysterical giggle escaping as she dashed a knuckle against her wet eyelashes. "I always thought a much better name for a girl would be Australia."

Though her eyes were as damp as Lucy's, Asia chuckled, then snuggled against Lucy in a gentle half hug. Warm tears splattered like spring rain on Lucy's arm. She couldn't tell which were hers and which were her sister's.

Fifteen

The interior of Atlanta's fabulous Fox Theatre was breathtaking, the lush reds and golds, intricately detailed Moorish facades, and twinkling ceiling lights calling to mind the enchantment of Arabian fairy tales. This had been one of Lucy's favorite places in the city ever since she was old enough to attend her first performance here of *The Nutcracker*. For a period during her childhood, it had been an annual treat for Marianne to bring both the girls.

Tonight Lucy was here for another ballet, one not quite as festive. She, Cam, and Monica were scooting into their loge seats, ten minutes from seeing a renowned traveling company perform a bittersweet love story. Monica, one of Lucy's single coworkers, joked that all she needed were ballet tickets to wrest Lucy and Cam from their significant others for a girls' night out. Dave was more a fan of rock concerts than fine arts; Michael enjoyed the symphony and some theater, but drew the line at extended sequences featuring men in tights.

"It always seems magical here," Lucy murmured to Cam as

they shrugged out of their jackets. "I may be almost thirty, but I still believe anything could happen. As my friend, you're not allowed to laugh at that, by the way . . . plus, I could easily toss you off the balcony."

Cam held up her hands. "Hey, no laughter here. These are great seats, aren't they?" They overlooked the stage and the orchestra pit, where musicians were warming up.

In her head, instead of scales and tuning pitches, Lucy heard the tiptoe strains of "Dance of the Sugar Plum Fairy."

Asia, what happens now that they've killed the Rat King?

The prince takes her to a magical land in the next act. You'll see, Blondie.

Will I like it?

Asia had always favored the slow, sophisticated pas de deux; Lucy loved Mother Ginger, with the children tumbling out from under her full skirt.

The music playing over Lucy's memory suddenly became discordant, and she blinked, realizing that she was witnessing not the Christmastime show of her youth but the tumultuous opening of tonight's story. Try as she might to concentrate on the talented dancers onstage, memories of her and Asia crowded from every rung of the multilevel seating. The time when Asia was in college and brought Lucy to see *Cats* for her birthday, but they were only able to afford tickets way up in the nosebleed section. They'd been here as recently as last February for Monty Python's *Spamalot.*

That had been shortly after her sister had completed treatment the first time, hoping it would be the last time. The two of them had laughed like hyenas through the "He Is Not Dead Yet" number and whistled under their breath with "Always

Look on the Bright Side of Life." Remembering, Lucy felt her eyes grow hot and dry. She knew rubbing them would only start a downpour.

Applause jolted her; the curtain was closing. She'd taken her eyes off the stage for one second, and she'd missed an entire act. The clapping seemed thunderous, disorienting, and the stadium seating and spacious interior sent her head spinning in a moment of vertigo.

This theater had always filled her with awe. Every time. She'd never walked through the doors and taken the place for granted, well aware of its history and that it had almost been torn down decades ago.

How could she maintain that kind of appreciation for a *building*, no matter how beautiful, yet go weeks, months, even years at a time taking people for granted?

Throughout the wedding planning, there had been instances when she'd wanted to stop taking calls from her own mother. During her one bitter argument with Michael, she'd not only neglected to cherish him; she'd actively wanted to kick him in the shins. And Asia . . .

From the moment Lucy had entered the world, her big sister had been there, protecting her, encouraging her, befriending her. Even though Lucy had experienced moments of worry that her sister might not survive breast cancer, even though she'd shed tears over the possibility on more than one occasion, it wasn't until this split second, with applause ringing in her ears like some sort of indictment, that it truly hit her.

There could come a day when Lucy's life didn't include Asia. When Lucy would get home from a moving performance, reach for the phone to tell her sister about an amazing solo, and not remember until she started dialing that there would be no one to answer. Until now, that possibility had been an abstract; on this particular clear night at the very end of November, reality pulverized her.

Her throat burned, and her attempts to breathe felt like raw clawing. She had to get out of there.

"Cam." Her voice was a broken whisper as she scrabbled for her coat. "Tell Monica I'm sorry . . . gotta go." Then she was moving toward the aisle before her friend could stop her or, worse, ask why.

They'd met at the theater in separate cars. Some instinct of self-preservation propelled Lucy to her vehicle, even though, if someone has asked for the row and numbered lot her car was parked in, she wouldn't have known. Later, she might reflect that she shouldn't have been driving in her condition. But Michael's apartment was close by and she needed to flee.

By the time she reached his complex, her body was racked with sobs. And by the time he opened his door, she was crying so hard no sound came out, just harsh, choppy breathing.

"Lu— Jesus, love." He stepped into the hall, wrapping his arms around her. "Is it Asia?"

"Yes." Then, realizing what he'd meant, she shook her head wildly. It took her another few seconds to find her voice again. "I mean, no. She hasn't . . . There's b-been no ch-change. Unless you've heard something from Mom or the hospital that I haven't."

For a moment she thought she might compound her embarrassment by heaving the contents of her stomach. She was hardly aware of Michael taking her by the elbow and leading her to his couch. They sat motionless for an indeterminable time, him merely holding her. A tissue box appeared as if by magic, probably saving him from having to burn his shirt later.

His voice was low and even, the pitch one that a cautious person might use with a traumatized animal. "Can you talk about it now?"

"Talk, maybe. Make sense, no." She was a sopping rag wrung viciously dry. "You're right about me. I fall completely to pieces." Patsy Cline had made it sound less pathetic than it felt.

"Lucy." An unformed apology hung in the air.

"It's okay. I am a mess."

"You're taking on your first mortgage in less than a month. You've been busy planning a wedding. Your sister is seriously sick. Any one of those would qualify you for a stress break-down."

She sniffed. "You forgot holiday shopping. Parking at the mall could drive a person right over the edge."

He said nothing, just running his fingers through her hair as they sat facing each other, leaning against the back of the sofa. Then he straightened. "Wait a minute, you had tickets to the theater tonight."

"Yeah. The last show I saw there—before tonight—was with her. Asia. It's become real to me," she said slowly. "You know how kids can't wait for it to be Christmas? As soon as Halloween kicks off the fall and winter holidays, even while you're thinking about all the candy you got, you're looking ahead to Thanksgiving and knowing Christmas is around the corner, but it feels like for-*ever* until it comes. Eventually you get to decorate the house and put up the tree, but it's still long, agonizing days until Santa arrives. Then it's Christmas Eve and you're so close you can taste it, and that's the worst waiting of all. When you first proposed to me, it was like that.

"I knew it would feel like an entire lifetime before the wedding because I wanted it so much, but I still planned to savor the anticipation. But as every day passes and the wedding gets closer . . ."

He frowned, the vertical lines appearing above his nose making him no less handsome, just very studious. "I'm not sure I follow."

"Every day that passes brings *me* one day closer to marrying you, something I've dreamed about. One of the happiest moments of my life. What are those same passing days bringing Asia closer to?"

"Ah. The unpalatable truth," he said, "is that every passing day brings us *all* closer to death."

She flinched. "You certainly know how to put a positive spin on things."

"Sorry."

He was right, though. No one lived forever. And no one could predict the future. Some patients were told they had months to live, only to confound the medical community by sticking around for another few decades, while patients who had the "good" kind of cancer, statistically curable, could die with no warning. Hell, she herself could be mowed down by a MARTA bus tomorrow.

She looked him straight in the eye. "Can I—can you keep a secret?"

"Of course."

How did she say this, any of the stuff that was really bugging her, all the inappropriate, politically incorrect things she had no business feeling? All of the stuff that, for whatever reason, seemed determined to work its way out of her tonight?

"I'm not *just* worried about Asia dy—" She couldn't honestly be superstitious enough to think that voicing the possibility would cause it, could she? "Obviously, that's what upsets me the most. But something's been bothering me since this last time she went into the hospital. God, she's looked so miserable. She tries not to hold her side in front of me, but I know it hurts. And she's lost so much weight. She's . . ."

Weak. A shadow of the vital big sister Lucy had always known, though it seemed like a betrayal to think it.

Lucy swallowed. "What if . . . what if when it happens, I'm *relieved?* I hate seeing her go through this. Again. I hate the not knowing. I hate dreading the next test and the next potentially bad announcement. What if she gets worse? It's like walking around with this bladed pendulum of death swinging back and forth over your head, and you never know when it's going to be close enough to just slice through. And that's what *I'm* feeling. What the hell is it like for *her?* Do you think there will come a time when she'll want to give up? Knowing Asia like I do, I can't imagine that. But then, I can't imagine trying to keep up a semblance of a normal life with everything that's happening to her, being done to her. If she gets tired, am I supposed to provide support by encouraging her to keep fighting, or am I supposed to assure her it's okay *not* to?

"I'm scared that before this is all over, before she . . . what if before that time comes, part of me, deep down and subconsciously, actually wants it to happen? Wants this all to be over? If I feel like that, even for a second, then after she's

gone, I don't know how I'll live with myself. I know it's irrational and stupid, so you don't have to tell me, but if I get
the news and any part of me is relieved, I'll feel like I killed
my sister."

"No, darlin'. No." He left it at that. It wasn't as if he had
answers to these dark questions.

Strangely, though, she felt better for having asked. And to
her shock, she realized she wasn't crying. She stood, feeling
as though she'd been emotionally cramped for too long and
needed to stretch. Her surroundings took on more clarity. Michael had been packing. She noticed neatly taped cardboard
boxes with their corresponding rooms written in thick black
marker.

He was making better progress than she was. She'd thrown
a couple of things in boxes, then realized she'd packed stuff she
still needed and had unearthed it.

"I'm sorry," Michael said, joining her. "You came here to
talk, and I have no idea what to say."

"That's kind of . . . nice," she admitted. "It's reassuring that
you don't always know everything." But maybe he wasn't the
only one she should be talking to about this.

The horrible image of her father's shoulders shaking on
Thanksgiving day crowded her mind. Lucy took a deep breath.
At twenty-eight years old, she needed to be a grown-up. If
Asia died, this family would be missing the glue that largely
held it together. Could Lucy help fill the gap?

She walked toward the stack of flat, yet-to-be-assembled
boxes Michael had leaned against the wall and started folding.
No one would ever be able to fill the gap. This was her sister,
not a loose tooth. But Lucy would be all right eventually; she'd

need to be in order to help her parents be all right. She owed Asia that much.

Michael handed her the packing tape as she creased the flaps into place. "You want to stay here tonight?"

"If you don't mind." She kept a spare toothbrush in the bathroom and a change of clothes hanging in his closet. Her sneakers and a pair of extravagant heels she never wore because they hurt her ankles were tossed on the two-tier rack between his brown loafers and running shoes.

"You want to come to bed, or stay up talking some more? Or we could put in a DVD," he offered.

Actually, she was finding solace in the mindless physical activity of packing. "Is there anything I can box up for you? I'm too edgy to sleep or even concentrate on a movie."

"I'm like the worst boyfriend ever. You come over for a shoulder to cry on, and I put you to work."

"It's okay." She tipped her head back, smiling up at him. "I'm all done crying."

Out of the frying pan, into the doctor's office. After Thanksgiving, lab techs had run a number of tests; then Asia had finally been sent home. Now here she was with Dr. Klamm, trying to absorb the results of those tests. She'd been patting her hands alternately on her legs until Lucy turned to look at her, drawing Asia's attention to what she was doing, and how sore her thighs were from the perpetual motion. She vowed to sit still, only to find herself a few minutes later tapping her fingers on the chair's arm.

"When will we start the new treatment?" she asked, glad

Lucy was here to help remember all the information. Asia was trying, she really was, but her mind kept shutting off in strange places, as if to protect her from information overload.

"Next week," he told her. "That will give your body a few extra days to gain strength."

So that they could start making her sick again in order to make her better. There'd been a test with radioactive dye, and after Dr. Klamm had seen the pictures, he'd followed up with a biopsy. The cancer had spread. She'd read enough to know that the liver and lungs were the most common organ sites for metastases. So far her lungs remained clear, but there was a tumor in the liver. To try to get rid of it, to try to prevent more like it, they were adjusting her chemo regimen—high doses several times a week and stem-cell reinfusion.

She was going to have to take an indefinite leave of absence from work. It had been coming, what with the two separate stints in the hospital and her increasing inability to concentrate, but it pissed her off. Apparently she'd have some extra time for checking out DVDs on that service Brandon had signed her up to receive.

Brandon. Calling him after this was going to be difficult. She exhaled in a thready sigh, and Lucy reached across to hold her hand.

Her sister was the one who said good-bye to Dr. Klamm for both of them and even remembered to ask some questions Asia had mentioned earlier in the car. *Lucy, all grown-up and taking care of me for a change.* Asia's smile was bittersweet. It was a blessing that Lucy didn't need her anymore, but it sucked a little bit, too.

They were silent as they walked to Lucy's car. Once there,

Lucy turned the keys in the ignition and immediately adjusted the heat. Asia was almost constantly cold, and she didn't think the little knobs and buttons on the VW dashboard were going to fix that.

Lucy sat back in her seat, looking toward the ceiling. "Where to? You want to go to my place and watch me pack and remind me where I set the tape down, because I lose it every three minutes? Or we could go to your place and play Parcheesi. Or I could drop you off and let you nap. Or we could just play hooky, do something silly while the rest of the poor slobs are sitting in their cubicles, hating their bosses."

"Is Parcheesi that card game you play in teams?"

"You're thinking of pinochle."

"Right."

The synthetic fabric of Lucy's Windbreaker rasped against the car's upholstery as she angled her body toward the passenger seat. "I know this is going to sound like an asinine question, all things considered, but are you okay?"

"You mean aside from the progression of cancer into my liver and having to give up my job?"

"Aside from those."

Asia turned her head, wishing she were limber enough in the small space to tuck her knees under her, the way she would when she'd been younger, curling herself into a ball. Gathering herself that way seemed to center her strength, made her feel more powerful. She'd spring out of the position ready to take on anything; she just needed those few moments.

"I don't know. They always say it's the not knowing that's the worst. At least we have a plan, right? I've been e-mailing the girls again. They've been sending encouragement about the appointment today and the test results. Deborah has a friend whose doctors were able to completely eradicate liver tumors with intensive doses of 5FU, Adriamycin, and Cytoxan."

A chemo drug called FU. Fitting.

"It isn't hopeless," Lucy said, her voice full of calm certainty.

Asia's heart swelled. When had her kid sister become such an adult? Lucy refrained from making promises not even skilled surgeons could guarantee, but she wasn't wringing her hands in terror either. "No, it's not hopeless."

"So did we decide where I'm taking you?" Lucy asked. "Any more loitering, we're gonna end up looking like suspicious characters."

This parking lot had probably seen it all: embraces of joy, tears of sorrow, ranting at the sky about the injustices of it all, prayers of gratitude. "Home, James."

Lucy doffed an imaginary cap. "Very good, sir."

The quiet was comfortable after all the talking to doctors, the beeping and whirring of machines, the footsteps of shift-change nurses waking her to take vital signs. Hospitals had to be the worst place on earth to try to get any rest. So when Lucy asked if she wanted to listen to anything on the radio, Asia shook her head.

Not far from her place, however, there was something she needed to say, even if it disrupted the calm. "Lucy, I have a confession to make."

Her sister slid her a curious glance, waiting expectantly.

"I don't have a will."

"You're kidding!" Lucy quickly followed with, "I only mean because . . . well, you're the professional who helps people with their assets and portfolios. You're the type to always get renter's insurance and make . . . provisions."

She was. But until that first moment when breast cancer had become part of her life, death had never entered her mind. She'd barely been thirty-two, with no dependents. Once her mortality had become an actual issue, she'd balked at the "responsible steps." It had probably been negligent, and she counted herself lucky that none of the paperwork she'd put off had turned out to be necessary yet. But before, it had seemed like the wrong time. Even the most skeptical of doctors admitted that the power of mind over matter could aid the healing process, so she'd refused to entertain the possibility of death.

Some might call that denial, but so what? It had helped her cope at the time.

"I have to make arrangements," she heard herself say. "Not just a will, but all of it. There are decisions I don't want to leave to others. It wouldn't be fair to you."

Their car edged a few inches too close to the other lane before Lucy corrected. "Okay, now you're worrying me. We agreed there's a good chance of improvement, right?"

Definitely, but even remission—her goal—could be temporary. "I'm not in a hurry to go anywhere, Luce, just thinking it's time to be proactive. Ignoring a risk doesn't make it less real."

"You're right."

"And let's just say, I mean, in the event of a worst-case scenario someday? Mom was the one who picked out Granpy Swenson's last suit, and you *know* she and I don't have the same fashion sense."

A smothered laugh burbled out of Lucy. "Okay, so a will and an outfit. *Not* that you'll need either anytime soon."

"Right. And details about the ceremony, too," Asia mused. Would she want an open casket to give people that final chance to say good-bye? Some would take comfort in it. Or would she rather have a few pictures of herself present so people could remember her however they wanted, preferably with hair?

It was surreal, thinking about these details. As if she weren't really herself but hovering over another woman, seeking to help her understand her choices and give her sound advice, the way she would a client. of course, she knew a lot more about the NASDAQ than she did about cemetery plots.

No cemetery, she decided impulsively. As picturesque as some of the nicer ones could be, she couldn't shake the idea that they were full of dead people. Besides, if there was a grave, well-meaning visitors would leave flowers. *Ugh.*

"There's something else, Luce."

"You wouldn't want to spend the hereafter in uncomfortable underwear?"

Asia grinned. "Think Saint Peter lets people through the gates if they meet their maker going commando?"

"Imagine the poor people who go during sex. Wouldn't *that* be an embarrassing way to arrive—as naked as you came into the world?"

"But happy. I always thought sex sounded like a nice way to go. Except for the poor bastard left behind. You could turn someone permanently abstinent that way."

Lucy snickered.

"Maybe Mom's been right all these years," Asia said. "There's *definitely* something wrong with us."

"Well, confirmation class never covered the appropriate undergarments for heaven, so it's natural to wonder."

Somehow, talking about it, making light of it, had shrunk the white elephant in the room. At least now she knew that, should things get worse, they *could* talk about it.

∾

> From: "Thayer R."
> To: [BaldBitchinWarriorWomen]
> Subject: Thank you!
> I really appreciate all the good thoughts and encouragement from both of you on the house sale! We've had it on and off the market so many times, been so close to sealing the deal, only to have it fall through, that I feel like the albatross is finally gone from around my neck and I can breathe. Asia, tell your sister my fingers are crossed that everything goes smoothly with her house closing this week!!! And thanks so much for letting me whine about the hiccups along the way. I love knowing you guys are there when I need to vent, but then I feel so petty after I hit send. So the new owners were making me crazy over carpet installation and plumbing questions—that's hardly anything compared to other problems in the world, right?
> Thayer

Asia reread the message, knowing the apology was for her, understanding the rationale behind it. *Who am I to complain about boyfriend troubles or the furniture store delivering the wrong order when other people have cancer or HIV or alarmingly complicated pregnancies?* But stress didn't work that way.

From: "Asia Swenson"
To: [BaldBitchinWarriorWomen]
Subject: Re: Thank you!
>>then I feel so petty after I hit send<<
Don't! It may be the big things that make headlines or get
scrapbooked or appear to draw people together—or di-
vide them. But, honestly, it's the little things that make up
life. While it's nice to occasionally stop and get perspective, if we start acting as if we aren't entitled to be disappointed over minor setbacks and daily upsets, then we rob
ourselves of the opportunity to celebrate equally "small"
victories and moments of joy.
Congrats again on the house sale,
Asia

She sat back against the bed pillows as her words disappeared on the unseen electronic route that would take them
almost instantly to her friends. Asia was part of a generation
that often took computers and the way they shrank the world
for granted, but honestly, it was a damn miracle. Anyone who
thought computers were making the world less personal had
obviously never reached for a keyboard at two in the morning
when she couldn't sleep, racked with fear or uncertainty, and
sent out a cry for help that netted immediate results. One of
the women she knew from the gym had tried her hand at online dating and caught some good-natured ribbing from other
gals. Asia hadn't considered the situation any of her business,
so hadn't really formed an opinion, but she certainly understood how, when used safely, the medium could help lower
artificial social barriers.

From: "Deborah Gene"
To: [BaldBitchinWarriorWomen]
Subject: Re: Thank you!
Well put, Asia! The government building where my husband works once had this high-alert day where they froze
the place for a few hours, not letting anyone in or out and
not letting calls in or out either. I was scared. But that night
I yelled at him about leaving his dirty clothes on the bathroom floor instead of putting them in the hamper. You'd
think I would have taken longer to bask in my gratitude
that the alert turned out to be a false alarm, but no, I was
all about the grungy boxers on a floor I'd just mopped the
day before. Is it just human nature to gripe?

   I don't think so. I think sometimes we blow up about
the little things because it's easier. Because it's a pressure valve. We let off a little steam over things that
aren't crucial so that when the critical shit hits the fan,
we don't blow up. We maintain control when it counts
the most.
Deb

From: "Asia Swenson"
To: [BaldBitchinWarriorWomen]
Subject: Little things
Can I tell you guys a secret no one knows, not even my
family? Well, Dad knew when I was a kid, but I never out-
grew the phobia. I'm terrified of spiders.

   She shuddered just typing the words, casting a glance toward
the textured plaster ceiling. Anything that could hang upside

down and drop on a person with no warning... Was it any wonder she loathed and feared them? Especially in Georgia, where some of the large ones *jumped*. In their girlhood, Lucy had addressed the problem promptly, because whenever she saw a bug in the house, she popped a jar on top of it, slid an index card underneath, and let the sucker free outside. If it had been up to Asia, she would have squashed every last eight-legged visitor in their house, except that squashing required her to get close.

> Just a little over a month ago, around Halloween, I was going into this grocery store and saw a big black spider, but I thought it was fake, part of the cobweb decorations they'd set up around the door. When it suddenly moved toward me—and I'm not proud of this—I almost wet my pants.
>
> How stupid is that? I have metastatic cancer. I've had countless chemo treatments. What the hell could one stupid spider do to me that even compares?

And yet, in a strange and admittedly creepy way, it was comforting that the lifelong phobia was still there. It was like, *Hey, cancer, you can screw up my life and take my hair and interrupt my Thanksgiving, but you can't fundamentally rob who I am.*

Not unless she let it. It was what Brandon had been trying to tell her. Cancer might define a lot of things about her life right now, but it wasn't the sum total of who she was.

She closed her laptop and reached for the bedside lamp. Then, grinning defiantly into the darkness, she slipped into her easiest sleep in weeks.

≈

Smiling as Michael held her car door open for her—the small gallantries counted—Lucy quickly settled into her seat. Georgia might not set record-breaking lows for December cold, but the intermittent wind had a bite to it. She watched as the man she loved rounded the front of the car, looking every bit as handsome as the day she'd met him. *Mine.*

Once he'd climbed in on the driver's side, she grabbed him by his blue-striped tie, leaned over the parking brake, and kissed him. Hard.

His lips parted in a combination of eagerness and surprise, and she traced them with her tongue, tasting him, reveling in both the familiarity and the . . . if not newness, precisely, then the passion she'd missed. They hadn't stopped touching each other, but it had been a while since she'd felt this responsive. Without meaning to, she'd given something up; now, her body humming with liquid pleasure, she wordlessly conveyed her intention to reclaim it.

When he finally drew back, he looked dazed. "So an hour with real estate agents initialing a thousand pieces of paper really does it for you, huh? I find myself wishing this car had a much bigger backseat."

"We own a home together!" With every call regarding wedding plans, with every premarital counseling session they had with Pastor Bob, her future with Michael became more real. But this . . .

"I know." He laced his fingers through hers, squeezing. "I'm excited, too."

"You know what I want to do?" she asked, so happy she was practically vibrating with uncontainable joy.

His eyebrows rose. "No. But I know what I'm *hoping* you want to do."

Her expression was half smirk, half admonishment.

"Don't give me that look," he said. "*You* planted one on *me*. A kiss like that would have a saint thinking lusty thoughts. And I am no saint, darlin'."

Maybe not, but he'd certainly been patient and forgiving lately. It had been weeks since they'd made love, and he hadn't complained, pressured her in any way, or made jokes about how the honeymoon was over before they even had the wedding. She just hadn't had much of a libido, although she'd tried. She really had. The last time, she couldn't relax enough to enjoy what was happening. She'd struggled to explain afterward that she'd been okay with just *his* enjoying it, because it made her feel closer to him to provide that, but she'd wound up making herself sound like a martyr. He'd snuggled with her and fallen asleep, and nothing further had been said about the awkward moment.

Looking at the way *he* was looking at *her* sent heat through her veins. She'd been embarrassed about their off night, but now she had very vivid ideas of how they could put that behind them. What was the saying about getting back on the horse? So to speak.

"Since we both took today off work," she said slowly, "I *was* thinking about Christmas tree shopping. Buying our first one together. For our place." *Our.* She loved how that sounded.

Finding the perfect tree to take home and decorate had been one of the most sentimental parts of her holiday since she'd first seen *A Charlie Brown Christmas*. It was a tradition for the Swensons to go together to a Christmas tree farm, spend way too long debating which one to get, and then take turns with the hacksaw until they'd cut it down.

"I think I've changed my mind, though," Lucy said with a wicked grin. *Now* she was thinking about seducing him in the middle of the day, eager and unashamed in the light. "You've corrupted me, Mr. O'Malley."

"Music to my ears. Is my apartment closer, do you think, or your house?"

"No, no. Aren't you aware it's good luck to make love in every room of a new home?" The place was ready for them to move in, although in order to do that she really needed to finish packing. *Not today.*

"I look forward to making love to you in that house, often. But without the benefit of any furniture or sheets or, to be quite honest, condoms?"

She pointed to the megastore across the intersection. "Carries everything from wine to mattresses. Why not make a quick stop, then go straight to the new house and make sure these shiny keys we were just given actually work?"

He chuckled. "See, this is why I love you. You're brilliant! I'm just sorry no one's selling Christmas trees in this particular parking lot, or we could indulge all your fantasies," he added as they drove across the street.

"We'll save tree shopping for later." Her need to make love with him, to renew that physical bond and truly feel connected again, had already eclipsed her moment of seasonal nostalgia. "The other, being alone with you, that's more important. If we split up inside, we can both grab different supplies and get out of here that much sooner."

"No." He turned his head toward her as he parked the car, his eyes so bright with love it made her chest ache. "Being with you *is* what's important."

With any luck, the fact that this chemo regimen was kicking Asia's ass also meant that it was kicking the cancer's. Even though she was lying perfectly still, her joints throbbed—her elbows, shoulders, knees, ankles, fingers, toes. She had a whole new sympathy for anyone who suffered arthritis. But mostly, all of her ached. Her *eyelids* hurt. What was that about?

"I'm not loving the new chemo," she told her sister, trying to move her lips as little as possible.

"That's what Mom said, although I bet you would have used more colorful words to describe the feeling."

Asia knew that Marianne, and her worry after seeing Asia in bad shape last night, was why Lucy was here on a Thursday instead of at work.

"That's not true," Lucy had protested. "I had a built-in few days off for moving into the new place. I'm actually getting more work done here because I have my laptop. The house doesn't have Internet up and running yet. So, see, I'm not baby-sitting. I'm mooching your wireless connection. And don't feel bad about my not moving right now. Michael and some of his burlier friends have it all under control with the rental truck today. He and I will get the smaller stuff, like lamps and clothes, in manageable chunks. We both have our individual leases until the end of the month."

Asia was beyond wishing she could help them move in, but when would she feel well enough to at least walk through

Lucy's new house? She barely had the energy to stand through a shower or decorate her own two-foot fake Christmas tree. The thought made her wince, thinking of Marianne casually mentioning yesterday that maybe this year would finally be the one she talked George into buying an artificial tree. Asia knew that her mother was trying to compensate for Asia's inability to participate in the annual tree hunt.

"Artificial trees are so much more practical," Marianne had said, not meeting her daughter's eyes. "Of course, we'd still want you and Lucy to come decorate it."

Until now they'd had a long-standing tradition: Each year, Asia cast the deciding vote after they'd searched from lot to farm to independent grower, all four Swensons cradling cups of cocoa and remarking on the cold, even though anyone who'd ever experienced winter north of the Mason-Dixon would deem them wimps.

Asia, you agree with your old dad, right? It just wouldn't be Christmas without that great evergreen smell.

Asia, please remind your father that we live in a suburb, not a ball stadium with a retractable roof.

Asia, don't you think that if we took this puny discount tree, we'd have enough money and ornaments left over for a second rescue tree, too?

Lucy always wanted to adopt some pitiful thing that probably wouldn't get a home otherwise, while George habitually forgot the size of his own home and expressed manly appreciation of fourteen- and sixteen-footers. They all pretended not to hear Marianne's reminders that if they just invested in an artificial tree, there would be no pine needles to clean off the carpet and they could spare themselves the annual trek.

Except that the trek had always been the point. Whatever spruce or fir they ultimately took home was incidental.

Asia sensed rather than saw Lucy studying her. "I'm not asleep, if that's what you're wondering."

"Sorry, was I hovering?"

"Nah, just radiating vibes of sisterly concern. Mom mentioned last night that they'll probably buy a fake tree."

Again, even though she wasn't directly watching Lucy, who sat at the foot of the bed, she could gauge her sister's reaction. Squirming ... the mattress wiggling was a big clue. "Those plastic trees have their benefits," Lucy said.

"I've really put a damper on the holidays this year, haven't I?"

"Asia! Don't say that. Look, even if they get the artificial one, we'll all go over next week to spend an evening decorating it, right? That's the important part." Lucy flopped down on the bed so that she could meet Asia's eyes. "And I think you should invite Brandon."

"Yeah?" It was pure chance that his path hadn't crossed her parents' before now. After all, he'd run into Fern and Lucy at the hospital and, once, just missed Morris.

Asia wasn't hiding her relationship with Brandon from Marianne and George; it was just that it seemed rather odd, amidst all the other drama, to announce, "Mom, Dad, I have a boyfriend!" Not to mention that it made her feel about fifteen. Then again, the barely PG-rated kisses she and Brandon had mostly been limited to might be on par with the dating life of a teenager.

"I'll ask him," she decided. In fact, since he'd made no mention of seeing his family at Christmas, she was a bit chagrined she hadn't thought to do so earlier.

"Good! You've always been more ... private than me, but you don't want to shut us out, right?" When Asia pretended to think it over, Lucy glared. "That was rhetorical."

Asia flashed a brief grin. "You know, you really don't have to stay. Brandon's coming over after work to check on me."

Lucy shrugged. "It's no trouble. I can let him in."

"Um, actually, I gave him a key."

"Oooh?"

"You and I both know that if I'm having a *really* rough day, even answering the door is taxing."

"Well," Lucy said softly, "hopefully these wonder drugs you're on will do their thing quickly, you can go off them, and you won't have so many rough days."

Wouldn't that be nice. Asia was getting too worn out to voice it, but she was sure her sentiment was clear.

"Don't feel like you have to stay awake to keep me company either. I probably should have parked my keister in the living room so you can rest."

"Not keeping me up. Too restless to sleep well."

Lucy snuggled in against some pillows. "You used to read to me to help me fall asleep, remember?"

A tired smile flitted at the corners of Asia's mouth. "I remember."

"I don't see a book within reach, but there's one I know by heart."

"What's that?" Asia asked, her eyes closed.

Lucy began a low-key recitation of "'Twas the Night Before Christmas." The last part Asia was able to focus on before her thoughts began to splinter and drift was the clatter on the lawn. Lucy could never remember the names of the reindeer, and Asia sleepily regretted that now she wouldn't get to hear what her sister came up with instead.

$\mathscr{e}$

When Asia opened her eyes again, prompted by male and female voices, it felt significantly later. Afternoon shadows stretched long across her room, disappearing into dark corners. At first, not quite awake, she figured she was hearing Lucy and Michael. Then she warmed in recognition. Brandon. She was smiling before she was even fully awake.

"Hey," she called through the open door. Even though her voice was gravelly, she could tell it was stronger than it had been earlier. The nap, however long, had served its purpose. "You guys talk about me all you want, but be warned, I can hear you."

Lucy stuck her head in the doorway. "Then you know we were talking about the wedding, you egomaniac, and not you at all. I was just on my way out, actually. Glad you woke up so I could say good-bye. Brandon, take good care of her."

His profile backlit in the doorway, he nodded to Lucy but kept his eyes on Asia. "Always."

She felt well enough to relocate to the sectional sofa so that he could tell her about his day while he threw together a quick dinner for them. He always insisted that, really, he was getting the best end of this deal, since, in exchange for pressing a few buttons, he received free food. Free, home-cooked, Southern food.

They were almost ready to eat when someone knocked at her door.

Brandon glanced toward her. "You comfortable with me answering that?"

Boy, she hoped it wasn't either of her parents. Although she'd been thinking earlier that it was mere happenstance that they hadn't met Brandon, now that she'd decided to formally invite him to the Swenson home next week, this wasn't how she wanted the introduction to go. Then again, Steph had phoned and said she might drop by, depending on how her own chemo regimen left her feeling. They were no longer on the same dosage cycle and didn't get to see each other as frequently.

"Sure," she told Brandon. "Go right ahead."

They both gaped when he admitted Morris Grigg.

Morris grinned at Brandon, seeming not displeased to have caught the younger man off guard. "I see the rumors are true." Then he sobered and crossed the room to take Asia's hand. "And how are you feeling?"

"Sheepish, right at the moment." Not every day your boss showed up unexpectedly at your house and found you with your coworker boyfriend.

"Don't be. If anyone should feel that, it's me. I didn't have the good grace to call first. But I had something I wanted to discuss with you. You received an invitation to the Christmas party this Friday?"

She nodded, gesturing that Morris should feel free to have a seat on the long sectional. "I would love to go, but . . ."

"Quite understandable. Jason and I doubted you'd make it, which is why I've come to share his important announcement."

Curious, Asia raised a brow.

"Jason and I and everyone else at the senior level have agreed that starting in the new year, we will begin honoring our most top-notch employees—those who give their all and get results without sacrificing warmth or integrity—with the annual Asia Swenson Award of Excellence."

Her mouth dropped open, and she blinked rapidly, not wanting to turn all emotional in front of the man who'd been both a personal mentor and a respected authority figure. "Sir, I don't . . . Did you know about this?" she asked Brandon over Morris's shoulder.

He shook his head, appearing as dazed as she felt. "Not at all."

Morris looked smug. "We're saving it as a secret for this weekend, but thought it only fair that if you couldn't attend, you hear it first. of course, if you feel better, please do join us. That invitation extends to the *two* of you, you know. We'd love to have you both there."

She wanted to hug him for the tacit approval in his voice.

Morris grinned. "Wait until my wife hears how I turned out to be a matchmaker. of course, Peters, you realize that when Asia is feeling one hundred percent again, she'll give you a run for those clients we temporarily reallocated."

Brandon's smile was distinctly proud. "Of course."

After he'd shown their boss to the door, Brandon joined her on the couch, dropping his arms around her.

"The Asia Swenson Award of Excellence," he mused. "Has a nice ring to it."

Feeling ridiculously sentimental, she recalled her first interview at MCG, her first desk in an oatmeal-colored cubicle, and how she'd slowly worked her way up to an office with actual windows. Fern had been her first hire, although Morris had rubber-stamped her choice, of course. She swallowed a thick knot of emotion. She would miss the office if she didn't go back, but thinking of all the people she'd met there over the years, she knew the company and clients were in good hands.

"They named an award after me." *Wait until Mom and Dad hear this!* They'd be so proud ... and she needed to call them anyway to ask about bringing a guest next week. She craned her head toward Brandon and adopted a playfully haughty tone. "I must be very special and important. Top in my field, really."

He leaned in to kiss her. "Well, I could have told you that."

Sixteen

"Asia Swenson?" A woman in colorful scrubs was standing in an open doorway, consulting a clipboard. "The doctor can see you now."

Brandon cleared his throat and squeezed Asia's hand. "You sure you don't want me to go in with you? I'm happy to wait here. Just wanted to make sure you know I'm serious about lending moral support."

"I'm sure." She was glad for his presence but could do this part alone. In a way—a way she didn't like to dwell on—it felt as if she'd come full circle.

She'd asked Brandon to drive her to the oncologist's today because Marianne and Lucy were having a mother-daughter lunch together and then the final wedding dress fitting. It was bad enough that Asia had cast a pall over the bridal shower, then Thanksgiving. She'd elected to keep this appointment to herself. If her increasing abdominal pain and fevers turned out to be nothing, they never needed to know about it. If they turned out to be . . .

The memory of Lucy's earnest request that Asia not shut them out ignited a spark of guilt. Maybe she should have been more frank about the doctor's concerns that the new treatment wasn't doing its job. *No, it's Christmas. And Lucy's only weeks away from getting married.* The instinct to protect died hard.

Asia winced at her mental word choice.

"Good luck," Brandon said. He'd yet to let go of her hand, though. She loved that about him.

She tried to say, "Thank you," but wasn't sure any sound emerged. Maybe she just didn't hear it over her thundering heartbeat.

The nurse made some minor small talk as they walked down the long corridor, but nothing she said about the weather or the holiday season made this feel like any less of a forced march. Asia couldn't help laughing when she saw the open door to Dr. Klamm's office. How many times had she been here?

She deserved an honorary desk, or at least a chair with her name stitched across it, like on a movie set. And, while she was at it, her own parking spot at the hospital. She and her family *had* to have purchased one by now. Maybe that was what she should say when people asked her what she wanted for Christmas—gift certificates for hospital parking.

"Ms. Swenson?" The nurse gave her a bemused half smile, as if wishing she were in on the joke.

"Nothing. I . . . It's nothing."

"Dr. Klamm will be right with you."

In fact, the nurse nearly collided with him when she turned to go.

"Asia, hello." The man's eyes softened as he studied her, not quite the caring yet professionally detached facade physicians wore as automatically as surgical masks.

Just looking at him, she understood the news wouldn't be good. But hadn't she already known? She'd come here today, asked Brandon to be the one to bring her, expecting to hear the worst. Only, until now, that was how she'd been thinking of it: the worst. A vague term that didn't include specifics. She would have preferred to live another fifty or sixty years, but had accepted that wouldn't happen. So how long did she have? Would she see another Christmas with her family? Watch her sister walk down that aisle? *I promised her. I promised her I'd be there.* She'd never broken a promise to Lucy.

And she didn't plan to start now, no matter what Dr. Klamm told her.

"Why don't you have a seat?" he invited gently.

She wanted to draw herself up and say stoically, "That's all right; I'll stand," as if she were one of those old movie cowboys unafraid to stare down bad guys, betrayal, or bullets. Which was ridiculous, because she was freaking *terrified*.

She slid into a chair. "The chemo hasn't shrunk the cancer in my liver?" Huh, she sounded almost calm. Denial? Shock?

"No, Asia, I'm sorry." As compassionately as possible, he laid out the medical facts, but her conscious mind kept drifting in and out, reminding her of when she was a kid and Marianne had played the piano downstairs late at night. Asia would fall asleep slowly, over the space of several songs, dozing for a few bars here and there and during pauses between pieces so that it was all one long, lulling medley.

Her cancer was still spreading. She'd not only failed to beat the enemy back; she was barely slowing its conquest.

"So . . . what now?" She thought of her friend Char. In Asia's limited experience, death was rarely easy or pretty. She suspected that one day it would get ugly for her. But Char had made herself so sick fighting so valiantly. Was Asia supposed to keep trying this, that, and the other? For what? Could the doctors say they thought she still had years? Or at this point was she bargaining for months? Weeks?

Please, God, let it be more than weeks.

Dr. Klamm paused, his gaze meeting hers without flinching. "We can continue treatment, Asia, but it's up to you what you want the goal of that treatment to be."

"I have to live to see my sister's wedding." The words poured out of her, urgent and desperately hopeful. "It's in January."

"I didn't mean to give you the impression that your time . . . That is to say, you still have some. Possibly as many as six months, if you want to experiment and see if we can find a treatment that slows the cancer."

But he couldn't guarantee even that much, because at some point it would stop being just about cancer and become an issue of organ failure. She thought again of Char. Was Asia not as brave as her friend? As unpalatable and surreal as the thought of death was, Asia couldn't stomach the idea of experimenting with even more potent chemotherapies.

Her assistant, Fern, had taken fertility drugs in order to have her beautiful baby boy, and there'd been a number of side effects from the hormones. At an office baby shower, one woman had asked Fern if she'd thought it was all worth it.

"Absolutely." Fern had beamed, cupping her hands over her very swollen tummy. "But . . . would I still be glad I'd tried if it hadn't worked?"

Asia had never *enjoyed* chemotherapy, but she'd approached it with spirit, wanting to soldier on and recognizing it as a valuable part of her arsenal. Had it been worth it? For hundreds, probably thousands of people, absolutely. It had saved lives.

Hers, it seemed, would not be one of them.

"We can't know for sure if different chemos would even help?" she asked.

"No," he admitted. After all, if they could predict that with certainty, she wouldn't have already undergone several types that *didn't* work.

"Should I do it?"

He hesitated. "That would not be my . . . personal recommendation, but we will honor your decision. And there are people you can speak with, brochures you can read before you decide."

She foresaw her "Cancer and You" library adding a "Hospice and You" wing.

"If you opted to stop chemotherapy," he added, "you would still be entitled to medical treatment. Pain management, palliative care. There are choices available that would not extend your life the way chemo theoretically could, but they should help you live with the disease and perhaps temper its effects."

Without the poisonous chemo drugs being pumped into her body, would some of the discomfort ease? The disease did its own damage, of course, but what if she stopped using so much of her energy to put up a fight and reinvested it in herself and whatever time she had left? At some point it had to stop being about fighting for her life and become about living that life.

"You didn't come here by yourself today?" Dr. Klamm asked.

"No. No, I have someone waiting for me." Someone special, someone she was pretty sure she'd fallen in love with over the past three months. Someone whose company she might be in better shape to enjoy if she gave up the most hard-core of her treatments. But was giving up in her nature?

Could she simply let go? Was she tired enough? Human beings—all species, as far as she knew—came preprogrammed with survival instincts whose main goal was to simply stay alive. Did openly acknowledging that cancer had won constitute even more of a defeat than death?

That's pride talking, a stupid basis for decision making.

Sure, at the back of her spinning mind was some half-remembered poem about not going gently, but screw that. The poet wasn't the one sitting in her chair, and she owed him no apologies for not having it left in her to rage. Her emotional reserves were currently leaning toward *cry, curse,* and *question.*

In Dr. Klamm's estimation, she was looking at a matter of months. The end of her life.

Just as no poet could fault her for any decision she made now, nor could anyone else make it for her. Not the well-educated and sympathetic doctor across the desk, not the handsome man sitting worried in the waiting room, not the family who'd rallied around her, trying to act as if her cancer weren't a black cloud over their own lives.

For possibly the first time since she'd come into this world, and despite her extreme gratitude for having found Brandon, Asia Swenson felt truly alone.

ᶜ∫

"You just look so beautiful." Marianne sniffed as Lucy turned slowly, checking the seamstress's handiwork from all angles.

"It's this dress," Lucy said in awe. It made her look fantastic. If she could get away with it, she'd wear the dress everywhere: work, church, to get the mail.

"It's not only the dress," Marianne protested. "You're glowing."

Probably from all the sex. Caught off guard by her own observation, Lucy lowered her head, resisting the urge to press her hands to her blushing cheeks. Something had changed between her and Michael since they'd moved under the same roof. He joked that it was her appreciation of the manly way he'd handled the giant U-Haul truck.

She hated to deflate his ego, but she suspected the difference wasn't about him, or even the new home. She'd changed, and their fight had been partially to thank for that. Even the simple act of having been angry with him, letting herself feel entitled to the emotion, was new for her. Despite what he'd intimated that night, having emotions didn't necessarily make her fragile; they just made her . . . her.

Somewhere along the way she'd stopped feeling quite so apologetic for being herself. She was imperfect: She would never be a size two; she was always going to cry at greeting card commercials; and, yes, she was selfish enough to wish there were more days like this, when she was allowed to focus on the thrill of her upcoming wedding instead of everyone tip-toeing around the topic of Asia's ever-present illness.

Yet Lucy had embraced all of that.

"Mom, thanks for today," she said. "It was really nice to spend the time alone with you."

Marianne's eyes welled with tears—like daughter, like mother. "Oh, sweetie. I can't believe my baby is all grown-up and about to be married."

Lucy hugged her mother, almost nervous about doing so in the gown, but if the dress couldn't withstand some heartfelt congratulations on her wedding day, she was in trouble. Once she had returned to the dressing room and was changing back into her street clothes, she heard Marianne blow her nose. She grinned. She and her mother were sure to be sobbing messes at the wedding, which would probably set off Cam and Asia, too. Lucy was glad they'd decided to have the photographs taken before the ceremony.

In the VW, Marianne turned to her daughter almost shyly. "Are they expecting you to put in some afternoon hours at work, or would you like to come with me to do some Christmas shopping?"

"That sounds nice, Mom, but I'm afraid I have to get you home. Michael and I have an appointment to see Pastor Bob later. It was originally scheduled for tomorrow, but . . ."

"Betsy Dunaham," Marianne said sadly. The eighty-year-old woman, a longtime member of the congregation, had suffered a stroke. "Yes, I read in the bulletin that services for her would be held tomorrow. Bob probably spent the morning visiting with her daughter. He was such a comfort when my own parents died."

There was a reverent silence, a moment of remembrance for those who had passed.

Marianne's head jerked up. "I suppose Bob . . . I'd never thought about it."

Lucy absently hit her turn signal. "Thought about what?"

"N-nothing." The way Marianne's lower lip trembled might have made her look endearingly young if she didn't also look so vulnerable. "It's nothing, dear."

Asia. Lucy's mind connected the dots; Marianne was wondering if, should Asia die, Pastor Bob would be the one to officiate at her funeral. *Marrying one daughter and burying the other?* With effort, she tried to push the thought away.

But maybe she shouldn't. Lucy had been given the gift of a day with her mother, uninterrupted and unexasperating; maybe the best way for Lucy to repay that was to let her mom discuss her fears.

"You were thinking about Asia?" Lucy asked.

Marianne bobbed her head several times, her hands pressed tightly together in her lap.

"Do you . . . want to talk about it?" They didn't have much experience with serious discussions. Lucy's questions about "When will I get my period?" and "What's the meaning of life?" were always filtered through her much older sister. Funny how six years didn't seem as big a difference as it once had. She'd considered Asia a generation removed from herself, one that was infinitely cooler and infallibly knowledgeable.

"Today was supposed to be about you," Marianne said.

Whether her mother meant that or it was just an easy excuse to avoid a difficult subject, Lucy was touched. "Thank you, Mama. But you always taught us to take turns. It was time to focus on me earlier. Now it would be all right to think about—"

"Your sister?"

"About you. I haven't asked lately how *you're* doing with everything." *Or Daddy.* One step at a time.

"Women's Bible study at the church," Marianne began, pressing her hands to her cheeks, her voice quavering. "We have it every week, and it's so bizarre. Enid Norcott is in my class, and she showed us one of the pew bows she made for you. It's beautiful. As everyone's filing in and pouring their coffee, half the women are coming up to me asking how Asia's doing, telling me she's in their prayers or that their daughter-in-law will be dropping off some fresh-baked bread for her. Then the other half crowd around wanting to know how the wedding plans are coming, what kind of dress I'll be wearing as mother of the bride, and that I checked to make sure it doesn't clash with what Bridget is wearing. I stand there, urgently hoping we can just get the lesson started, and not knowing whether I'm supposed to feel happy or sad."

Lucy's heart squeezed. "I know exactly what you mean. But I think we're allowed to be both, Mama."

"And guilty?"

Survivor's guilt? That was the term Lucy had heard for people who'd come away from fatal crashes unscathed while other passengers were killed. She supposed it also applied to the healthy loved ones of someone who'd died from an illness, but she hesitated to use the expression with her mother, since Lucy wasn't trying to imply that Asia had one foot in the grave. "How do you mean?"

Marianne stayed quiet for so long, Lucy didn't think her mom would—or could—answer. Then, finally: "What if this is my fault?"

"What?" Lucy's head whipped around, and she stared at

Marianne for a moment before her mom, out of lifelong habit, chided, "Eyes on the road, please!

"Susannah Graham's daughter works as some kind of medical tech," Marianne explained, "and she was telling Susannah about a-a gene or something that's hereditary in females. What if *I* passed along something that made Asia sick? What if . . . what if she's not the only one who gets cancer?"

Lucy was aghast. *She means me.* Honest to God, it had never even occurred to her. She'd mentioned to her own doctor when Asia was first diagnosed that her sister had breast cancer, and the doctor had said that, with cancer in the immediate family, Lucy might want to start getting mammograms earlier than most women. But that was it.

"It would be one thing for me to get it," Marianne said. "I've lived a full life, been blessed with two beautiful daughters I got to raise to adulthood, and that father of yours, the only man I've ever loved."

"And we all appreciate everything you do for us. Just in case we didn't say thank you enough for the costumes you sewed for elementary school plays or the food you've cooked over the years."

"That's another thing! All these new findings about how this might cause cancer, or such and such might help prevent it. I should have made you girls eat more broccoli and brussels sprouts."

In an ironic counterpoint to her mother's hysterical words, Lucy swerved the car into the parking lot of a restaurant where the lunch special was locally known as "heart attack on a plate" and deep-fried cheesecake was an actual dessert selection. Cheesecake. Deep-fried. But Lucy couldn't finish this conversation *and* trust herself to get her mother home safely.

She might not apologize as much for her emotional limitations these days, but at least she needed to recognize them as a potential threat to other drivers. "Mom, no. You can be as upset as you want about what Asia's going through. It would be ridiculous to pretend it's *not* upsetting. But you can't blame yourself. Even the doctors can't accurately explain or predict the cause or the outcome, and they've had years of education in the field."

"Logically, I know you're right," Marianne whispered. "But logic doesn't help."

"Surprises are a part of life," Lucy told her mother. "I know it seems flip to call cancer a surprise, like it's a birthday party for a teenager. It's nasty and maybe somewhat predictable in certain cases, but even if you're expecting to get the diagnosis, I imagine it's still an ugly shock."

"Again, I don't disagree with you," Marianne said, shredding a tissue she'd pulled out of her purse. "But how are we supposed to just be okay with never knowing?"

This from the woman who'd spent years dragging Lucy out of bed every Sunday morning so they wouldn't be late for church. "Faith, I suppose. You've told me it's not our place to understand everything, but to trust God."

"That's before it applied to my daughter having cancer!"

Lucy actually smiled, not sure it was appropriate to be amused by her mother's wry confession but unable to help herself. "So yours is a selective faith?"

"When it comes to my *children*, damn straight." Casting an apologetic glance skyward, Marianne added, "Not that I've ruled faith out. I'll never stop praying for either of you girls. But I get angry, too. Some patients recover fully and doctors can never explain why, so why not my daughter? Where's her miracle?"

Lucy wanted to say maybe it was coming—for all she knew, it was—but she hesitated. Where was the line between faith and false hope? Maybe if Asia really were dying, they should be happy she was going to a better place.

Were they all being selfish, wanting to hold her here on this earth while she was clearly suffering?

But she's alive.

Suffering, like surprises, was sometimes a part of life. The flip side was the fiercely sweet moments, from the rush of a first kiss to the simple beauty of a sunrise over the water. The unexpected discovery of two people falling in love. The insignificant and fleeting joy of a gorgeous butterfly landing on a little girl's arm. The shocking thrill of a woman discovering she was pregnant after medical experts had concluded she couldn't conceive.

Marianne cleared her throat. "Thank you for stopping the car, dear. I wouldn't want your father to see me like this. I have to be strong for him."

Lucy wasn't sure whether that comment made her want to laugh or cry. She'd always assumed it was her big bear of a dad who supported Marianne, but what she'd witnessed on Thanksgiving reminded her that relationships were rarely that simple.

"You and I are going to have to help him," Marianne said, her voice quavering slightly but sounding more pragmatic now. "It kills him that there's not more he can do to keep the two of you safe."

You and I. The words formed a small glow inside Lucy. That was the other part of life, the part she cherished most deeply, even if she hadn't stopped to think about it often enough before Asia got sick. Through the awful discoveries and the happy surprises, the one constant were the people around you who helped you cope and celebrate. Flawed people, maybe, but Lucy was grateful for them nonetheless.

Brandon had taken one look at Asia's face back at the oncology center, and his own face had fallen. As he started the car, he managed to say, "I'm so sorry," before her tears started, small, bitter hiccups and salty streaks down her cheeks. He had said little, just given her the space to grieve.

Now he steered her into her apartment. "Couch?"

"Bed." Once they got there, she met his eyes. "Would you lie down with me for a little while?"

He kicked off his shoes. "For as long as you want." Tucking an arm around her as if she were fragile—or precious—he brought the warmth of his body close to hers without putting any of his weight on her.

She echoed his earlier sentiment. "I'm sorry."

"For what?" He seemed startled. "You don't have anything to apologize for."

"I should have tried harder to push you away." She was glad she *hadn't,* that he was here and solid and comforting her when she needed it most, but wondered if that made her

self-centered. "I should have tried harder to make you understand."

"You never made any secret of the situation. You all but
threw it in my face every time I turned around. I made my
own choices."

"And now you'll be hurt because of them."

When she'd first been diagnosed with the mets, she'd wondered if it was better to brave it alone, without a partner or
lover, if having one would merely add to the emotional bag-
gage. Now she knew it did. Brandon, however, seemed to be
getting the shit end of the deal. As soon as she had the thought,
a ghoulish chuckle ripped through her.

"Something funny?" He propped his head on his wrist.

"Well, I was lying here feeling sorry for you. And then I
remembered—Hey, wait a minute, *I'm* the one who's dying.
You're really not sorry that you let yourself get this close, now
that you know how it's turned out?"

"Nothing's done as of tonight. There are still days and
memories ahead."

Christmas. The wedding. She turned, burrowing her face
in his chest. Neither of them spoke for a while, although occasionally he stroked his hand over her back.

"You've changed me, Asia. I love my job, and I'll always love
it, but what the hell is wrong with me? Watching you with Lucy,
I've realized how much time I've let slip by without seeing my
own sister. A little thing like the ocean shouldn't get in the way
of families, and it's a lot easier for me to go there than for her
to pack up kids, a husband, and a German shepherd. And my
dates were . . . dinners at trendy restaurants where we compared
schedules and mutual acquaintances. I don't even know if the

last woman I was seeing realized my mother was dead, much less thought to ask me about it. Remember, I told you I see the silver lining in the way *Casablanca* ends? Even though he has to let her go, he's a better man for having loved her."

"Thank you," she whispered, leaning into the rhythm of his heartbeat beneath her cheek. "I love you, too."

If the last few months had made her more capable of saying that to someone—of saying it to Brandon—then maybe there were, indeed, silver linings.

Seventeen

Asia dozed fitfully that afternoon, but her dreams were more disturbing than being awake was painful, so she finally slid out from between Brandon's arms and left him a prominently placed note saying that she needed some air, he shouldn't worry, and she'd be back very soon.

Even though she didn't acknowledge a specific destination in her mind when she climbed into her car, it didn't take her long to recognize her route. Night was falling, but streetlights decorated with greenery and red Christmas bows twinkled at her in the dusk. The main sanctuary's brick tower stood massive against the horizon, taller than any of the surrounding buildings. As the half hour struck, the low, full sound of church bells pealed.

Asia had always believed in God, hoped He had a sense of humor, and trusted in His basic goodness. Maybe she should be turning to Him now, but she felt more like a woman who'd come to pick a fight.

Her hands fisted around the steering wheel, she looked for a parking space in the church's crowded lot. Inside, children, choir members, and possibly sheep would be rehearsing for this year's nativity pageant. With any luck, Pastor Bob would be in his office and available to talk. If Asia were honest with the man about how she felt right now, would he absolve her, telling her God understood her fury? Or would he chastise her because she'd had thirty-four good years, more blessings in her life than countless others ever received?

While she doubted that the wise and caring man who'd known her all her life would be that sanctimonious, she lingered in her car, just in case. If she was already on God's bad side, she couldn't afford the black mark against her soul that would surely come from popping a preacher in the nose.

She actually didn't want to hit anyone; she wanted comfort. A promise that somehow it was all going to be okay. A freaking cross-stitched platitude, maybe. She glanced toward the church. It was now clear she wouldn't find what she needed in a hospital, and she wished she had back the days she'd spent there. Would she find what she needed inside this building?

As she got out of her car, everything took on the grainy quality of a badly digitized film—her own movements at the wrong speed, the colors of the sky off by a shade. She half expected someone to call, "Cut!" Maybe they could take it from the top. Maybe she could make different choices, go straight to the total breast removal instead of wasting time with a partial procedure that hadn't worked. Notice Brandon sooner, instead of waiting until she was so sick she could barely participate in a real male-female relationship. Accept his invitation to dinner the first time he'd asked. Better yet, make the invitation herself.

"Asia?"

She started, so surprised to hear her own name that for a

moment she thought this was a dream. Maybe someone was trying to wake her up. Or . . . She stopped in her tracks beneath the cathedral's shadow and looked upward.

"Asia, I thought that was you." The voice, unmistakably Lucy's, was coming from her left.

Feeling foolish, Asia turned. "Hey. What are you doing here?"

"We were just seeing Pastor Bob," Lucy said, her hands linked with Michael's.

"That's where I'm headed."

"Oh?" Lucy frowned. "He didn't mention you'd be coming in."

"This is an impulsive visit," Asia managed. "I'm hoping he can fit me in."

Lucy waited, as if expecting more explanation.

"Guess we shouldn't keep you," Michael said. "See you at your parents' on Saturday?"

"For the tree decorating?" Asia nodded. "Wouldn't miss it. I still can't believe Mom talked Dad into an artificial one, though."

"They're very practical," Lucy said in a tiny voice.

"I suppose they are." Despair crescendoed so loudly inside her that she knew Lucy and Michael must hear it. Asia imagined the choral director stopping everyone inside, trying to ascertain *where* that sour note was coming from.

"See you there," Lucy said.

"See you." Asia remained rooted to the spot. They all stood awkwardly, waiting for nothing in particular. Finally she shuffled forward on the path, going in one direction while her sister went in the other.

Eighteen

They took the steps to her parents' front porch, illuminated by the light Marianne had turned on for her guests tonight and by the tiny red and green lights George had woven through the railing. Behind Asia, Brandon was carefully watching to ensure she didn't lose her balance. Although if she didn't know better, she might think he was stalling.

She stopped, asking over her shoulder, "Are you nervous about meeting my parents?"

"That's not the part that . . . No." He studied the ground intently.

"Does it upset you that I haven't told them about my doctor's visit?" It was a huge burden she'd placed on him, making him the only one to shoulder the responsibility of that knowledge.

After Christmas. She'd tell her family after Christmas, preserving the holiday but still giving them a couple of weeks to digest the news before Lucy's wedding. If this was to be her last Christmas, she refused to spoil it with news of advanced, untreatable cancer. After being robbed of Thanksgiving, she *deserved* this.

Brandon's smile was sad. "No, I understand. I just—"

The front door opened, the scent of cloves and cinnamon wafting out as Marianne delicately cleared her throat. "We thought we heard a car door close, but then no one rang the bell. I thought I'd better check to make sure everything was all right."

"We're fine," Asia said impishly. "Just out here necking in the shadows."

"Asia Jane!"

"Yeah," Brandon chided behind her. "Asia Jane! I'm Brandon Peters. Nice to meet you, ma'am."

"Never mind the 'ma'am'; you call me Marianne. I'm this one's mother." She shot a final reprimanding glare at her daughter. "Come inside. We were about to pour some mulled cider and make hot cocoa. Lucy's been eyeing the bag of marshmallows since she got here. I tried to tell her she needs to be careful if she wants to fit into that wedding dress."

"I do not!" Lucy protested from the living room. She sat on the couch, unraveling bubble paper from around Christmas knickknacks. "I've lost four pounds. The move-in diet: lugging everything around and getting so busy unpacking—"

"Unpacking?" Asia whispered, sitting next to her sister. "Is that what you kids call it these days?"

"—you forget to eat," Lucy concluded, shoving at Asia's knee and trying not to laugh.

Michael had stepped away from the strands of lights lining Marianne's carpet—he'd apparently been conducting the annual check to find and replace blown bulbs while George hung stockings—to shake Brandon's hand. Now he arched an eyebrow at Lucy. "Not to mention the delayed dinners because some people didn't label their boxes and we can't find half the kitchen utensils."

"I take it that someone is you?" Asia asked Lucy as their mother disappeared into the kitchen where the cider was simmering.

"It will all balance out genetically," Lucy informed them pertly. "I'm slightly disorganized—"

"Slightly?" Michael echoed.

"—and *he* alphabetizes his movie collection. Within subcategories, no less. Cross the two of us and there's a chance our kids will turn out normal. Hi, Brandon, nice to see you again."

He grinned. "Always a pleasure."

"I don't alphabetize my movies," Michael said sheepishly. "Although she is right about my arranging them by category."

Lucy snorted.

"That way," he continued, "when my wife says something like, 'I'm in the mood for a comedy tonight,' I can find one in seconds."

Looking pleased at the *wife* moniker, Lucy blew him a kiss. "Gotta love an obliging man."

"Only thinking of you, dear."

Asia rolled her eyes. "And that's officially the closest I ever want to get to other people's foreplay."

A crash jarred her attention to George, who'd dropped the resin replica of a gingerbread house that was traditionally set in the center of the mantel.

"Oops. Sorry, Dad." Asia suspected that when Lucy and

Michael did delight everyone by having babies, her father would like to imagine his beloved grandchildren sprang fully formed from the cabbage patch. "Have you, um, met Brandon?"

Their mother had emerged in the doorway at the sound of one of her collectibles hitting the floor. "You haven't properly introduced this young man yet? Honestly, Asia."

"She's off your case now about the marshmallows," Asia muttered out of the side of her mouth. "Consider it an early gift."

Lucy nodded her head once, carefully staring straight ahead.

"What are you girls up to over there?" Marianne asked. "And don't even *bother* saying, 'Nothing,' because you look . . . Actually, Asia, you look quite nice tonight."

"Beautiful," Brandon agreed, bending to pick up the ornamental house and hand it back to George.

"Thank you." She'd paired a silky violet blouse with black slacks. She also wore the wig Lucy had helped her find and dangly gold earrings. But maybe people weren't remarking on her clothes. She'd brushed on colored lip moisturizer and was happy with her own skin tone tonight. She looked . . . healthy. She thought it came from having had a few days to make peace with her decision.

"So, are you feeling better?" Marianne asked, her voice full of optimism. "The new chemo is working well?"

Flinching, Asia exchanged looks with Brandon. While she didn't intend to break the bad news during the season of glad tidings, she didn't want to outright lie, either. How cruel would it be to let them think she was getting better?

"Actually, Mom, I'm . . . taking a break."

"A break?" Marianne parroted, her hands going to her hips in a don't-you-play-games-with-me-I'm-your-mother gesture.

Staying out of the dialogue for the time being, Lucy stiffened on the couch.

"You know how sick the chemo can make me, and the hospital was a lousy place to spend Thanksgiving. So I'm not going to have any treatments for a little while. I want a Christmas with my family."

Marianne chewed her lip, obviously tempted by the thought that they could relax and enjoy the holiday without worrying about negative side effects, but suspicious that this "break" would harm her daughter in the long run. How could Asia explain kindly that the long run had ceased to be a concern?

"Do you need help carrying the mugs of cider, Mrs. Swenson?" Brandon offered, sidling toward her in a way that seemed more like natural charm than calculated intervention.

"I told you to call me Marianne," she tutted. "But, yes, an extra pair of hands would be very helpful."

Thank you, Asia mouthed as he glanced in her direction from the doorway.

Her father, she noticed, was watching her intently but said nothing, merely lifting a strand of lights to help Michael conclude his inspection.

Lucy was more stubborn. "Would this be a temporary break?"

"It's Christmastime, Blondie." The softness of Asia's tone made it no less unyielding. "Let it go."

Her sister froze.

Then, as if nothing had happened, Lucy stood to grab another box of ornaments that needed to be unpacked before the tree decorating. They worked in wordless tandem, placing ornaments from years past on the table and making sure they all had hooks or loops of yarn.

"Okay," Marianne said, bringing a tray into the room, "I have a few mugs of cider poured. Who else wants hot cocoa besides Lucy?"

Lucy stood. "I'll come supervise marshmallow distribution."

For the next hour, everyone continued to make jokes and position stocking holders and unwrap both store-bought limited-edition ornaments and homemade contributions, like a miniature wreath that seemed to be made of spray-painted pretzels laced together with faded ribbon. But Asia couldn't help noticing her sister barely said a word directly to her, or even looked at her.

"We should put on carols," Marianne said to no one in particular.

Asia and Lucy both stepped away from the tree.

"I'll do it," Lucy said, staring over her sister's shoulder.

"Luce—"

Lucy rounded the corner into the other room, where the main stereo was set up. Last Father's Day, she'd enlisted Michael's help in hanging small speakers in the corners of the front room so that the music could be enjoyed there as well. Asia followed her sister, although she honestly didn't care whether they ended up listening to Nat King Cole or "Grandma Got Run Over by a Reindeer."

"Don't," Lucy said, not bothering to turn as she rifled through her parents' music collection.

"You have to—"

She rounded then, her eyes blazing. "You don't get to tell

me how I *have* to react to news like this. News you weren't even going to share."

"Of course I was." *Eventually.* "Just not tonight, okay? Maybe we can talk tomorrow."

"Girls, we need another opinion in here before we can start hanging these ornaments. The tree is listing to the side," Marianne complained.

They heard the lower tones of their father saying that the tree was just fine.

"Lucy, come tell me what you think," their mother implored.

"On my way, Mama." Her voice sounded normal enough, but the hand she had wrapped around a Bing Crosby CD shook as she glanced back at Asia. "Tomorrow."

"I'm not completely insensitive," Lucy said as she barged into the apartment, tossing her purse down next to the front door. She'd tried to decide what to say the entire way here, but the more she thought about it—the more she tried to accept that her sister was going to die—the more pissed she'd become.

"Hello to you, too," Asia said, coming into the room from the kitchen, drinking from a plastic Six Flags cup that had been through the washer so many times the only reason Lucy recognized the logo was because she had a cup at home exactly like it.

"I'm known for being *overly* sensitive," Lucy said. "So, of course, I understand why you didn't want to tell everyone last night, but you could've called me first. I'll bet you didn't just find this out, did you? I had a right to know."

That sounded moronic out loud, but dammit, she didn't ever want to be sucker punched like that again. They'd been having so much fun and then there'd been that moment when it all shattered like one of her mother's blown-glass German ornaments beneath someone's shoe.

"You had a *right*?" Asia's voice rose. "Grow up, Lucy; this isn't about you."

Lucy reeled, the impact of her sister's condemnation stinging her. "Of course not! It's very rarely about me. It's always been 'Asia made the honor roll' or 'Asia got asked to the prom by the hottest guy in school' or 'Asia has cancer.'"

Asia slammed the cup down on top of the nearby entertainment center; clear liquid sloshed over the top. "And you're what, *jealous* of my fatal disease? Because, trust me, I didn't ask for it! And I didn't ask for the extra attention from it."

"I realize that! I'm not stupid." Lucy fought for control of her temper, but it had been on a low simmer all night, and hitting the boiling point was inevitable. Maybe she should have confided in Michael, but she couldn't. This was between her and Asia. "I know it must blow in a million ways I'll never even comprehend, but this is hard on more people than just you."

"No shit. You think I'm somehow magically unaware of that? You think that doesn't weigh on me every time someone takes me to an appointment, every time the doctor gives me lousy news and I have to figure out how to tell people I love? You don't think it makes me feel even worse when my *dying* disrupts someone else's day?"

"Their day?" Lucy could feel her entire body shaking. "Their *day*? It's going to disrupt my entire life. You're my sister. You're supposed to be the first person I tell when I find out Michael and I are pregnant. You're supposed to tease me about waddling and getting fat. Our kids are supposed to grow up together."

"I know." Asia's voice was choked.

"You're the strongest person I've ever met. People beat cancer. I've heard the stories; I've met survivors! What the hell's wrong with your doctors?"

"It's not their fault, Luce. It's no one's fault."

"Well, it needs to be *someone's*, because I'd like to rip their fucking head off!"

All righty.

There didn't seem to be much else to add, and the silence rang in Lucy's ears. It had that unnatural, post-rock concert quality. Asia's neighbors had probably all dialed the police to report a domestic dispute and possible acts of violence. And when the hell had she started crying?

Lucy cleared her throat. "I, um . . . So, is this astounding display of maturity the reason you didn't want to tell me?"

Asia half laughed, half sobbed, shaking her head. "I wanted you to have Christmas."

"I love you for that. But you're starting to piss me off."

"I gathered." Asia slid down to a sitting position against the wall.

Lucy walked toward her. "I told you we want to be part of your life. You say you're trying to protect people, which may be true, but you shut me out. Let me be a part of this."

Asia's head flopped tiredly in Lucy's direction, her expression skeptical. "Of *this*? Are you sure?"

"You're my sister," Lucy repeated, a good deal more gently than she had before. "I'm really sorry I yelled. That was so much worse than when I fought with Michael. I don't ever want to fight with anyone again."

After a beat, Asia said, "We could kiss and make up if it would make you feel better. But no tongue."

"Ew." Lucy scooted away from her. "That was so wrong."

"It really was."

"So." Lucy studied her, trying to force her brain to process the truth of the situation. The funny thing was, she'd thought she would accept this better, had been prepared for it because Asia had seemed so weak, her pallor alarming and her eyes clouded. Now, she looked ... good. There was a disconnect that made it even more difficult to mesh Asia's temporarily improved appearance with the fact that she was actually worse. "What happens now, medically?"

"The doctors help me manage my pain and do everything humanly possible to keep me kicking for this wedding I have to be in. After that, I'm signing DNR papers. Dr. Klamm gave me some paperwork for an advance directive."

Something inside Lucy clenched painfully. Her soul, possibly. "I'm a selfish bitch. I don't know what I was thinking, busting in here and reaming you out like that."

"That's all right. *I'm* an overprotective know-it-all. And you yelled for the same reason I yelled back. Pastor Bob says God will forgive us. Currently, I'm working on trying to forgive Him." She pointed toward the ceiling, making it clear that her *him* was not their pastor.

"That's why you were at the church the other night," Lucy deduced. "Do you think when it's time to tell Mom and Dad, Pastor Bob should be there?"

"No. If they see him, they'll be freaking before I can even

get the explanation out and assure them that I've made my peace with this."

"Have you?"

Asia exhaled, resting her forehead on her palms. "I will. Promise me something?"

Lucy swallowed. "What do you need?"

"Take custody of Al when I'm not here to water him anymore. And make one of those requests. You know, 'in lieu of flowers'?"

"You don't want flowers?"

"Hell, no. I'm only showing up at your wedding because you went with silk."

"So what's your 'in lieu of'? Money donated to a charity?"

"You don't think asking for cash seems tacky?"

Lucy's laugh was strangled but heartfelt. "Mom would be so proud. We're speaking of, I assume, your funeral, and you're worried about good Southern manners?"

Asia shrugged. "Between you and me, ever since that first wrist-eating corsage Johnny Hart got me for homecoming, something about flowers has always struck me as a little creepy. I'd like the good-bye to be . . . happy. Like the bon voyage on cruises. Don't they throw confetti from the deck or something?"

"I've never been on a cruise."

"Seems I recall confetti from old *Love Boat* episodes."

Is this what they'd been reduced to, *Love Boat*?

Good evening, I'm Captain Stubing. . . . I'll be your funeral director.

"Do we get a discount if we buy those tiny wedding bubbles in bulk?" Asia asked. "Maybe people could just blow bubbles. That's cheerful, and there wouldn't be any confetti to clean up."

"Asia!" *Great.* Not only had Lucy's girlhood notion of throwing rice fallen by the wayside, but Lucy would now associate the bubbly farewell outside the church with her sister's funeral. Her eyes watered. "Thanks. Now I have to return hundreds of lace-decorated bottles of bubbles."

"Sorry." Asia drew a deep breath. "You'll help me tell them, after Christmas?"

"Of course." She couldn't imagine how on earth their parents would cope. It was so fundamentally *wrong* that George and Marianne, who'd already buried their own parents, would have to bury one of their children.

"Lucy? Don't let them put me in the ground. Just in case something happens before I get all the arrangements—"

"You still have time," Lucy interrupted. *Don't you?*

"Just in case," Asia reiterated. "You'll find a place to sprinkle my ashes, won't you? Somewhere beautiful."

"Somewhere perfect," Lucy vowed, having not the slightest idea where that would be. But she'd find it.

"Don't wear black. You put it on sometimes because you think it's slimming," Asia fussed, "but you're a colorful person. You should wear bright florals and funky earrings that command notice."

"Florals? I thought flowers creeped you out."

"You make them work. Speaking of plants, don't let Mom and Dad do the artificial tree next year."

"They own one now," Lucy said. "It might be hard to talk them out of it."

"Then drag them along to buy a live tree for you and Michael. Don't let them give up family traditions. If they stop doing the stuff we all did together, if—" Her voice broke.

If the customs the four of them had shared disappeared, it would be as if Asia had disappeared. Not just from their active lives, but from their shared memories, their collective love for her. No, they'd always love her, but it was disconcerting to think that one day they might possibly get *used* to being without her.

"I promise," Lucy blurted.

"Thank you. You want to hear something funny?"

The emotional strain in her sister's voice made Lucy doubt very much that she was about to laugh.

"The cr-cremation scares me more than the dying. Isn't that dumb?"

Pressure filled Lucy's chest, trying to work its way up in her throat and leak out her eyes. Was this what good-bye felt like? Fear of flames and absurdist speculation about bubbles at the memorial service? *I can't let her go yet.*

Asia squeezed her hand. "It's okay, Luce. This is my Everest. I'm ready . . . and I hear the view's spectacular."

Nineteen

It had been Lucy's idea for everyone to spend the night at her parents' house on Christmas Eve.

"Like a slumber party," she'd told her parents the night of the church pageant. "So we can all get up early and see what Santa left us."

George had smiled across the kitchen counter at his wife. "When should we break it to her that you and I were the ones up all hours assembling toys?"

"Shush," Marianne had told her husband, sprinkling one last teaspoon of rosemary into the Crock-Pot. "Lucy can believe in Santa for as long as she wants. But, sweetheart, I thought you and Michael wanted to host Christmas at your house this year. Your first one in the new place."

If they only had this Christmas left with Asia, Lucy wanted it to be here, in the tradition of dozens of Swenson Christmases past. "I was being overly ambitious. We still have so much unpacking and minor handiwork to do. We're just not ready.

I'll have everyone over for a New Year's dinner, if that's all right with you."

"Of course," Marianne had said. "You and Asia can sleep up in her old room, because it's the biggest, and share the queen-size bed. Brandon can have the guest room; Michael can have your bedroom."

Should she find it exasperating or hilarious that her mother had so deftly ensured that Lucy would not be sleeping in the same bed as the man she was about to marry, the man with whom she lived, for crying out loud?

"I plan to combat the platonic atmosphere," Lucy told Asia over the phone, "by strategically hanging mistletoe all over the house. And pouring people lots of drinks."

Her sister hadn't been kidding, Asia noticed with some humor on Christmas Eve. As they all cajoled Marianne to play carols for them on her grand piano, Lucy kept freshening the woman's bourbon punch, a family recipe and holiday favorite. Asia had decided to enjoy a few drinks tonight herself. She eyed the frosted glass bowl on the side table, then glanced at Brandon. He looked fantastic tonight, his eyes appearing darker because of his navy cashmere sweater, which was so soft she was tempted to run her fingers over it every chance she got.

"Can I get you more punch?" she asked. Not that she was trying to get the man drunk, but it would be better if neither of them was stone-cold sober when she asked him the question she had in mind that night.

Hoping to take advantage of her comparatively good days while she still *had* good days, she wanted to make love. It had occurred to her that she could take the coy route, offer herself up as his Christmas present—although certainly not under her parents' tree—but she wasn't 100 percent certain that he would want to take her up on it. That he'd want her. Would lovemaking further complicate their short relationship? How would he react to her postsurgical body? No lover had seen her naked since her mastectomy, and the cowardly part of her insisted that maybe it was better to remember sex as it had been before her current condition.

It's not the sex I want—it's him. If she were going to bring that up later in private discussion, she definitely needed at least a mild buzz.

"Asia?"

"Huh?" Heat flooded her cheeks as she realized Brandon was staring at her. *Right.* She'd asked him if he wanted a drink; then she'd zoned out, thinking about sex and how long it had been since she'd had that kind of physical intimacy, and she'd totally ignored his response. *Very suave.*

"Tell you what," he offered. "You stay here, and *I'll* get us fresh drinks."

Meanwhile, Marianne had allowed herself to be ushered to the piano bench. As a girl Asia had sat there with her, turning the pages.

"If I play, you all have to sing along," Marianne said. "It's only fair. Any requests?"

Brandon handed Asia a glass of chilled punch and smiled. "I'm in favor of any song I don't know the words to so that I can spare you all my voice."

"Wait, wait." Lucy gestured exuberantly with her own glass. "I seem to recall, before you and Asia started spending so much time together, that she mentioned you singing at an office holiday party. Seems she was *quite* taken with your karaoke number."

Asia's face warmed all over again. "I don't remember saying that, exactly."

Michael leaned on the edge of the piano, pursing his lips. "You sure she was taken with his singing, darlin', or the man himself?"

From the corner of her eye, Asia saw that Brandon was preening at these revelations, and she mock-glared at her soon-to-be brother-in-law. "Watch it; it's not too late for me to extract your present from beneath the tree, you know."

Lucy gave a muffled squeal like a thirteen-year-old who'd just remembered she had good news. "We are going to do one present tonight, right? That's the deal?"

Brandon tilted his head. "You guys got to open gifts on Christmas Eve? You're so lucky. My mom used to threaten us within an inch of our lives if we even shook the boxes before Christmas morning."

"We always got to pick one special gift each on Christmas Eve, then everything else the next day," Asia explained. Her mind drifted in random sequence to featured gifts she'd received. The year she'd been absolutely begging for a personal headphone stereo/tape player. She groaned, thinking of iPods and feeling old. Did music companies even make audiocassette tapes anymore? One year she and Lucy had both received fairy princess dolls. Asia had displayed hers on a bookshelf so that its perfect dress and hair were never mussed; Lucy had dragged hers everywhere she went and, if Asia wasn't mistaken, had even attempted a home perm.

She blinked. Although she hadn't thought of the doll in years, she thought it might still be up in her room.

"So can we open a present later?" Lucy pressed.

Asia backed her sister up. "It is tradition."

Exchanging indulgent looks, Marianne and George both nodded.

"Carols first, though," Asia pleaded. She hadn't heard her mom play in a long time and missed it.

Her mother smiled at her. "You still know all the words to 'All I Want for Christmas Is My Two Front Teeth'? She sang it once for an elementary school recital, Brandon, and she was *adorable*. That was the holiday season she really was missing her top two teeth. Come to think of it, we must have pictures of that in one of the albums."

Photo albums? "Let's focus, people," Asia said quickly. "Drinking and singing."

Lucy, however, had long ago had all of her baby pictures shown to Michael; now a wicked gleam entered her eyes. "That's right, Brandon. You've hardly seen any of the family photos, have you? In the eighties—"

"Your gift is getting returned, too, little sister. Which is a shame," Asia threatened, "because it was a good one."

"How about 'Silent Night'?" George suggested, clearly realizing they were getting nowhere fast by soliciting suggestions from the younger generation.

As they all huddled around the piano and tried to remember verses past the first familiar one, their 'Night' was slightly off-key and faltering, but the sound of their voices together produced a warm glow within Asia's chest. It wasn't a glamorous celebration by any stretch, but it was such a perfect moment in time—to be surrounded by people she loved, people who were smiling and there for one another, had been there for her through the hardest fight of her life.

I made the right decision. It came to her with such certainty that she let go of her breath in a whoosh, relief popping through her. She appreciated their being with her for the fight, but it was time to stop fighting and just enjoy.

Which she did through three more songs, laughingly ignoring Brandon's whispered suggestions that she tackle the breathy "Santa Baby" in a solo performance.

"Not a chance, Peters."

"It should be on your list," he huffed. "Right under hula dancing."

"We have very different ideas of how this list should be shaping up," she teased. Then she thought of what she wanted to do, if he was up for taking their physical demonstrations of affection beyond the usual kisses, and reconsidered. Maybe their lists did overlap.

Marianne yawned, warning that the bourbon punch was going to have her out cold soon, and if they wanted to each open a present tonight, they should do it now. Reverting to the same role she'd cheerfully seized since she was seven, Lucy had them sit down while she navigated the pile under the Christmas tree and put together a variety of selections for everyone.

"Brandon, you're our guest, so you first. There look to be three packages under here for you." She held up an oblong box with green-and-gold foil wrapping. "This one's from Asia; the smaller square is—"

"I'll take Asia's." He winked in her direction. "She keeps threatening to reclaim everyone's goodies before they can open them. If I get mine out of the way, I can annoy her without fear of retribution."

Lucy laughed. "Maybe I'll open mine from Asia, too!"

Brandon unwrapped his box and grinned at the executive putting set she'd purchased online. Since she'd been admonished to avoid crowds for most of the holiday season, she was exceedingly grateful for Internet shopping.

"I love it," Brandon told her. He handed it over for George to examine, and the two men chatted golf while Lucy distributed more boxes.

Asia was sure Brandon would actually use the set, but, more important, she was sure he recognized it as a commemoration of their first outing together.

Michael opened a small square from George and Marianne, which turned out to be a "First Christmas in Our New Home" ornament for him and Lucy. George puffed up in masculine appreciation over a set of precision power tools from his future son-in-law. Then Marianne chose a gift bag from both of her daughters. Inside, for her crystal collection, was a sparkling figurine of a mother with two daughters kneeling on either side, listening as she read. For the eyes on each otherwise unadorned piece, the artist had used the birthstones of Marianne, Lucy, and Asia.

"It's gorgeous," Marianne exclaimed. "Tomorrow I'll have to find just the right spot to put it. Thank you, girls!"

Lucy tore into a box from her sister and pulled out rich red fabric. As she lifted it, it became clear she was holding a dress with a vee neckline and a flirty hem. Not overtly sexual, but vivacious in a way that would complement her blond good looks. Michael's jaw had already hit the floor, Asia noted with satisfaction, and he was practically drooling, clearly envisioning Lucy in the dress . . . and back out of it.

Asia smiled. "It's the kind of thing you would stop in front of when we window-shop."

"But never actually have the guts to buy," Lucy protested with a self-deprecating chuckle.

"That's why it's a gift. I knew you'd never get it for yourself, even though you should. You've got the curves to pull it off, baby girl."

"Thank you. If you haven't already picked out your gift to open, I have something I want to give you." Lucy handed over a plain white envelope.

Inside were three tickets to *The Nutcracker* ballet just after Christmas. *Me, Lucy, and Mom.*

Lucy met her eyes. "When I realized it normally runs through December and not just until the twenty-fifth, I thought the three of us could go together, like we used to."

One last time. Her throat too tight to speak, Asia bear-hugged her sister, and they wiggled over closer to include Marianne in the embrace. Not long after, the elder Swensons declared that they were turning in and retreated to the bedroom at the back of the first floor. The other bedrooms were all upstairs.

While Lucy and Asia debated whether to pop in a seasonal movie, Brandon excused himself to call his aunt and uncle and wish them a merry Christmas; he planned to phone his family in Germany when he got up tomorrow. His nephews would have already opened all their toys and could make full reports.

Michael stood, too. "I'm going to take a quick shower, give you girls some time to talk."

He hadn't said anything directly to her about it, but Asia suspected he knew her situation. Lucy would need someone to talk to—just as, it had turned out, Asia needed Brandon—but Michael was discreet.

"I'm gonna go upstairs and put this dress on a hanger," Lucy said. "Want to come?"

"Yeah, I wanted to check something in our room anyway."

While Marianne had changed the wallpaper and comforters so that Lucy's and Asia's bedrooms no longer looked exactly like the provinces of teenage girls, she'd left most of the belongings and furnishings undisturbed. Mostly, Asia took for granted that her room at home had always been here waiting for her, but now it touched her. Marianne could have turned it into a sewing room, sold forgotten knickknacks and possessions for a few bucks on eBay. The fairy princess doll, with her flowing gold locks and silver-spangled taffeta skirt, sat in pristine condition atop the exact shelf Asia had chosen for her more than two decades ago.

Lucy looked over her shoulder. "I remember that doll!"

"You loved yours. Take mine and put her aside in case you guys have a daughter. Give her the doll when she's old enough to be excited about it. To be played with," she added firmly, waiting for Lucy to nod her agreement. "Not left on a shelf, but loved and dragged around and given baths in the sink. And, even though I already said it, thanks again for those ballet tickets. I can't wait to go."

"Me, either."

Asia inhaled. "At the risk of undercutting any sisterly bonding we just shared, how do you feel about my kicking you out for the night?"

Lucy arched an eyebrow. "But wherever shall I go?"

Asia laughed. "This room's at the far end of the house, and the guest room Brandon's staying in is right over Mom and Dad's. I wanted to talk to him for a while and don't want to disturb their sleep."

"Very thoughtful of you," Lucy said drolly. She bent down over her already unzipped duffel bag and pawed through the contents. She unearthed two plastic flutes. "There's a bottle of champagne in the fridge. I was thinking of surprising Michael in my old room, but you might need them more than I do."

"You're sure?" *Perfect.* She'd invite Brandon to see where she'd grown up and share a private holiday toast. What happened after that would be up to him, but she was resolved to at least make her desires clear.

Who said you had to wait until January to make resolutions?

From: "Asia Swenson"
To: [BaldBitchinWarriorWomen]
Subject: Happy New Year!
I hope you guys both did something fun to ring in the New Year earlier this week. We had a low-key celebration at Lucy's beautiful new house; then Brandon spent the night here. Being intimate with him is unusual (boy, that doesn't sound very sexy, does it?), unlike any experience I've had with a man before. I don't want to overshare, but we've never shirked from being honest. Thayer, thank you for your candid comments on what your own love life like was

after diagnosis, and for the tips you've shared on what two people might enjoy when conventional lovemaking is no longer possible. My own libido might be too far gone to ever really have a "sex life" again, but the stolen time with Brandon was special and I'll be forever glad we had that, even if, in the future, we stick to holding each other.

The holidays here have been wonderful, but very busy. I know I've slacked off in e-mail lately, and I've been touched to get your messages checking on me. As you may have worried after my brief and somewhat vague responses, yes, there was news. Not the kind one hopes for. There are new tumors invading organs, and the doctor thinks we're defining my life now in terms of months. What's that so-called emotional response? The five stages of whatever? (Or is it seven? I can never recall.) I feel like I'm going through them every ten minutes.

One moment I want to cry (and have), and the next I feel like picking a fight (which I've done so far with my pastor and my sister and once a pharmacist, to whom I immediately apologized when I remembered the guy controlled how well I would feel for the rest of the week). Other times I feel almost accepting, which probably just means I'm too tired for the other steps. Lucy helped me tell my parents. We presented it as my not being a candidate for "cured," which we reminded them we'd pretty much known already. And I told them I wasn't quitting treatment, per se, just changing my approach and not doing the really aggressive chemo anymore. Honestly, I feel better already.

I don't know if the improvement is even physical. Maybe it's psychosomatic? I dreaded the increased chemo and the not knowing so much that now I'm in a better place emotionally. of course, who knows how long that will last? When I'm within shouting distance of the point of no return, will I start playing the what-if game, wondering if it's too late to barter a few more days with modern miracle drugs? The pain is constant, but tolerable. Dealing with that will become a more pressing issue, too, but for now, I'm trying to enjoy Brandon, and Lucy's wedding next Saturday. I'll e-mail you guys pictures—she's going to be a lovely bride.

I'm still trying to decide on some resolutions. The reality—and I've had time to try to adjust—is that I probably won't be here to see the next new year. But that doesn't mean I shouldn't set some goals and try to achieve them while I still can, right? You know how they say, "Today is the first day of the rest of your life"? Maybe someone else in my position would see that comment as paradoxical, but right now, it has never felt more true to me. Brandon's made some noises about a quick trip to Germany. There are some people he'd like me to meet, and I've always wanted to visit another country!

You probably won't see many more posts from me. I'll try to pop in from time to time with a hello or a photo or a question, but I feel restless. Did either of you ever have life lists? Like learn to knit or make balloon animals or climb Mount Everest? Obviously, there are some things that are permanently outside my scope. But there are others I can attempt, even if I bomb spectacularly. (I've already tried hula dancing. Mark that one down in the "lousy" category, but I had more fun failing at it than I ever imagined.) So I'll be busy, hopefully, unless things take a serious turn for the worst, in which case you won't hear from me for obvious reasons.

If there's big news, either I'll post or Lucy will. Meanwhile, I love you both. I never would have made it this far without you.

Asia

Twenty

Lucy rolled over, dimly aware that this wasn't her bed and that a strange sound had awakened her. Happy excitement flooded her. This was the hotel room where she and Asia had come after the rehearsal dinner! This was the night before—or morning of—her wedding.

"Go back to sleep," Asia said in a stage whisper. "Sorry I woke you."

Propping herself on her elbow, Lucy brushed hair out of her face and squinted through the dark to try to see her sister. "You okay?" It had been coughing that woke her.

"Yeah. I was having some trouble breathing, but I'm fine now."

"You sure?" There was a moment of silence, and Lucy wished she could see her sister's expression better. Was she really all right?

"I could get you a glass of water from the bathroom," Lucy offered. "I have to go, anyway."

"That sounds nice. Thanks, Luce."

Lucy padded across the luxuriously thick carpet, experiencing a zing when she thought about coming back to this hotel later, to the honeymoon suite. As a married woman. By the time she returned with the water, she was too excited to sleep. She glanced at the glowing green numbers of the digital clock on the nightstand.

"It's morning! I wonder if the sun's up yet?" She went to the window, drawing back the thick curtain. Still dark. *Still* being a particularly accurate description, as far as she could see; it was as if time had stopped, not even clouds moving across the suspended sky.

Asia had the clock in her hand. "Should be daylight soon enough."

"Want to watch it with me?" Lucy asked impulsively. "We could go out on the balcony."

For a second Asia said nothing. Lucy couldn't fault her for the lack of enthusiasm. After all, it was January. Sitting on the tiny excuse for a balcony in the predawn cold simply to anticipate the sun's rise over a hotel wasn't exactly a postcard moment. But this was Lucy's wedding day—everything was infused with an extra romanticism. What better way to greet a new chapter than by cuddling close to one of the most important people in her life and watching the promise and warmth of a fresh day spill over them?

"All right." Asia sighed. "I suppose I could keep you company long enough for the sunrise, but then can we catch another hour or two of sleep before we have to be anywhere?"

"Absolutely! I'll shower first so you can rest longer," Lucy promised, already pulling the comforter off her bed. Asia's cap and fleecy blanket were always with her these days, but any additional warmth would be good for her. "Thank you for doing this," Lucy told her as they huddled into a two-seater patio chair, swathed in layers of blankets.

"Well, it is your wedding day. So I'm humoring you," Asia grumped. "But now we're square. No making me do the hokeypokey or the Macarena or throwing the bridal bouquet at me later."

"Deal." Lucy wouldn't target her sister with the fake flowers anyway. It seemed taunting. Besides, the only flower she thought Asia would appreciate was the single bud Brandon had spontaneously lifted from a table at the rehearsal dinner and tucked behind Asia's ear, the petals a pale contrast to the dark wig Asia now routinely wore. For a woman who'd gone so far as to describe flowers as creepy, Asia had looked perfectly content at his easy, affectionate gesture. And had kept the rosebud on the hotel nightstand while she slept.

Brandon was a great guy, but with no official affiliation to the family. Lucy hoped he didn't drift away when ... She hoped they could stay friends, and had even told him that this week when they'd had a second alone. She'd been afraid it would cause an awkward lull in the conversation, but he'd hugged her and said he'd definitely keep up with her and Michael.

"I'm nervous," Lucy admitted in a whisper, watching the edges of the sky fade to gray.

"About the ceremony, or about actually being married?" The yawn punctuating her question made her sound no less genuinely interested in the answer.

"About everything."

Through the overlaps of cotton and fleece, Asia's fingers

found Lucy's and squeezed. "You'll be fine, Blondie. Trust me."

They sat quietly, holding hands, and Lucy was aware when Asia's went lax in sleep, just as her uneven breath deepened into a rasp. Streaks of pink appeared on the horizon, reaching toward them as Asia's fingers slid down and away.

Watching alone, Lucy tilted her face to the oncoming gold of the sky, imagining she could feel each tendril of warmth on her skin even through the chill of the air. It was a shame Asia missed the silent, Technicolor triumph of daylight once again overcoming darkness, but Lucy knew her sister was with her in spirit.

Walking carefully in the square-heeled sling-backs, holding the railing for extra balance, Asia followed her sister down the winding stairs to the old church, the original section of the building that had been renovated and added onto countless times over the past century. This charming and spiritual pre-ceremony ceremony had seemed like a much better idea, Lucy had confided, *before* she'd realized it involved navigating a narrow staircase in her bridal gown.

Since Lucy, Michael, and their photographer had chosen to overrule the "groom shouldn't see the bride" superstition and have the majority of their pictures taken prior to the wedding, Pastor Bob had suggested this special touch. In the back sanctuary, a room big enough for only a modest altar, a few pews, and gorgeous stained-glass windows, he would perform Holy Communion for the bride and groom and their immediate families. Michael, his siblings, and both sets of parents were already waiting inside. Asia would go ahead of Lucy, and the bride would get her entrance, Michael lifting his eyes and seeing her in the dress for the first time.

It'll knock his socks off. The stylist that morning had concocted a formal—but not sleek or stiff—updo that made Lucy's hair look as if it were spun gold. Her makeup was barely noticeable except that it made her eyes sparkle even more and her lips full and pink and healthy. Asia ran her tongue self-consciously over her own mouth. She had a blister that her mom had assured her they'd covered well. Other than that and the shadows beneath Asia's eyes, she felt she looked pretty spiffy, all things considered.

They stopped in the cramped hall.

"Ready?" Asia asked.

Her sister's hands trembled. She'd remarked on the walk to the stairwell that she now understood the purpose of the bouquet. It gave a nervous bride something to clutch. But she'd left the flowers behind in order to receive communion.

Lucy smiled gamely. "Ready as I'll ever be, I guess."

Don't I know that feeling.

Asia walked inside, meeting her mother's gaze first and forcing a smile through the tears that suddenly threatened. She doubted any of the Swensons would make it through this day dry-eyed.

Unlike the much larger gathering that would take place in a couple of hours, there was no music for the sacrament. No organ or trumpet to herald the bride, just the sighs and heartbeats of immediate family, and Michael's intake of air when Lucy entered the room.

She was the last to join them at the front, and Pastor Bob

gave the happy couple a moment to exchange nonverbal dec-
larations of love before opening with prayer. After he'd blessed
the day and asked for God's will and wisdom in their marriage,
the preacher glanced from Marianne to Lucy to Asia, his familiar deep voice clotted with emotion.

"Your family, within the bigger church family, has certainly
been a . . . Well, I'm honored to have known you. We've seen a
lot together, and I anticipate many more memories and special
occasions to come. I hold each of you very dear."

Asia grinned at him, relieved he could still say that to her
after the vitriol she'd spewed in his office. There were some
words you probably weren't supposed to use in front of a man
of God, but Pastor Bob had assured her he'd heard them all
before and that his place was not to judge.

The photographer had asked to be present in the small
sanctuary, thinking its intimate environment and colorful
backdrop—sunlight streaming through the bright blues and
burnt oranges of the stained-glass windows—would be picturesque. His request had been categorically denied. Not
every instant of a person's life was meant to be captured on
film or logged in journals, documents, and medical records.
Some of the most important moments were simply meant
to *be*.

However, that still left the photographer plenty of shots
in the church atrium, a quick one on the front steps before
the wind disrupted anyone's hair, and many more in the main
sanctuary, which Enid Norcott had turned into a silk-and-
greenery-festooned fairy tale. If Asia's cheeks hurt from smiling, she could only imagine how her sister would feel before
the end of the day.

"Is Brandon here yet?" Lucy asked, standing to the side and watching as Michael posed near the altar with his parents.

Asia had noticed him talking to one of the O'Malley brothers a few minutes ago. "He's here. I haven't really talked to him yet, but he waved." And mouthed a quick *wow* at her, which always lifted her spirits.

"Well, I want a picture of the two of you," Lucy said. "Make sure the photographer gets one. For now, I need one more of you and me."

"Another one? Luce, we've had one with you and me, us with Mom, us with Mom and Dad, us with all the bridesmaids, us—"

"Hey." Her sister thumped her on the shoulder. "As the maid of honor, aren't you *required* to take orders from the bride?"

"With that attitude," Asia teased, "you'll be lucky if I don't lead a mutiny."

Lucy held up a single index finger and pouted. "One picture. That's all I ask."

When the photographer had snapped everything on his must-have checklist, Lucy signaled him to follow her.

I have to get one of these puffy white gowns, Asia thought with a grin. Something about it imbued the wearer with the power to boss others around and still seem inherently feminine and lovable.

Lucy's choice of location was one of the newer stairwells, carpeted in royal blue and leading up to the choir's rehearsal room. "You'll have to go up above me," the bride instructed, spreading her skirt in explanation.

They definitely wouldn't fit on the same step. So Asia sat

one rise past her sister, leaning sideways against the wall with Lucy in front of her, the bunched handfuls of satin arranged around her making her look like a little girl playing princess. Remembering countless afternoons of dress-up and taking Lucy trick-or-treating, Asia grinned.

"Probably the most genuine smile you've given the photographer all day," Lucy kidded. "But I personally am sick to death of beaming for the camera. I was thinking something more like this." She blew out her cheeks, widened her eyes, and crossed them.

"Very attractive." Asia turned toward the camera with her own variation of Deranged Monkey Face and the flash popped, the photographer shaking his head at them as though they'd abandoned all sense of decorum.

"All right," Lucy said. "Better freshen up my makeup and see if there's one final way to use the restroom. I think it's about that time."

"Yep."

Soon Doreen, the church's wedding coordinator, was herding them into a line outside the main sanctuary.

This was what everything had been leading up to, and Asia knew she'd always cherish the day. The ushers had escorted all the special guests to their seats. Michael and the groomsmen waited up front with Pastor Bob.

Music swelled, and Doreen reached for the sanctuary doors, admonishing them, "Big smiles, ladies!" as if they were a high-school cheerleading squad. In response, Reva and Rae, both looking even more flawless than usual, lifted their chins and pulled back their shoulders. Asia made the mistake of glancing toward Lucy at that moment, and as soon as their eyes met they both began to giggle. Asia tried not to make any noise, but her body just shook harder.

She had to get it under control! Reva and Rae were already headed down the aisle, and Cam was preparing to go next. Then it would be Asia, followed by Lucy on their father's arm.

Lucy angled her body forward a fraction. "You're not going to be laughing hysterically all the way down, are you?"

"I'm not making any promises," Asia said.

George cleared his throat. "You girls."

Lucy snickered. "I know, Daddy. We're impossible."

"No. You're amazing, and I'm proud of you."

The simple statement raised a wealth of emotion in Asia's chest, and she turned back toward the sanctuary, not wanting to dissolve into a puddle.

He kept his voice low. No one more than a foot from him would be able to hear his whisper over the music, but his words reached both his daughters. "Your mama's darn near perfect, but y'all don't ever listen if she speculates she went wrong with you somewhere. My opinion, there's something very *right* with the both of you."

Swallowing the lump in her throat as she proceeded forward, Asia couldn't agree more. That something was love. Thank God she'd had so many reminders of it in the past month, so many small moments that had demonstrated how important it was to love and let yourself be loved. The pews on either side of her were full of people who brought that idea to life, relatives and longtime family friends and, among them, Brandon looking dashing in his suit. Gratitude—no, *joy*—spread through her like warm sunshine as she walked through the sanctuary. From the satin-bow pew markers to the candles twinkling near the altar to, of course, the many, many silk flowers, every adornment was meant to convey a sense of celebration; at this moment, Asia's feelings were completely in tune with her surroundings.

She beamed as she neared the front, passing her mother and Michael's parents and approaching the railing where the other bridesmaids waited. Sure, she could wish that she'd been more naturally open, like Lucy, or that she and Brandon had developed their intimate relationship much sooner, but it was never too late. Every day brought a fresh chance to appreciate what she had while she still had it, to pause midclimb, not worrying about reaching the top or what would happen when she got there, but simply enjoying the beauty of the journey.

Simply enjoying her life.

Photo by Lee Isbell of Studio 16

Tanya Michna is summa cum laude graduate of University of Houston–Victoria. Her first writing-related job was there in college, and she's been writing professionally ever since. She lives with her husband and two children outside Atlanta, Georgia.

Necessary Arrangements

Tanya Michna

This Conversation Guide is intended to enrich the
individual reading experience, as well as encourage us
to explore these topics together—because books,
and life, are meant for sharing.

A CONVERSATION
WITH TANYA MICHNA

Q. At its heart, Necessary Arrangements *is the story of two sisters. Do you have a sister?*

A. I do, a younger sister who lives nearby. We've spent the past three decades getting each other into trouble, bailing each other out of trouble, getting each other into more trouble—each of us grateful that there's at least one other person around who shares the same, er, *unique* sense of humor. We've both been known to laugh at the wrong time, especially if we happen to make eye contact, but the ability to laugh has seen us through some difficult moments and helped us create some great memories.

Q. So was the relationship between Lucy and Asia based on yours with your sister? Do you draw on the people around you for characters in your books?

A. Not really, no. The stories I tell are fictional, and my characters don't represent real-life counterparts, although my experiences may shape my perspective and the stories I tell. My family has lost women to cancer; I hope any personal emotions I was dealing with while writing about Asia and Lucy deepened the story. In my books, however, I've written about other situations that bear absolutely zero resemblance to my life and were cobbled together through imagination and research. In fact, for me, getting to write about different types of people, choices, and locations is one of the exciting parts of being a writer.

Q. Did you always know you wanted to be a writer?

A. Yes. Correspondence with former teachers and diary entries I wrote as early as age seven confirm that even as a kid, surrounded by classmates who aspired to be astronauts and veterinarians, I knew I wanted to sit isolated in my office after sane people had gone to bed, wrenching my thoughts onto a computer screen and arguing with myself about how to word a sentence. Okay, *technically,* there was a phase in kindergarten when I wanted to be a princess, but even then I would have written royal memoirs.

I've been an avid reader as far back as I can remember. With all that books have meant to me, I can't imagine a more fulfilling occupation than providing stories for fellow book lovers. Plus, there was no chance of my ever being qualified for a job that required advanced mathematical skills, mechanical aptitude, or any navigational ability.

Q. Asia's story is bittersweet. Did you ever think about giving her a more traditional happy ending?

A. I did consider it, especially when I found myself sobbing at the keyboard at three in the morning. After all, I love happy endings! Numerous cancer patients, including some I know personally, do achieve remission and are eventually considered cured. However, that isn't Asia's journey, even if I'd wanted to tell it that way. Hers isn't about overcoming an obstacle in the conventional sense. Her journey is about going through one of the most negative and frightening situations I can imagine and not only reaching an acceptance, but actively finding the positive, even changing herself for the better. Though life can throw difficult and cruel challenges at us, I believe there will always be love and hope and moments of simple but surprising beauty, too. Asia is able to find those.

Q. Did you have to do a lot of research for this book?

A. More than for any other writing project I've ever done. I talked on the phone and through e-mail to cancer survivors and medical professionals. I read a stack of reference books followed by various personal journals and online blogs. What stuck with me more than technical terms or current drug research was how incredible people are. Some readers may question whether Asia copes with her situation with an almost unbelievable amount of grace and spirit. But my fictional account would pale in comparison to some of the awe-inspiring tales of real-life patients, what they've been through, and the positive influence they've had on others around them.

Q. In the story, Asia mentions to Brandon that she doesn't want to regret not having seen new places or not making the time to try new things. Do you have a "life list," minor or major goals you hope to accomplish?

A. If you'd asked me last year, I would have said that the major goal in my life was to get both of my children successfully potty-trained. It seemed an elusive quest worthy of Don Quixote at the time! Now, however, my kids have mastered this toddler rite of passage. My ongoing daily goal is to be a good mother, but I have smaller, more specific dreams, too. I want to go to Europe. I lived there as a kid, when I was too young to appreciate anything I was seeing; my degree is in history, and I think it would be fascinating to visit some of the places I've studied. A few months ago, my husband and I actually did go to Italy for the first time, but I was there for only a matter of days. I'd like to return for a longer period and see more countries.

I also have a bizarre desire to one day stand up in front of a crowd and sing. I think it must come from those moments during my favorite musicals when I'm blown away by a soloist, a single person onstage sharing an emotional experience with an entire theater full of people. Considering the popularity of karaoke, I could theoretically achieve this singing goal without much trouble. But since I really can't sing, perhaps it's better if I stick to writing as my way of sharing and evoking emotions.

Q. So, are you working on a new novel now?

A. As soon as one book is done, I always start something new, whether it's a short story or full-length novel. The manuscript I'm writing now is quite different from *Necessary Arrangements,* although family still plays a very, very important part. I think that, just as readers often have certain styles of books they like to read over and over, authors have certain themes they feel called to revisit. Thankfully for me, there are countless variations on universal themes, and I look forward to exploring them.

QUESTIONS FOR DISCUSSION

1. Lucy and Asia Swenson, both sympathetic characters with their own distinctive strengths, are also opposites in many ways. Which sister did you relate to more, and why?

2. Throughout the story, flowers represent different things to different people and in different situations. Is there an item in your life whose meaning has altered over time?

3. Discuss how Michael and Lucy's relationship is different from Brandon and Asia's. How are the two relationships alike?

4. What character do you think changes the most during the course of the book?

5. Asia wishes once or twice that she started falling for Brandon sooner. What do you think would have happened if he'd asked her out when she was healthy?

CONVERSATION GUIDE

6. The saying that every cloud has a silver lining is a cliché, but it can often be true. Has anything good ever happened in your life as the direct or indirect result of a crisis?

7. If you had to make the decision Asia faces at the end of the book—fighting for more time or making the most of the little time left—what would you choose and why?

8. Do you have a list of things you'd like to do, try, learn, or see during your lifetime? What is on that list?